TRANSITION

by
Paige Walker

COLLEGE BOY
PUBLISHING
"We Breed Bestsellers"

Young Adult Fiction/Fantasy/Horror/Love & Romance

ISBN: 978-1-944110-35-2

Published in Dallas, TX, by College Boy Publishing. College Boy Publishing, LLC is a division of The College Boy Company & ArmaniValentino.com. To order wholesale or bulk orders of this book, please contact the publisher directly at collegeboypublishing@gmail.com or 972-383-9234.

Autographed copies of this book may be ordered directly from www.PaigeWalkerAuthor.com. Please allow up to 7-14 Business Days for delivery. Wholesale www.collegeboypublishing.com

Paige Walker is available for book signings, workshops, panel discussions, consultations, and radio & television interviews by emailing collegeboypublishing@ygmail.com or by calling 972-781-8404.

Printed in the United States of America

08 09 10 11 12 PWAV 5 4 3 2 1

TRANSITION

by
Paige Walker

Disclaimer

This is a work of fiction. Names, characters, businesses, places, events and incidents are either the products of the author's imagination or used in a fictitious manner. Any resemblance to actual persons, living or dead, or actual events is purely coincidental.

Edited by
Armani Valentino & Rose Barlow
for College Boy Publishing

Published for print & digital distribution by
Armani Valentino

Inside Designed & Setup by **Armani Valentino**

Creative Direction for Cover by
Paige Walker & Armani Valentino

Cover Design by **iHor**

TABLE OF CONTENTS

Prologue

"It was one of the best and worst days of my life. I never expected things to spiral out of control like they did...I never expected any of this."

Prologue

There is nothing, nothing at all, and nothing for a long time. My world isn't just black; it's gone. I can't feel, I can't see, and I can't hear. There is nothing. I am nothing. Am I dead? I can't tell if I am dead or not. Did he kill me? I don't know what's going on or where I am. Maybe I'm dead and this is what death feels like. It feels like nothing.

TRANSITION

Chapter 1

I wake up to the best day of my life.
The sun brightly streams into my room from my
bedside window. It's a beautiful sunny day. *Thank
goodness.* I love the sun. I hoped that today would
be sunny. It's September 5, 2014, my eighteenth
birthday. *Today, I become an adult*, I think to
myself. A sigh slips from my lips. The only down
side about today is school. Even though it's my
birthday, it's a Friday, and I still have school. I wish
I didn't have to go to school today. *I wish I could
just have the whole day to myself.*

TRANSITION

I live in a small town called Rosenburg, Colorado. It's a modern city that houses many diverse residents. Whenever you go outside, you can see houses, trees, and mountains. Rosenburg is a densely forested city. Regardless of the trees and forest, it's a beautiful city. I can't imagine living anywhere else. I love my home, I love my family, and I love my friends. *I love my life.* From where I stand, my life is perfect. *Could it get any better than this?*

"Nichole! Wake up honey!" my mom yells. I can hear her walking up the stairs to my room. She knocks on the door but doesn't wait for a response before she opens it.

I pull my purple comforter back and sit up in the bed as my mom walks into my room. Kathryn Roberts, my mom, is a beautiful and figured woman with flawless light brown skin. She has pretty dark brown eyes that most men find themselves lost in. My mom has plenty of admirers but her heart belongs to my dad. My dad would say that he didn't have a chance when he first saw my mom because her eyes hypnotized him. He called it love at first sight. My mom's hair is dark brown and really long. It extends almost to the middle of her back. She has always been so beautiful to me. Sometimes I would find myself looking in the mirror to see if I looked just like her. I want to be as beautiful as her. I'm pretty, but I never believe that I am as pretty as her.

"Happy birthday, honey," she says with a smile that could stun people into silence. My mom has her casual attire on today. She is wearing light blue jeans, a black blouse, and her black fluffy house shoes. She had pulled her hair back in a low ponytail with no strand loose. She looks dressed for a relaxing day at the house. Most likely, she isn't going to work today. When she dresses like this, she stays home.

CHAPTER 1

"Thanks, mom," I reply, as she walks toward my bed to give me a hug. My mom and I have always been very close. We always understood each other and we never had any real serious arguments. If we hadn't been mother and daughter, we would have been best friends. I could tell my mom anything.

"I know it's your birthday but you still have to get dressed for school." She places her hand on my head and smoothes back my hair. Her hand drops and then she walks toward my room door and turns around to look at me. "When you get ready, come downstairs because I made your favorite for breakfast." She walks out of my room and back downstairs. I can hear the wooden staircase creak as she makes her way down.

I get out of bed swiftly and walk up to the purple-framed mirror that hangs on my closet door. Almost everything is purple in my room. It's my favorite color after all. I stare at my reflection in the mirror. *I don't look any older.* I know people rarely see drastic changes in their appearance on their birthday but I really would like to see some. I know growth happens gradually and throughout life. So when someone's birthday comes around, they could never really see how much they have really grown.

I continue to stare at myself trying to find something that is completely different from yesterday. Of course. I won't find anything. *Nothing's different. Nothing's ever different.* I look into my bright green eyes. My dad would always tell me that my eyes were his gift to me. My eyes were a gift from my dad but my dark brown hair came from my mom. I run my hands through my hair in an attempt to tame it. My hair is curly. It's always curly. For some reason having a Caucasian father and African American mother produces curly hair in their offspring. I am mixed and like most mixed kids I've met, I have curly hair.

I open the double doors to my closet and pull out a long peach maxi dress to wear to school. It's my eighteenth birthday and I am going all out with my wardrobe today. I put the dress on and it hangs perfectly on my body, accenting the curvaceous body that my mother passed down. The dress falls effortlessly to the floor but barely touches it. It has a round neckline and an elastic belt enclosed in it that encircles me just below my bust. I finish off the outfit with some jewelry pieces and sandals that I had bought specially for the occasion. I walk out my room and turn left towards the bathroom to finish getting ready. By the time I am finished, my hair hangs beautifully in loose brown curls; I am wearing natural toned make-up and just a little lip-gloss. I turn in a circle observing myself in the bathroom mirror. *Nice outfit, Nichole*, I think to myself. *Time to go eat breakfast.*

...

When I enter the kitchen, I go and sit next to my eleven-year -old sister, Tiffany Roberts, at the breakfast bar. My sister looks just like me. It's as if we are twins born years apart except for the fact that her eyes are hazel and mine are green. I adore my little sister. Tiffany and I don't always get along but we love each other. I could tell she looks up to me because no matter what, she takes anything I say literally. Therefore, I have to watch what I say around her at all times.

"Good morning, Tiffany," I say as I lean across the chair to give her a hug and a kiss on the cheek.

My sister is wearing her school uniform. She has on a red collar shirt with a khaki skirt, and red baby doll flats. Tiffany has brown hair also and it is pulled back in a curly ponytail. Every morning she tried to get her hair to lie flat on

CHAPTER 1

her head, like mom's hair, but her hair would always curl up and escape its confinement.

"Good morning, Nicky," she replies. "Happy Birthday!"

"Happy Birthday sweetie!" My dad chimes in. "My first born is all grown up and becoming a young adult. I don't know how I'm going to live with myself!" My dad plasters a huge megawatt smile on his face. "Why can't I shrink you down back into a little girl?" I laugh at his melancholy tone. "You're old enough now that you can buy lottery tickets and cigarettes but if I see a cigarette in your hands, young lady, I will lock you up for the rest of your life." My dad jokes but I know he is serious.

I shake my head at him; my dad knows I would never use or buy cigarettes. Jake Roberts II, my dad, is a handsome Caucasian man with curly black hair and green eyes. He has a medium build and is somewhat tall. He is at least taller than all of us. He is wearing black dress pants and a white button down shirt that is tucked in. He is always dressing professionally. It's his style. I would catch him wearing similar outfits on weekends even though he doesn't have work. He works as an optometrist and feels that he has to look professional all of the time.

"Thank you," I say as my mom places my favorite breakfast in front of me. I love chocolate chip pancakes, turkey bacon, and eggs. Yum. I love food so much that I should be fat but I'm not.

My family likes to go all out for each other's birthdays. Whenever it's one of our birthdays, we always make the whole day special. The first thing we do is make the birthday girl, or in my dad's case the birthday boy, their favorite breakfast. My mom does most of the cooking except for when it's her birthday. My mom is an excellent cook. Sometimes, I help her cook so that I can learn a thing or two. In fact, when it's her birthday, I do all the cooking. My dad can't cook to save his life.

After fixing their own plates, my parents sit at the breakfast bar with Tiffany and me. My dad sits down in the chair beside me, and my mom sits down in the chair beside Tiffany. We talk about our plans for the day and laugh at my dad's ridiculous jokes about becoming an adult. His jokes are more corny than funny but I think that's what makes them funny.

Once we finish breakfast, my family begins singing the happy birthday song. They place a large red velvet cupcake with cream cheese icing in front of me. The cupcake has a single candle lit on top of it. I take a deep breath and blow out the candle. My wish is that today will be the best day of my life. *Today will be the best birthday ever.*

···

Tiffany and I leave the house after breakfast to head to school. Ever since I got my driver's license, two years ago, I always drive her to school. I pull up at Rosenburg Middle School and park so that my sister can get out and head to school.

"Bye, Nicky," Tiffany says as she gets out the car with her silver backpack. "See you later!" She closes the door and runs off to her friends. She doesn't even give me time to respond.

My morning ritual is to drop off Tiffany and then to pick up my best friend Casey Neal. Casey is a pretty girl with cream skin and raven black hair that is very long and silky. She would have been Snow White if Snow White ever existed. She is of normal height, not too tall but not too short

CHAPTER 1

either. She lives just a block away from Tiffany's school. When I pull up to Casey's house, she runs out the door.

"Happy Birthday," she screams as she hops into my baby blue Prius. "Oh, here is your birthday present." She hands me a tiny box. I open the box and inside is a BFF charm, with crystals all around it, made for a Pandora bracelet. Did she also get me a Pandora bracelet, because I don't have one?

"Thanks, Casey, it's beautiful but I don't have a Pandora bracelet," I murmur. *I could probably make a necklace out of the charm.*

"Well, if you ever get one, you have a charm for it." I place the gift in my back seat and start driving toward the school.

"I've got the perfect dress for your birthday bash tonight," she says suddenly. "It's what you would call a little black dress of perfection. Well, it's green but you get what I mean." *The little green dress of perfection... hmmm?*

I'm having the biggest party of the year tonight. It is going to be at a club called Nightside. How my parents pulled off booking the club, I have no idea, but everybody is super excited about going. I am excited about going. I gave an invitation to everyone at school, which includes both the people I know and don't know. It even includes the people I don't like or that don't like me. The party is strictly invite only and everyone has to bring their invitations to get in. I will also have a guest list at the door because I know a handful of people are going to lose their invitations.

"As long as you're cute and I'm cute, that's all that matters," I say as we approached the school.

"Oh, so Nate doesn't have to look cute?" she asks with mock sarcasm.

TRANSITION

"Well, Nate has to be dressed to impress also," I respond.

Nate or Nathaniel Blackwood is my gorgeous boyfriend. We have been dating for almost a year. He is one of the most popular guys in school. I swear we are destined to be together forever and we are madly in love with each other. My parents aren't sure about him. They think he is a bad boy but have relented because they think he is just a phase I am going through. The bad boy phase, I guess. Nate and I have the perfect relationship. We have never had any sort of argument, which is great, but Nate still has some jealousy issues. If a guy even looks in my direction, Nate gives him a piece of his mind.

Nate isn't very muscular but he is really strong. Sometimes I think it is crazy how strong he is but I don't think too much of it. Nate has a pale skin complexion but it suits him. He also has short black straight hair that's always styled sloppy but in the cutest way. His eyes are as blue as the ocean. I could drown in his eyes. No matter what his features are, they all complement each other to make one good-looking man. Most of the girls in school have a huge crush on him but he only wants me. *Only me...*

Nate and I met a year ago, when he first arrived at the high school. He and two other guys, who are now his best friends, had just moved to Rosenburg. He told me that his parents just wanted to relocate and start fresh somewhere new. This town is nice and quiet and he says they like nice and quiet. I have never met Nate's parents but he says they are just always busy and that one day I will get to meet them. Nate used to tell me that when he saw me on his first day of school, he knew instantly that I was the one for him. He said I looked beautiful and smelled like cinnamon. The cinnamon

8

CHAPTER 1

part was strange but I think he was just imagining that I smelled like cinnamon. I wore perfume but I never bought cinnamon perfume. We have been inseparable since the first time we saw each other. *I love Nate.*

We arrive at the school at eight forty-five in the morning. Rosenburg High School is one of the biggest high schools around. Classes don't start until nine so we have time to socialize with other friends and associates before we head to class. Casey and I aren't the most popular girls in school but we are likeable and easy to get along with so that gives us a substantial amount of popularity.

When we arrive, Nate is sitting at a bench in front of the school with his two friends John and Tyler. Everybody at school likes to hang out on the outside benches and tables before school starts. Nate looks over when we pull up in a parking spot. A huge smile forms on his lips when he sees me. He stands and walks toward me.

"I'm going to go talk to some friends, and give you two some privacy," Casey says when we get out of the car. She gives me a knowing look as she walks off. She always feels like Nate and I are inappropriate when we are around each other, so she always makes a hasty retreat. I personally wouldn't say we are inappropriate. I guess being constantly around each other and making out can be inappropriate but we are in high school. Who doesn't make out in high school?

Casey is almost never in a relationship due to her distrust of men and when she is, it always ends before it begins. She would always give me some excuse, saying she broke up with the guy because he probably was going to cheat on her soon or something like that. She thinks that she is avoiding heartbreak by ending her relationships before her heart could get broken. I think it has something to do with her father cheating on her mother and leaving her, her two older brothers, and her mother to start a life with another woman. When I try to talk to her about it, she says 'no man is trustworthy, I mean look at what my own father did.' She swears that the day she meets a trustworthy man, will be the day she falls in love. She doesn't think that day will be anytime soon.

"Hey babe," Nate says sweetly as he approaches me. He swiftly kisses me on the lips. "Happy Birthday." *Those lips...*

"Thanks," I reply, as I lay my head in the crook of his neck while he embraces me in a loving hug. Nate is six feet tall and when standing my head is just slightly below his chin. We are a perfect fit.

"I will give you your birthday present tonight after your party," he says as he releases me slightly so he can look at my face. I nod. *Tonight...*

"So I told my parents I was going to spend a night at Casey's house tonight after the party," I say quickly. I look down at my hands to avoid his eyes.

Nate and I are planning to get together after my party, at his house, so we could express our love to each other in a way I never have before and I am full of nerves about it. It's my idea of course. He will always tell me that there is no rush; if I want to have sex then we will but if I don't he respects my decision. I think that is sweet but I also think that he might be using those words to make me want to even more. Who doesn't like a sweet, respectable man?

"When the party is over, I'm going to drop Casey off at her house and then make my way to yours." *...and then we will spend the whole night together.*

"Are you sure you still want to come over?" He looks at me searching for withdrawal.

CHAPTER 1

"It's fine if you decide to change your mind. Even though I don't want you to change your mind." *I don't want to change my mind either.*

"I'm sure." This is what I want after all.

"Okay" he looks back at his friends for a moment and they gesture for him to come over. I follow his gaze and frown. Couldn't they spare him for a longer period of time? He turns back to face me. He looks as if something is funny. "My parents will be gone, so there will be no interruptions. We will have the house to ourselves." I smile. "I'm going to go and see what these guys want. I'll see you at lunch." He gives me another kiss and is off to his buddies.

I start walking toward the school passing groups of students laughing and making jokes. Some people yell happy birthday and I smile and thank them on the way as I walk to the school. I look back at Nate and his friends. They are laughing. *He could have spent the rest of the morning with me. It's my birthday after all.*

"So, no making out this morning, I'm impressed," Casey says with sarcasm. She has to run to catch up with me as I walk into the school building.

"Ha ha, your sarcasm brings me joy," I say as I nudge her in the arm. "One day I will be teasing you about making out with your boyfriend."

"Ahh yes... my imaginary future boyfriend. You know, I want my future boyfriend to look like Tyler, Nate's friend, handsomely beautiful. A beautiful man that I can trust."

"Why don't you just date Tyler?" I tease her. Tyler's history with girls is not a good one. He is known for brea-king hearts.

TRANSITION

"I have to be able to trust him. I cannot have a relationship with a guy I do not trust, and Tyler is nowhere near trustworthy and will never have a chance with me. Especially with the string of broken hearts he's left at the school. He's just... so cute." she says dreamily. "Oh, and I love the color of his skin. I think it's so pretty. I want my children to have color in their skin even if their color isn't as rich as his." Tyler's handsome with a caramel skin complexion and brown eyes like chocolate. *Chocolate and caramel.* Casey has always wanted mixed children. She would always talk about how all races should mix so that we all get unique colors to our skin. "Don't get me wrong, I like my skin color, I just want to be able to have children with various complexions. A rainbow of children." I stop walking and stare at her. *Is she serious?*

"So, you're going to be one of those women on TV who has had twenty children with fifteen fathers of various races.... just so you can have mixed children with a rainbow of colors?" I ask. "Don't ask me to babysit for you.... cause the answer is 'No!'" I start walking again.

"Of course not, one father.... with twenty children" she says with certainty. I look at her and we both start laughing. We made our way to our lockers to get our books for class. We were able to get side-by-side lockers for our senior year by begging the secretary at the front desk until she got sick of us. "Ok, so I'm not having twenty children." Good to know.

The bell rang just then; we both say our goodbyes and scurry off to our classes. Casey and I had been best friends since elementary school. We are destined to be each other's maid of honor and godmother to each other's chil-

CHAPTER 1

dren in the future. I can't imagine life without my best friend. She is more than my friend. She is my family.

My first class of the day is Spanish II. I walk into class and sit down in my normal seat. I sit in the middle of the classroom. I don't like sitting at the front or too far back. I like Spanish. It is a language that I have always wanted to learn. It isn't the only language though. I want to learn at least two more. I feel that it's important to learn different languages so that I am able to communicate with others. I am glad to have a teacher whose first language is Spanish instead of a teacher with Spanish as their second language. It makes it easier to learn.

I don't have Spanish with Casey or Nate but I do have it with my friend Amber. Amber can be a little over dramatic at times and she is a big flirt. We aren't as close as Casey and I are but we are still friends. Casey and Amber don't get along well. They aren't even friends, but just because they aren't friends doesn't mean Amber and I can't be friends. Amber is a pretty girl with tanned skin and she has way more curves than I do. Her hair color matches her name. Amber sits in the desk to my left. I look over as she sits in her seat.

"Well hello, birthday girl." Amber flips her shoulder length amber-colored hair off her shoulder as she looks at me.

"Hey Amber, are you coming to the party tonight?" That's a stupid question. Knowing Amber, she wouldn't miss the party for anything.

"Am I coming to the party tonight?" She has a look of shock on her face. "Of course I am! What kind of question is that? Your party is going to be the party of the year!" Amber put a smile on her face and looks behind my shoulder. I turn to see what has caught her attention. There is a guy staring at me. I look back at Amber; she is still smiling. I shake my head.

"Looks like you have an admirer. His name is Landon, go talk to him," she says. I sigh.

"I'm not interested, Amber, you know that."

She rolls her eyes. "…but he's so cute, and you're never interested." *I'm never interested because I have a gorgeous boyfriend named Nathaniel.*

"Then you date him. I only have eyes for Nate." Amber is always trying to hook me up with guys that like me. She is the opposite of Casey. She dates too much and trusts too easily.

"Yeah, I know. I don't even know why I try. You and Nate are going to get married one day." *One day…* I smile.

"Yeah, we are, and if you stop trying to push guys on me, you can be a bridesmaid."

"Are you bribing me, because it's working?"

I laugh. "So, are you bringing a date to the party or are you flying solo?" She gives me a look that says 'don't bring sand to a beach.'

"No, I'm not bringing a date. I'm flying solo so I can dance with who I want and flirt with who I want."

The teacher starts class and our conversation ends. We could have kept talking except when students are caught talking in Spanish II, they are required to hold a conversation with the teacher in Spanish. *Ugh… I did not want that.*

The day goes by smoothly. I get a lot of birthday wishes from almost everybody in school, even from the teachers. Right before lunch, I get a pretty mean look from a girl named Rebecca. There is no way she is wishing me a happy birthday because she can't stand me. She is blonde and beautiful and one of the most popular girls in school.

CHAPTER 1

The reason she doesn't like me is because I am dating Nate. She wants my boyfriend and she can't have him. I still invited her to my party and I am sure that she will be there. No matter how much she doesn't like me, she and her friends aren't about to miss one of the biggest parties of the year.

I'm walking to my locker when I suddenly stumble and drop all my books on the floor.

"Shoot…" *Why am I so clumsy?* I bend down and start to pick up my books when someone walks up to me.

"Let me help you with that." I look up and see Aaron.

Aaron is one the best-looking guys at school, besides Nate that is. He is muscular with bronzed skin, probably from playing football in the hot sun. He is also the school player but that doesn't stop girls from falling all over him. He has been trying to get with me since forever but I never fall into his traps.

"Oh…thanks but I got it." He better go before Nate sees him.

"Nonsense let me help you. It's your birthday after all. You shouldn't be carrying your own books." Aaron and I stood up. All my books are in his hand when Nate walks up.

"What do you think you are doing?" I look at Nate and he looks furious. He knows Aaron is up to no good. *Oh no…*

"I'm helping the pretty lady with her books." Nate looks at me.

"I dropped them and he was helping me pick them up." Nate looks back at Aaron.

"Look I'm not someone you should be pissing off, so if you don't mind, give me my girl's books and back off." Nate takes my books, quite forcefully, from Aaron. Aaron walks off backwards with his hands in the air and a smile on his face. "Come on baby, let's go to lunch," Nate murmurs.

...

At lunchtime Nate surprises me with bouquets of happy birthday balloons and red roses. They are my pre-gift according to him. All the girls in the cafeteria look a little envious but they are trying hard to hide it. Casey gets the whole cafeteria to sing happy birthday to me and reminds everyone about the party tonight. Then Amber gets up and tells everyone to bring a gift and to not show up empty handed like free loaders. Casey gives Amber an annoyed look.

Classes went by quickly after lunch. Only a handful of people came up to me throughout the day claiming that they lost their invitation. I wrote their names down so I could make sure they are on the guest list. If they thought I would give them another invitation so that they could bring a party crasher, they were mistaken.

After school Casey and I head to my car so we could head home. Over my shoulder I hear my name being called. I look back and see Nate running over.

"I'll meet you at the car," Casey says. "Give me your keys and I'll start the car." I hand the keys over to her and turn towards my boyfriend. He is carrying something in his hand.

"Hey babe, what's up?" I ask with curiosity.

"I've decided to give you your present early," he says with a smile. In his hand he holds a black satin box. He hands me the box and I open it. Inside it is a beautiful necklace. The necklace is a thin string of what looks like diamonds. I am in awe and speechless as I stare at the beautiful piece of jewelry in front of me. *It couldn't be real... could it?*

CHAPTER 1

"I'm speechless, Nate." I don't know what to say. "Thank you."

"They are real diamonds you know," he says with a smug look on his face like he just bought me the world.

"Oh my... how could you...oh my," I can't believe he has gotten me a real diamond necklace. This must have cost a fortune. *They are real.... oh my.*

"I want the best for my baby." He leans in toward me and gives me a lingering kiss. "I'll see you at the party and by the way I can't wait for tonight," he whispers against my lips. He turns and leaves to get in the car with his friends.

They are riding home in his friend John's car today, which is some kind of black sports car with dark tinted windows. Nate's friend John always creeps me out. He has Black wavy hair and cream skin like Casey's but his eyes are so dark that you can't tell the color. They are almost black looking. He is a short guy but he is big and muscular like he lifts weights every day. I never understood why they are all friends. I mean Nate and Tyler I understand, but when you add John into the equation it is odd. Nate and Tyler are full of life and John is like a gloom over them. He never truly fit in with everyone else. It is just something about him that makes people feel on edge. I don't even think I've seen him smile or laugh...ever.

I watch as the guys drive off and then turn to walk to my car where Casey is waiting.

TRANSITION

Chapter 2

Before heading to my house, I drive to
Casey's house so she can get her dress and accessories
for the party. Casey's house is a medium sized house
made of reddish brown brick. I always like how on the
outside of the house it looks small and modern, but on
the inside it looks huge and high-tech. Casey walks in
her house to gather her things while I wait for her in the
car. She walks out of the house with a small bag for accessories and a long dress bag. She hangs the dress bag
up in the car and hops into the passenger seat.

TRANSITION

"You got everything you need?"

"Yep let's go," she replies.

...

We walk into my house and stop in the kitchen to look at my party cake. The cake is huge. There are two parts to the cake. One part is made of cupcakes that are placed to form the number 18. The cupcakes are made of white cake with swirled purple and white icing. The other part is a regular square cake with white icing and an edible picture of me on it. Purple icing bordered the base and top of the cake.

"Nice cake," Casey says and I nod. We turn to leave the kitchen when my mom and sister walk in.

"Mom! Save me some of Nichole's party cake please," Tiffany says whining. My mom looks toward me expectantly.

"We will save you some cake alright," I say. Tiffany jumps up and down with delight. "Have fun at your friend's house tonight, Tiff." Tiffany nods.

"Hi, Casey," my mom says as she gives Casey a hug.

"Hi, Casey," Tiffany says with a smile.

"Hi, Mrs. Roberts. Hey Tiff," Casey replies.

"Why can't I go to the party, mom?" Tiffany says with mock disappointment. My sister just wants something to be mad about.

"This party is not for little girls, Tiff," my mom replies, "but when you turn eighteen, we can have a party like this for you, ok?" Tiffany nods her head in agreement.

"But just so you know, I'm not a little girl any more, mom," Tiffany says. *Here we go again....*

Casey and I make our way to the stairs. The conversation my mom and sister are about to have is going to last too long and we need to get ready. When we make it into my

CHAPTER 2

room, Casey closes the door quickly, turns toward me and stares.

"So...," she says. I know exactly what she is saying 'so' about but I want to play dumb.

"So... what," I reply, mocking the exact tone she had just given me.

"Sooo... are you and Nate really going though with this whole thing," she says waving her hand in no general direction.

"What whole thing, Casey," I say, pretending to be confused.

"Oh my gosh... stop playing dumb. Are you going to sleep with Nate or not," she asks with a hint of irritation because I am evading her question.

"That's the plan." I lay down on my queen-sized bed and cover my eyes with my arm. *I'm so nervous.*

"Well... use protection and... and... and well are you sure you want to do this? I mean, I know you love him and all but I just always have this bad feeling about him, like he's hiding something." Casey walks to the far wall of my room and sits down at my vanity desk.

"He's a good guy, Casey. Just give him a chance, all right? Of course I will use protection. I'm not stupid." I know Nate isn't hiding anything. Casey just doesn't trust him. I trust him. We tell each other everything. I know everything about Nate.

"I believe you, but I still don't think he is trustworthy," Casey says as she goes through my make-up bag that is sitting out on my desk.

"You don't believe any man is trustworthy, can we please stop talking about this?" I say a little irritated. *Let it go Casey....*

TRANSITION

"Don't be mad at me, I'm just looking out for you. Now… let's do our make-up."

"Ok…," I say and sit up on the bed.

"Since you're going to be experienced after tonight, when it's my turn, you can give me some pointers," she says as she puts on some brown colored lipstick. She is not wearing that color with her green dress.

"Whatever you say," I say quickly, willing this conversation about my future sex life to end. I jump out of bed and sit next to Casey at my desk to pick out my make-up for the night. Hmmm… red lipstick, I might wear that color tonight. *Maybe Nate will like it?*

I know Casey doesn't think I should trust Nate but the fact is, I do. I love Nate and he loves me. That is all that matters. I push all thoughts of tonight out of my head. I am really nervous about it but first things first, I have a party to attend.

···

Casey and I took forever to get ready and I am glad we have an ample amount of time to devote to our new glamorous looks. I am dressed in a sexy black halter dress that hugs my curves at every dip. It stops just below my butt but just above my knees. I chose a natural look for my make-up with red lipstick to make my look pop. My brown hair hangs freely past my shoulders in loose curls all around my head. My shoes of choice are red pumps and I also put on the diamond necklace that Nate gave me this afternoon. The attire for this party is semi-formal. It is like the prom before the prom.

"Where did you get that necklace?" Casey asks as she looks questioningly at the necklace Nate gave me. "Are those real diamonds?"

CHAPTER 2

"Yeah, they are. Nate gave it to me for my birthday," I say while admiring the necklace in the mirror. *Oh...Nate...*

"They are not real!" she exclaims. "Oh my gosh...he bought you real diamonds? How did he afford that?" I have no idea.

"I don't know." *I don't really care...*

"You don't think he..." She must think he stole it or something. *Of course I don't think he stole it!*

"No!" I say staring at her. "I don't think he stole it." *I don't think he stole it. He wouldn't do that. Would he?*

"Whatever you say...how do I look? I mean I know it's your birthday and all but I need to look good, too." She turned in a circle so I could see her whole outfit.

Casey is wearing a tight dark green sleeveless dress that accents the little curves that she has. She wore her hair straight and went for the natural look with her make-up also. She wore dark green pumps that have crystal studs all around them.

"You look cute," I say in approval. *We look hot... I hope Nate likes my dress...*

"Thanks, girl. We both do."

"Come on, we have to go down stairs to take pictures before we head to the party."

Casey and I both walk down the stairs toward the foyer so we can show my parents our outfits for the party. Tiffany has already left for her friend's house, so she would have to wait for the pictures to see what we wore. My parents stood waiting for us in the foyer by the front door so we could leave right after they got their pictures. When Casey and I made it to the foyer, my parents' faces lit up in a smile.

"You girls look so nice," my dad says. "I can't believe my little girl is all grown up," he says looking at me; he looks sad and happy at the same time. My dad is having a hard time with me growing up. I guess he feels like he's going to lose me, or something, just because I am getting older.

"You girls look beautiful," my mom says with a sob. "I remember when you two were so little, dressing up in princess costumes and now look at you." *Oh mom…*

"Thanks," Casey and I say in unison.

"Ok, let's get some pictures of you girls and then Casey can you take a picture of Nichole, her dad, and me?" My mom asks.

"Sure, Mrs. Roberts."

It took about thirty minutes for us to finish the photo shoot in the foyer. We have to have taken fifty pictures or more.

"Now Nichole, I know you're going to Casey's house after the party so call me when you make it there," my dad says. "Don't forget because I'll worry. You know that there have been a few people going missing lately. One of which was one of your classmates." He's talking about Ashley Fortune. "I know not many of the missing people were in this area when they vanished but I want to know you're safe, ok?"

"Yes, dad," I say.

"Yes, Mr. Roberts," Casey says shortly after.

Ashley Fortune was a girl who went to my school. She was also Tyler's girlfriend at the time she went missing. He and her family were devastated when they could not find her. She went missing almost a year ago and still to this day no one can find her or her body. The fact is no one knew if she was alive or dead. Tyler had to go see the school counselor for about six months because his parents were afraid he

CHAPTER 2

was depressed. I didn't know Ashley personally but I did see her every day since she was Tyler's girlfriend, and Nate and I were dating at the same time, but we were never really friends.

It is about eight-thirty at night and we have to head to the club before the doors open for the party at nine. My parents are in a separate car than Casey and me. Casey turns the radio real loud as soon as I start driving. She wants to get in the zone for the party.

"This is going to be the best party EVER!" Casey yells over the music. "Maybe I'll give Tyler a dance...who knows?"

"Huh?" I had to turn the music down to hear her better.

"I said, maybe I'll give Tyler a dance." I look over at Casey.

"I think you really like Tyler."

"I like him but he's not for me. A dance isn't going to hurt anyone though." I can tell Casey thinks of this party as a once in a lifetime opportunity. Why not give the boy she has a crush on a dance? I know at the end of the day she isn't going to go any farther than a dance with him anyway. *Tonight is going to be the best night of our lives.*

TRANSITION

Chapter 3

We arrive at *Club Nightside* at five minutes to nine. I pull my car into the parking space on the side of the club by my parents' silver BMW. The club is a huge one-story building. It is black on the outside with red double doors at the entrance that are blocked by a red velvet rope. Above the doors is a well-lit neon red sign with a black border that reads NIGHTSIDE. There are a couple of locked doors on the side and back of the club but the employees only use those. Outside, lights circle around the club so that the parking lots aren't pitch-black.

TRANSITION

At the entrance there is a security guard with a clipboard that contains the list of people who forgot their invitations. My parents walk inside ahead us while Casey and I stop in front of the security guard whose name is James.

"Hi, James, I'm the birthday girl, Nichole."

"Hello, Ms. Nichole, Happy Birthday," he says.

"Thanks, I just wanted to confirm that you know that if the guests have their invitations, they are allowed in but if they don't, they can't get in unless they are on the list." No party crashers.

"Ok, Ms. Nichole, I will make sure nobody gets in unless they have an invitation or are on the guest list." I start to walk inside when I remember that I have extra names to put on the guest list.

"Oh, I almost forgot," I say quickly. "Here are a couple more names to go on the guest list." I hand him the list. "If they are already on your list, that's fine. I'm just making sure they will be able to get in because they lost their invite." James takes the list from me.

"I will add these names to the list. Have a great party," he says as he opens the door for Casey and me to enter.

The club is already booming when Casey and I walk in. The guests aren't here yet but who arrives at a party on time? I am even going to disappear for a while and make a fashionable entrance.

The club on the interior has black walls and floors to give it that secluded look. Colorful lights illuminate the dark space as they flash all over the place. There is a stage at the back center of the club. The DJ is set up on the stage with all his equipment. To the left of the stage are bathrooms, one indicating girls and the other boys. The doors of the bathroom are black and the light inside is dimmed so that the light won't offset the darkness. On the left wall, is the club bar, which is shut down, of course. The bar now houses the foods and the birthday cake for the party. In the front left corner of the club, near the entrance, is a big decorated crate labeled Gifts. The crate is decorated in bright purple and silver colors. Near the right wall of the club are tables and chairs for people to sit and eat.

"I'm ready to party! What about you birthday girl," Casey yells over the music. "Do you want me to wait with you for your big entrance?" *Did she even have to ask?*

"Yeah," I yell back answering her. "You're my best friend, of course I want you to make an entrance with me."

"What time are Nate and his friends coming?" I don't know what time Nate is going to arrive, but I hope he will arrive sooner rather than later. It didn't even cross my mind to ask him that earlier.

"I'm not sure, but I hope soon. Come on let's go wait in the office, it's already ten minutes past nine and people will be showing up soon." There is a door on the left wall, near the bar, where the owner's office is located. We are waiting there until a lot of people show up, so I can make an entrance.

"You think they would come this early?" I'm not sure if anybody would be here on time or not, but there are always a select few that are early birds.

"Some people will and some won't, everybody is different," I say as I shrug.

Casey and I begin walking toward the office. I make a gesture to my parents that we're heading there. My parents nod and continue to make sure everything is well organized. As we are about to walk in, two security guards and the owner walk out. The owner gives me a quick happy birthday before continuing with the guards for what I guess is some instruction about dealing with wild teens. The office we are waiting in is a contrast to the appearance of the club. It has white walls and white floors. There is a black leather couch on the back wall of the office, and near the front wall is a black desk with a computer and other equipment. There is a big black cabinet on the left wall of the office that matches the desk. The door has a small one-way window that allows us to see what is going on in the club. Casey and I sit on the black leather couch to wait.

"Waiting is going to seem like forever, Nichole." Yea it really is. *Why did I want to make a fashionable entrance again?*

"Maybe, maybe not," I say trying to sound nonchalant. I am anxious for the party to start but at the back of my mind I keep thinking about Nate and going to his house after the party. *Tonight is the night.*

The party doesn't get started until ten. Most of the guests arrive by that time. Casey and I are still waiting in the office getting ready to walk out. The office is basically soundproof, so we can't hear the music or the voices outside of it. *I wonder if Nate is here.*

Casey and I stare out of the one-way window at all the guests. Some of them are dancing and some are just standing around talking to each other. I don't see Nate but that doesn't mean he isn't here.

"It looks like the whole school has shown up," Casey says as we stare out the window. "Even Rebecca and her gang of followers are here. I guess she couldn't pass up a good party." I guess she couldn't pass up seeing Nate either, I think to myself.

CHAPTER 3

"I guess not." I am happy that so many people have shown up to my party.

"Are you ready to make your big entrance?"

"I need five minutes and then we will go in." *I'm just not ready to walk out yet.*

"Whatever you want, it's your birthday," Casey replies.

It isn't that I am nervous but I just want to wait a few more moments before my big entrance. Plus we need to call my mom so that the DJ will know to throw the attention on me. I am walking out to *Flawless* by Beyoncé. Beyoncé is one of my favorite artists and it's my day so it seems just right to walk out to that song.

"Call my mom, please," I ask Casey sweetly.

"All right... and here we go." Casey replies. She pulls out her phone and calls my mom. "Mrs. Roberts, she's ready for her entrance." *Here we go.* I watch as my mom walks up to the DJ to tell him that I am ready. The DJ starts to announce something that is probably an introduction to my entrance and Casey and I proceed to exit the office.

"...And here she is everybody. The birthday girl Nichole Roberts," the DJ yells over the sound of *Flawless.* Everyone claps as I make my entrance. I walk over to the stage at a steady pace. A lot of people are here but I still don't see Nate. However, what I do see are stacks of gifts in the back corner. *Wow, people are generous.*

Casey stays behind while I walk up the stairs to the stage. *Where is Nate?* I look out at everyone from the stage while the DJ hands me a microphone.

"Is everybody having fun?" There is yelling and whooping from the crowd. "I want to thank you all for coming out to my party." The crowd cheers and the DJ turns the music almost all the way down so that I can speak.

"Looking good, Nichole," someone yells but I can't tell who it is.

"Thank you! You all look nice tonight! Before we get this party going again, I want to also thank you all for all the generous gifts. I really appreciate it. I hope you all have a good time because I know I will. I'm going to give the mic back to the DJ now, so let's get this party started!"

Everyone cheers and began yelling "let's party" and the DJ starts up the music again. I smile from ear to ear as I leave the stage to go dance with my peers.

I dance, Casey dances, and I even think I see my mom getting down in the back of the club. Everybody is having so much fun. This is going down as the best party of the year!

I dance with Casey for a while and then we drift with the other guests and dance with them. After a little while, Amber walks over to dance with me.

"Nice party girl!" She yells over the music. Amber is a good dancer. We could both move with the music. Amber is wearing a one shoulder, tight plum dress. She looks good and from the glances she is getting from some of the guys, she has a couple of admirers at the party tonight.

"Thanks… you look cute!"

"I know right! Thanks, girl!" Amber and I continuing dancing together all the way through to the next song. "Where is Nate?" Amber says finally. "I thought you two would be booed up by now making an inappropriate scene on the dance floor!" I shrug my shoulders. I don't know where Nate is and I am starting to get angry about it.

CHAPTER 3

"I don't know but I'm not going to let his absence piss me off." It's already beginning to but I don't want to admit that.

Amber says nothing else about Nate being missing. We just keep dancing together until some guy from school pulls her away. She is certainly making an inappropriate scene on the dance floor. My Mom blanches when she looks Amber's way and I laugh.

At about eleven my mom walks on stage to say it is time to sing happy birthday to the birthday girl. I climb the stage as my dad brings my cake on stage with lit candles. Nate still hasn't arrived. *Where the hell is Nate?*

I am furious but it never shows on my face. I look at Casey and she just shrugs. She reads my mind. She doesn't know what to tell me about my missing boyfriend. I blow out the candles on my cake and wish I could be this happy all the time. Which, of course, means excluding how I feel about Nate not being here. *Just let it go and enjoy yourself.*

Casey walks with me to eat some food and cake. We are taking a break from dancing. Half the people at the party are either eating or dancing.

As well as cake, on the bar there is cheese dip, meatballs, fried chicken, a fruit tray, a vegetable tray, and an assortment of finger sandwiches. I am eating a little of everything. *I love food!*

There is no way I am opening presents tonight because I am having too much fun. After she ate, Casey goes to dance with some guy she has been flirting with. She thinks Nate and I are inappropriate? Well, she should see the way she is dancing with that guy. I walk over to the punch fountain to get some punch when the guy that was staring at me in Spanish class walks up to me.

TRANSITION

"Hey Nichole, I'm Landon," he says as he holds out his hand for me to shake it. He looks nervous. Landon is a good-looking guy and he seems nice, too. He always looks presentable wherever he goes. He is one of the smartest guys in school. He is probably going to be very rich some day.

"Hey Landon, I know who you are." He smiles shyly. "No need to be so formal." I shake his hand anyway not wanting to be rude.

"Oh, really... that's great and sorry," he says nervously. "You look beautiful tonight." *Aww... he's sweet. I think he might have a crush on me.*

"Thank you, and you don't look too bad yourself," I say quickly.

"Thanks..." There is this small awkward moment before he began to speak again. "Hey, I know you have a boyfriend but do you want to dance with me," he asks. *Do I?*

Hmm... *He's sweet. I haven't danced with a guy all night and Nate doesn't seem like he is going to show. One dance won't hurt. I mean it's not like Nate would kill me if I danced with another guy. He's not even here!*

"Sure, why not," I reply. I put my punch cup in the trash and pull Landon out onto the dance floor.

I know how to move when I dance. I'm not the best dancer in the world but I can get down. Landon is a decent dancer and it is easy to drift from song to song dancing with him. As we finish dancing to *Wiggle* by Jason DeRulo, I see Nate out the corner of my eye. It is twelve o'clock and he is just making it here. He looks furious but I'm mad, too.
I can't believe he showed up this late!

Chapter 4

Landon follows my gaze. He blanches when he sees the way Nate is looking at him and if looks could kill... Landon backs away slowly and then turns and walks away. I guess he's scared of Nate, but I'm not. Nate looks pissed but so what. I don't think Nate has any right to be mad at me. I mean we were just dancing. It's not like I am cheating and well... he hasn't been here for most of the party anyway. I mean the party is about to end in thirty minutes! I walk over to where Nate is standing at the back of the dance floor. I stand in front of him and say nothing. *He is the one who needs to explain.*

TRANSITION

"So you and Landon...hmmm... interesting choice," Nate says calmly. I cross my arms, look to my left, and I see that Casey is dancing with Tyler. So she got her dance with him after all. I turn back to Nate.

"It was just a dance Nate. Anyways, where were you for most of the party?"

"The boys and I stopped to get something to eat and just lost track of time. If for one second I thought my girl was dancing around with losers, I would have come straight here to eat," he speaks as if there is a hidden message that I am not getting. "And anyway that didn't look like *just* a dance. You were giving it your all." I was giving it my all but I was having fun!

"You think *you're* mad." I point my finger at his chest. "Well I'm furious, Nate." I put my hands on my hips. "I thought I would have you here all to myself. After all, it is my birthday." He stares at me for a minute and then relaxes a little. I am glad because he needs to cool down. He is the one at fault here.

"I'm sorry, you're right. I should have been here at nine when the party started," he says sweetly. *A little too sweetly, what is he up to?*

"You're not mad anymore?" I pause. "I mean I love how quickly you got over me dancing with Landon but this isn't like you," I say, stunned by how quickly this has all blown over. Nate has never been mad at me before but I've seen him get mad at others and it isn't a pretty sight.

"It's your birthday baby and I can't be mad at you for long on your birthday," Nate says as he pulls me out onto the dance floor. "Let's dance." *Finally*, I get to dance with my boyfriend.

CHAPTER 4

We dance for the rest of the party. There is no more talk of him not showing up or me dancing with Landon. Amber even comes over and says something about 'finally he made it' but we don't pay her much attention. Those last thirty minutes at the party are like a fairytale.

At twelve thirty everybody begins to leave the party except me, Casey, my parents, Nate, and his friends. People say their goodbyes and occasionally someone yells how this was the best party ever. Amber gives me a hug before she leaves.

"See you Monday, girl," she says and then leaves. Amber and I rarely talk outside of school so I will get an inquisition from her about Nate on Monday.

My parents pack all the gifts and left-over food up in their BMW with help from Nate and his friends. I'm not going to be able to open those until tomorrow. After the gifts are all packed up, we all clean up the club. It is nice for Nate and his friends to help. I guess he is trying to score points with my parents. It works. When we finish, Nate walks over to me to give me a goodbye hug.

"I'll see you at my house," Nate whispers in my ear. I nod my head in agreement and then he and his friends take off. Before Casey and I leave, my parents stop us at the door.

"Honey," my mom says. "Your dad and I just want to give you this gift to open before you go home with Casey." They hand me a small box wrapped in pretty wrapping paper.

I open the box and inside is a beautiful Pandora bracelet. *Casey must have known my parents bought me this.* The bracelet has five charms on it. One charm is a picture of my family and me, another is a picture of Casey and me, and there is also a shopping bag, a heart, and the letter N. I also have Casey's BFF charm to add to it later.

"There is room for more charms so you can add different things throughout your life," my dad says.

"Look, there's a picture of us...awww," Casey says.

"Mom, dad, thank you... it's beautiful... I love it," I say as I give both of them a bear hug. "I love you. Thank you for everything." I quickly put the bracelet on my wrist.

"You're welcome baby," my mom says. Then she starts to explain each charm. "The N is for Nichole, the heart represents love, the shopping bag is to represent your shopping addiction, the picture of you and Casey represents friendship, and the picture of you, Tiffany, me and your father represents family."

"It's the best present ever and I can add Casey's BFF charm to it too."

"Now you two get home safely, alright," my mom says.

"Yes, Mrs. Roberts, we will. Come on Nichole. *Twilight* marathon. My house. Now."

"Call me when you make it there," my dad says looking pointingly at me, then Casey."

"We will dad." Gosh, my dad can be so over protective sometimes.

We all leave the club at the same time and Casey and I make our way to her house. I know she is going to want to talk about what I am about to do, but nothing she can say will stop me.

"Now that we are alone, I want to hear you say that you are one hundred percent sure you want and are ready for this," she says the words slowly, making sure I understand her.

CHAPTER 4

"I am, and I will call you in the morning. As a matter of fact I will come by your house around noon so you will see that I'm safe and sound and no longer a virgin. Is that ok with you?" *She is not going to let this go unless I reassure her one last time.*

"It is as long as you promise to not spare any details." Of course she wants details.

"I promise, and I'm going to get Nate to hook you up with Tyler," I say with a smile.

"No you won't," she says sternly. "I do not want to date him. How many times do I have to tell you that?"

"Alright, Alright," I say. "I saw you two dancing." She stays quiet, deliberately ignoring me. "Fine! I'm going to stop butting into your love life." We pull up at her house. "Give me a hug," I demand. She leans over to give me a hug before she gets out of the car. "See you tomorrow. Oh wait, can you help me put your charm on my bracelet?" She puts the BFF charm on the bracelet and then gets out of the car.

"See you tomorrow and send me a text when you make it to Nate's house."

"I will." She closes the door and walks to her house. I call my dad to tell him we made it to Casey's and then I wait until Casey gets in her house before I head to Nate's house.

Nate lives a little far from Casey's but not too far. He still lives in civilization but just in the civilization where more trees exist. *Maybe I should give him a call.* I pick up my phone and I dial his number. The phone only rings twice.

"Hello." Nate sounds a little irritable. I hope his anger hasn't relapsed.

"Hey baby. Is everything alright? I'm on my way to your house. I should be there in ten minutes," I say hesitantly.

TRANSITION

"Aw hey babe," he cheers. "Ok, make it here safely. I'll be waiting for you." I blush at his words.

"Ok I will, I love you baby."

"I love you too baby, hurry and get here because you're making me anxious." *He's anxious for me!*

We hang up the phone. This is going to be the best night of my life. I had put on some lacy underwear under my dress so I can look sexy. I hope he likes it. I ride in silence. I am anxious myself for the night ahead. I make it to his house in a little over ten minutes and he comes outside when he sees my car approach. I send a quick text to Casey saying I made it to Nate's, while Nate walks to the driver's side of my car to open my door. *No turning back now.*

"Hey baby," he says as I get out of the car with my overnight bag.

"Hey," I say nervously. He laces his fingers with mine and we walk hand in hand into his house. I look up at his house. His house is small and plain. I wonder what the inside looks like.

When we walk in, I see Tyler and John sitting on the living room couch. I look questionably at Nate and he shrugs his shoulders. *What are they doing here?*

"The guys aren't going to bother us," he says quietly so that only I can hear.

"Hey Nichole," John says with a smile. *He never smiles!* What is up with him? "Nice party you had there." I look into his dark eyes. *Those eyes scare the daylights out of me, but he looks happy for a change.*

"Uhh…Thanks…John. I'm glad you had fun." Nate is going to answer for this.

Nate's house is small on the inside, too. I don't have any problems with small houses but the way he talked about

CHAPTER 4

his home, made it sound like it was some kind of small mansion. The kitchen, living room, and dining room, in Nate's house, are all in the same area. It looks like no one really lives here, at all, with the lack of furniture and house appliances. There is a TV, a couch, and a small dining table with three chairs. There are no pictures, decorations, and nothing to indicate that people actually live here. Nate leads me down the only hall in the house. There are four doors down the hall. The first door we pass on the right leads to the bathroom. The bathroom is empty looking too. There are two doors on the left that are closed. Those must be either his parent's room or a guest room because the second door on the right is his room.

In his room there is a bed and that is it. He shuts the door behind himself. I stand near the bed turned away from him. *His friends are here... I don't know about this.* I turn toward him and crossed my arms. I can't see my own face but I know there is a look of irritation on it.

"Nate, you said we would be alone," I say accusingly.

"We are alone, I don't see anyone here except you and me." He pulls me near him and he wraps me in a warm embrace.

"Well, we are only alone in your room, not in the house." He kisses me and when I don't respond, he lets me go.

"Come on, let's enjoy this moment we are having together," he pleads. "Take off your clothes for me." *So we're getting right to business?*

"I don't know about this anymore," I say. *There is no way we were doing this with his friends around.*

"What do you mean? You want this, I want this," he says seductively as he tries to pull me closer to him. I resist.

TRANSITION

No way... *There is absolutely no way I'm going through this while his friends are around.*

"No, Nate, we are not doing this while your friends are in the same house." *There I put my foot down.* If he loves me, he will understand.

His face goes from happy to furious in a second. He just stares at me in silence. "So you're going to be a tease then," he says icily. *A...what?* He did not just say that to me.

"Nate you can't be mad at me. Just respect my decision. I'm going to go to Casey's house and we can talk about it some more tomorrow or in this case later today." *He is scaring me with the look he has on his face.*

"You're not going anywhere, Nichole. You know I'm still pretty pissed at you for dancing with that Landon kid..." His voice sounds as cold as ice.

"... And you thought sex with me would fix how you felt," I say with sarcasm. He takes a step toward me and I take a step back.

"You know, Nichole, I liked you, really liked you but you knew I was a jealous guy. You can't be surprised that I'm angry." *Liked me?* That is all I heard.

"You're more than a little jealous, Nate, and what do you mean you *Liked me?*" *There is no way I am going to have sex with him now! Who does he think he is?*

"I mean what I said. I *liked* you. As in past tense, as in I don't like you anymore," he says with certainty. *What the hell?* "I thought I could see us together forever but once someone has pissed me off, I'm pissed off for good. I guess you can say I can hold a grudge forever." He laughs darkly. Warning bells go off in my head. *What is wrong with him?*

"I'm leaving, Nate, and don't call me. As a matter of fact, lose my number. I never want to see you again." I say

CHAPTER 4

with tears in my eyes. I head for the door but he blocks me. "Get out of my way, Nate." I struggle to get past him but he is too strong.

"Like I said before, you're not leaving." In that moment I see his eye color turn from blue to black and his face is full of rage. He grabs my arm tightly and swings me back onto the bed. I hit my head on the bed frame and tears begin to run down my face. *His eyes.... they look just like....they look just like...*

"What the hell is wrong with you, Nate," I yell. "What's wrong with your eyes!" *The eyes....his eyes are so black... just like...just like... John's...*

"Oh, didn't I tell you? My eyes turn black when I'm about to eat." I have a bad feeling that I am not going be able to leave this house.

"Get away from me, Nate," I cry. "Don't touch me and what do you mean your eyes turn black when you're about to eat?" *What is he talking about...there's no food in here! What is he about to eat?*

"SHUT UP," he yells loud, a little too loud. I'm sure his friends hear him. I wonder if they will come and see what's wrong and then maybe I can leave. *Maybe I can leave.* "Speak again and you'll regret it." *I will regret it?* I keep quiet even though I'm not sure what he is planning to do. He walks over and gets on the bed with me. I try to run but he pulls me back to the bed with amazing strength. *He's so strong.* My tears are in full bloom. I try to break free but I can't. I can't get away. *I just want to leave.*

"Let go of me," I scream. "Nate, let me go now! Get away from me!" I keep yelling but he is ignoring me and from the looks of it his friends are not coming to help. Tears run down my face.

TRANSITION

"You are so beautiful. Don't worry this will be quick," he says as he leans closer and moves my hair away from my neck. I don't want him to touch me! I am about to scream but he places his hand on my mouth. I bite into it as hard as I can drawing a little blood but he doesn't even flinch. He leans in closer as if he is going to kiss me on my neck. *Is he seriously still trying to be romantic?* "Such a waste," he says as he gently kisses me on my neck. What does he mean? *Please, I want to go!*

"What's a waste…," I say shakily into his hand. I feel a sharp pain on my neck and am about to scream when the world goes black. *And then there is nothing….*

Chapter 5

There is nothing, nothing at all, and nothing for a long time. My world isn't just black; it's gone. I can't feel, I can't see, and I can't hear. There is nothing. I am nothing. *Am I dead? I can't tell if I am dead or not. Did Nate kill me?* I don't know what's going on or where I am. *Maybe I'm dead and this is what death feels like. It feels like nothing.*

TRANSITION

How did I get to *this* point? How did this happen to me? One thing is for sure, the darkness feels like it is forever and never ending, I'm dead and Nate is my murderer.

After a while I begin to hear and see but everything is black, everything is blank. *Maybe I'm not dead, maybe I am.* I start to feel again. It feels like all my nerves are super-charged because I feel everything. There is plastic all around me and even though I can see, everything is black. I feel my-self hyperventilating from panic. *Where am I?*

I feel around but all I can feel is plastic. All I can see is darkness. I want to see the light. *Where is the light, where is the sun?* I become more aware. I feel around my surround-ings. *Am I in a trash bag?*

I need to tear out of this bag. I thought I would be weak from panic but when I reach out to tear the bag it tears effortlessly. *Well that is easy.* Dirt pours in on top of me as I climb out of the bag and out of the ground. *Why am I in the ground?*

It is dark and I am frightened. I think my heart should be racing as I look out to my surroundings but it isn't. *Why isn't my heart racing? Why isn't my heart beating?* I *am* dead! I am dead and in a forest. Why am I dead in a forest! I look around frantically. All I can see are trees. Trees are eve-rywhere and forest. The forest is everywhere.

I keep looking around in a panic. *Where the hell am I?* There's no way that I'm dead… my heart must be beating so fast that I just can't feel it. I was in the forest ground, in the middle of the forest, in a trash bag, and buried in the ground. *This has to be a nightmare.* I must have left Nate's house and fallen asleep in the car or at Casey's house. My eyes are wide as I look around. Everything is a blur until it isn't and then out the corner of my eye I see *her*.

CHAPTER 5

I whip my head around and focus on the figure of a woman far away. She has to be about twenty miles away but I can see her clearly as if she is right in front of me. My eyes aren't that great so how can I see her? She stares back at me. She has long black hair and a pretty face. Her skin and eyes are a soft brown. *At least they're not black*, I think to myself. I don't want to see any more black eyes.

The woman is fairly tall, about my height and she looks around my age, maybe a little older. She wears jeans and a tee shirt with a light jacket and tennis shoes. In an instant she is ten miles closer to me. *How did she move that fast?* It is like she moves with the speed of lightening. I remain sitting on the ground, stunned into place. Why is she in the woods? *Is she dead too?*

"You need to feed," she says. How can I hear her so far away? Her voice is as clear as if she were standing right in front of me. *Why does she want me to eat? I'm not hungry.* I just want to know how to get out of this forest and if I am dead or not.

"Did you hear me?" She asks stiffly. "You need to feed now. If you wait too long, you won't be able to control yourself." I have no idea what she is talking about and I still can't find my voice.

"Here... I'll help you," she says and in an instant she is directly in front of me holding out her hand trying to help me up. I recoil slightly. "It's just a hand. It won't hurt. What's your name?" I am still frozen in place with no idea how to talk. She lowers her hand when I don't take it.

"I'm Jade and you are?" So the strange woman now has a name, Jade.

TRANSITION

"Am I dead? Are you dead? Are…we…both dead?" I finally find my voice. She begins laughing. *Why is she laughing?* I don't find anything funny.

"Well I guess you could say that," she says with humor. So we are dead. I don't want to be dead. Sadness starts to grip me.

"So we're dead, in a forest? Why? Is this where all dead people go? Are you like my guide to help me transition?" She is smiling at me. *Why is this funny to her?* Maybe she has been dead for a long time and she finds it funny.

"You know, it's funny you used that word. *Transition.* No I'm not your guide and this," she gestures to our surroundings, "isn't where all dead people go. You have *transitioned* in a sense but you're not dead as in dead and gone in the world." *So she is crazy.* I guess if you meet someone in the woods, they are probably crazy.

"I. Don't. Understand." I say the words slowly, trying to convey the depth of my confusion.

"Do you know what you are," she asks suddenly. *What I am?* Yep, she's crazy.

"I'm a person…," I say slowly. I might have to break things down for her. "As in a human being. A female human being to be exact." She just stares. She looks as if she is about to tell me some grave news.

"No, you're not," she says staring down at me. I probably should get away from her. If she thinks I'm not a person then something must be wrong with her.

"So, if I'm not a human being," I say sarcastically. "What am I? Am I like a ghost or something?" She just stares.

"You're a vampire," she says confidently. *We just went from crazy to psycho.* Vampires don't exist. She is cra-

48

CHAPTER 5

zy and I'm crazy for talking to her. I stand up just then. She continues to stare at me.

"Do you want me to prove it to you… because I can." So she's going to prove vampires exist? Well, I guess I'll let her try and then I'm going to walk away from this crazy woman.

"Fine…prove it to me then." I can't believe I'm going to stand here and let her prove that vampires exist.

At one moment she looks kind and sweet and then the next, she looks scary. Her once brown eyes turn black. I stumble backwards on my feet and fall to the ground. *The eyes… her eyes….* They look like the eyes that are going to haunt me for the rest of my life. I scream. She opens her mouth and I see two of her teeth grow into fangs. Real Fangs! I hear a low growl in her throat.

"Believe me now?" she asks. All I can do is scream. "Be quiet! We are not the only vampires in the world you know!" She retracts her fangs and her eyes turn back to their normal brown color. *What the hell?* I want to cry but no tears fall. *I need to get away from her!*

"I'm not a vampire!" …but she must be.

"Yes you are. If you weren't I'd be tempted to feed on you, and as you can see, I haven't."

"How could I be a vampire," I start to freak out. "I'm dead, aren't I? Or is this a nightmare? I just want to go home! Why am I in the forest? Where am I?" I want to cry so badly but tears just won't fall. She comes closer to me and grabs my arm tightly. I pull back and break free.

"Don't touch me you psycho!" She stares at me.

"Stop whining and come on! You need to feed. I'll find you an animal because there is no way you're ready to feed on a human." *To…what…?*

49

TRANSITION

"FEED ON A HUMAN! Why would I feed on a human?" She starts walking and I stupidly follow. *Why am I following her?*

"Because that's your source of food. Now come on dammit. I'm only helping you because I just can't leave you here."

"Look, I can't be a vampire…alright…I just can't." She keeps walking and shakes her head. "I cannot be some kind of supernatural creature. I mean how do you even become a vampire?"

"We will talk about that after you have fed."

"I need to go home." I cannot stay here with her. *I still think she's crazy.*

"You cannot go home," she says as she stops and looks at me. "Firstly, if you did, you would probably lose control and kill your whole family." *I will not kill my family.* "…And secondly," she says slowly, "you don't age, you live forever. People will start noticing that you're not ageing." *I don't age? I live forever! Sounds like a nightmare disguised as a dream.*

"Do I shine in the light, also?" I ask sarcastically. She frowns. I still am not sure if I believe anything she is telling me.

"You watch way too much TV. I mean, I love the movie but do you believe everything you see on TV?" She starts walking again and I follow. "Look, we can talk more about it when we get to my house, but for now let's be quiet and find you some prey." We don't talk for a while. I just follow her as we walk through the forest. I don't know what has happened to me and maybe she does. Even If I don't think I am a vampire, I can't shake the feeling that she is

CHAPTER 5

right. I'm not going to put my family in danger just in case she is. I am losing my mind.

We walk for what seems forever until she stops. She points straight ahead of her and beckons me to look. About fifteen miles away is a grey wolf. She puts her finger to her mouth telling me to keep quiet. *What the hell does she expect me to do?*

She gestures for me to go to it. I guess she wants me to feed since that is the reason we are still out here. *How am I supposed to do that?* How am I supposed to catch a wolf without getting hurt? *How am I supposed to 'feed'?*

I guess she's fed up with waiting because in an instant she is gone from beside me. I see her go and grab the wolf with ease. The wolf doesn't have a chance. She must be strong. She is back beside me in a flash and with the wolf thrashing and growling in her arms.

"Bite it," she says. *Umm....no!* I shake my head no. "Bite the wolf," she says more forcefully. I bend down and bite the wolf on the neck. I think I did it right, because that's what the vampires in the shows and books do. Nothing happens. I lean back, look at her, and shrug. She sighs.

"You have to use your fangs and by the way, humans can bite into flesh if they tried." *I don't have fangs!* Why can't she understand that?

"I don't have fangs." *I don't want fangs.*

"Yes, you do. Here I'll bite it first and that should trigger your fangs to come out and play." She smiles. So this is a joke to her. My life is a joke. If I have fangs that means everything she said is true. It means that I can't go home to my family. If I have fangs, it means that Nate is a vampire and he turned me into one.

TRANSITION

I see her eyes turn black again and shortly after her fangs come out. I wanted to believe that it was a hallucination, the first time it happened. Now I know it is real. I watch as she bends down and sinks her fangs into the wolf's flesh.

My instinct kicks in and I can smell the wolf's blood. My mouth waters. I can feel my fangs protract in my mouth but I can't feel my eyes change. I'm sure the green color of my eyes has turned into the black color I now despise. I feel dangerous. *I feel strong.* She pulls away from the wolf. It's like nature takes over and before I know it I sink my fangs into the wolf's neck. I can feel Jade's eyes on me but I don't care, because I am feeling a hunger that I didn't even know I had. Everything she told me is true. *Unless this is a nightmare induced from watching a Twilight marathon.*

When I feel I have drained the wolf, I pull away from it. As soon as I sit up I feel my fangs retract. I look at Jade. "Ok, I believe you." Like I have a choice.

"Kind of hard not to isn't it," she says jokingly. She throws the wolf to the side. "Come on, let's go to my house. It's not far from here."

Chapter 6

I can't help feeling sad. I feel like I have just lost everything and gained something that I don't want. I want to yell and scream, but it is as though only one emotion is showing itself...sadness. I am sad and there is no denying it. *What will I do now?*

TRANSITION

I follow Jade to her house and I am grateful that she doesn't talk on the way. I have too much on my mind and I don't want to hold a conversation. What I really want is to be with my family. *Why did Nate do this to me?* Why couldn't he just break up with me like a normal boy? *He's not normal,* I think to myself. *He's a vampire.* I can't believe that I've been dating a vampire. How could I have not noticed he was different? I guess it is because he was totally normal...that is until he wasn't. I should feel angry right now but all my sad and scared feelings are taking over. What will I do now? What will my family do? *I wonder what they are doing right now.* I stop walking. They probably don't even know I'm missing or halfway dead in my case. It can't have been more than a couple of hours since I was crying in the room of my pissed off vampire ex-boyfriend. *What time is it?*

"What time is it? Shouldn't the sun rise at any moment?" I ask Jade.

"No, it's like one in the morning...why would the sun rise this early?"

One in the morning! It has been a whole twenty-four hours? My parents and Casey are probably freaking out right now. "Wow, I was out a whole day?" I can't imagine what my family is thinking. Jade looks at me questionably.

"You have been out for about four days," she says. *Four...days...* I know exactly what my parents are doing. They are planning search parties, yelling at Casey and Nate, putting up missing posters, and probably by now offering a substantially large reward to give anyone who finds me. My family is probably frantic.

I drop to my knees on the forest floor and start breathing heavily. I look out into the dark forest. *I've been gone four days!* I am *so* not ready to accept the fact that my family

CHAPTER 6

probably thinks I'm dead. I continue to stare into the forest as I clutch myself so hard that I feel as if my nails are going to pierce through my skin.

"Is that normal? Why was I out four days? What day is it?" I am slowly losing it. I don't want to believe that I have been missing for four days. I don't want to believe any of this.

"Yep, that's just how long it takes to transition." *Transition... I hate that word.* It is quickly becoming my most hated word. "...And it's Wednesday." *Wednesday!* I start shaking.

I need to see my family. I want to see my family. I need to see how they are doing. Maybe Jade will go with me. If I lose control she can stop me... *I hope.* I can't live without my family. I need them. I want to go home. I want to see my mom, my dad, and my sister. I really want to cry and if I could cry, I would be wailing.

"Get up," Jade says. "You can break down at my house, not in this forest."

"This can't be happening to me," I say hysterically. "I can't be a vampire! This can not be happening to me!" Jade crouches down in front of me and puts her hand on my shoulder.

"You have to pull yourself together. I know that this is all of a sudden and a surprise but you're not alone." Jade helps me to my feet. "Let's go."

We walk at my pace until we finally make it to a small cabin located in the middle of the forest. *Why does she live in the woods?*

"Welcome to Casa de la Jade," she says as if she is showing me around a grand house. The cabin is nowhere near grand. It isn't falling apart or anything but it is really old looking. The wood the house is made of blends in with the forest, probably for protection and camouflage. I can hear a creak not too far behind the cabin. This cabin is definitely fit for someone trying to stay away from the public eye.

Jade opens the door to the cabin and we walk in. *Do all vampires live poorly?* Nate's house is blank and bland, too. The cabin is made up of one room, one closet and a bathroom. There is a bed on the back wall with a burgundy cover and a white pillow on it. The couch in the middle of the room is black and leather. It is odd because it is the only modern piece of furniture in the house. A bookcase full of books is against the wall near the couch. *She reads a lot I guess.* I look towards the door that leads to the bathroom. It is directly across from the bed. *I can't live like this...*

"I know it's not a lot and I know what you're thinking... do all vampires live like this? No, not all vampires live like this. I just prefer to live out here but if I want to go do something in the city, around people, I go out." *She goes out...?*

"Oh...." All I can do is stare at her. She starts laughing.

"I don't live here all the time! I just come here when I don't want to be around people. Believe me, one day you will understand. I have a condo in Denver. It would take about an hour drive to get there from here." *Oh... so not all vampires live poorly.* "It's all high-tech in my condo... I like electronics." She sits down on the couch and I join her. "So what do you want to know? Wait, I still don't know your name or who turned you. I mean I saw the three guys who brought you into the woods and buried you but I don't know which one turned you." *She saw them?*

"My name is Nichole, Nichole Roberts, and you saw

three guys bring me into the woods and bury me?" This is news to me.

"Nichole is a pretty name and yeah I saw two white guys and one black guy." She saw Nate, John, and Tyler?

"Do you know them?" *Maybe she knows them.*

"No, not all vampires know each other. As a matter of fact we don't all get along that well. Not many would have helped you as I have." I wonder why she did then.

"Oh, well the one with the black straight hair and blue eyes was my boyfriend and I didn't even know he was a vampire." I proceed to tell her the story of what happened on my birthday. I tell her about the party and how Nate reacted at the party. When I get to the part about me being at Nate's house, she just shakes her head but she doesn't look shocked. "It was one of the best and worst days of my life. I never expected things to spiral out of control like they did. I never expected any of this." I put my face in my hands. How could this happen to me?

"So he didn't even tell you he was a vampire?" I look up at her and shake my head. "...And he got mad at you because you danced with another guy? I'm sorry that happened to you but to tell you the truth, not many of us get to choose this fate. How did you meet him anyway?" I sigh; I used to like telling this story.

"We met at school. When I first saw him, I thought it was love at first sight. I knew there were new students in school but I had never met any of them. I was walking down the school hallway, to class, when I caught him staring at me. He was standing by the lockers, leaning against them. I instantly knew he was a new student because I had never seen him before. I stopped walking after I noticed him staring. *Is he looking at me,* I thought to myself? I looked behind me because I was sure there was no way he was looking at me. He looked mesmerized, as he stared at me, and I was equally mesmerized. *This guy is gorgeous*, I thought, as he stared at me. He smiled at me and I swear it made my heart jump. I was frozen in place. He closed his locker and walked over to where I stood. He was still smiling when he held out his hand. We introduced ourselves and then he offered to walk me to class. We have been inseparable ever since. I mean we have been inseparable until now. Back then I didn't know his secret. Back then I didn't know he would kill me. I was stupid to trust him." I frown at how much detail I remember about the day Nate and I met.

"We are all stupid in love." I smile at Jade's comment.

"I thought it was, 'We are all fools in love.'" I am sure she has it wrong. She shrugs.

"It doesn't matter. You know the vampire that turned me was in love with me and I had never met him." I stare at her in shock. I wonder what that must have been like.

She tells me that one-day, about ten years ago, this vampire in New York was stalking her. She describes him as tall, dark and handsome. I am surprised she described him as such since he basically ruined her life. She says he followed her everywhere for two weeks. She didn't know what to do. One day, she says, she went out to dinner with her friends to a fancy restaurant. When she and her friends left the restaurant they started walking to a club that was two blocks away. The vampire that had been following her grabbed her and pulled her into an alley. Her friends ran after her but before they could get to her, the vampire turned around and killed all of them. He then turned around back to her. She says he told her that he wanted her and that he wasn't going to hurt her.

CHAPTER 6

She says she screamed as loud as she could but no help came.

"Then he forced me to drink his blood and he bit me," Jade says. "I woke up four days later, a vampire. He said he was following me because he thought I was so beautiful and he wanted to spend forever with me. He tried to control me and he wouldn't let me escape him. The only reason I got away is because he found some other girl that he wanted to be with." She laughs. "Vampire men are almost the same as human men. They leave you when someone younger and more beautiful comes along. After that, I spent most of my time alone." I can't smile at her statement about men. I am still too shocked by her story. At least in my scenario, I am the only person physically hurt. I feel bad for Jade.

"Why did you want to be alone?"

"I said I spent most of my time alone not all of it! I liked it better that way. Plus I had a really hard time adjusting to being a vampire. I wasn't able to control myself at times. Meaning, I have killed some people but I have never turned anyone. After a while I got used to being alone."

"That makes sense." I guess. *She killed some people?*

"I also know how hard it is going it alone. I want to help you. Ask me anything." She smiles. *I don't even know what to ask?*

"So Nate could be out in the daylight. Why is that?" She laughs.

"Like I said, you watch too much TV. We can go out in the daylight." *Oh...that's good.*

"Do we have special powers?" I blurt out the questions before I have a chance to think. It is a stupid question. Jade rolls her eyes.

"We can run fast, we're really strong, we jump high,

59

and we have heightened senses. If you ask me if we can read minds or predict the future, our Q&A is over," she says laughing.

"Is blood the only thing that sustains us?" This is a question to which I really want to know the answer. If I can abstain from drinking blood, I will.

"Well, the Chinese have made a blood substitute for us to drink." *Ha....ha...* She's trying to be funny.

"That's not funny," I say a little irritable. *I feel more than a little irritable.*

"Down girl, your eyes are turning black." *What? No?* "I'm just playing! You should have seen your face! I'm going to go to bed. You can sleep here on the couch and there are some covers and towels in the closet." She stands up, walks to her bed, and lies down under the cover. *So we sleep? That's good I guess.*

"I'm going to use your bathroom first." I need a moment alone.

"We don't use the bathroom!" Oh I didn't realize I hadn't needed to go. That's strange.

"I just want to take a look at myself." I need to see that I still looked like *me.*

"That's understandable...goodnight." I walk to the bathroom and close the door.

I don't look any different. I guess I thought my appearance would have changed. I am still wearing my party outfit. *I need clothes and soon.* I splash some water onto my face to wash away the dirt and use Jade's brush to tame my hair. I want to see what I look like when I am hungry so I force myself to believe I am. I watch as my eyes turn black and my fangs quickly come out. I gasp at myself and jump back when I see my reflection. *I look scary,* but like this, I feel my

CHAPTER 6

strongest. I retract my fangs and watch my eyes turn back green. I'm going to have to get used to this new *me*. I leave the bathroom and lie down on the couch. I cover up with a small blanket that Jade has graciously left out. She is already sleeping.

I know my best friend. She probably hates Nate. No one has heard from me in four days now. Casey is probably hounding on Nate because I am missing. I need to warn her about him. If I know anything now, it is that "angry Nate" likes to kill people. Well, since Nate is a vampire he doesn't need to be angry to kill people. He's a vampire; he's a killer by nature, I tell myself. *You're a killer.*

Tomorrow, I think I'm going to check on my family and warn Casey about Nate.

...

I dream that I am at home with my family. We are laughing and joking with each other. My mom made lasagna for dinner with garlic bread and green beans. The food is delicious and everything is perfect. The doorbell rings and my mom goes to answer it. She comes back and Nate is following her into the kitchen. I get out of my seat and run to hug him. He swings me around in a circle. When he puts me down, I look up at him. His eyes are black and he has fangs like a vampire. I look back at my family but they are gone. *Where is my family?* I look back at Nate and he says, "You are mine... forever." He pulls my head to the side and sinks his fangs into my neck. I scream.

TRANSITION

Chapter 7

I wake up with a start and rub my eyes.
I had the worst dream. It was so detailed and vivid
that I could have sworn it was real. I dreamed that
Nate turned me into a vampire and dumped me in
the woods. I open my eyes and look around my
room, only it isn't my room, it is Jade's cabin.
It wasn't a dream.

TRANSITION

I sit up on the couch and look over at Jade. She is still sleeping. I need to get home and see how my family is doing. *How am I going to find my way home?* I don't even know where I am, other than in the woods somewhere. I have been out for a full four days and today is Wednesday. Nate and his friends are probably at school so they won't see me. I get off the couch very slowly so I won't wake Jade. She said we have heightened senses, so I am just hoping that I can get away without waking her. But, as soon as I stand up, she wakes up.

"Where are you going," she asks as she sits up in the bed rather quickly. So I guess it's hard to sneak up on or away from a vampire. *I could lie...* but I decide on the truth.

"I'm going to check on my family." She gives me a look that says no I'm not. "Look, I'm not going to make contact. I just need to see them."

"You know," she says slowly, "Those guys just left you in the woods. If a vampire wants to make another, they just don't leave their, for the lack of a better word, "child" in the woods." I consider her words.

"What are you saying? You don't think that Nate meant to make me a vampire?" If he didn't, that means he was really trying to end my life.

"It's possible. He was probably trying to kill you and was being sloppy about it. He probably doesn't even know you're a vampire." *Sloppy*, I think to myself, *isn't even a word that would come to mind in connection with the word vampire.*

"How do you make a vampire?" Making a vampire must be easy if she says he was being sloppy.

"Well in order for a person to be turned, they have to have some vampire blood and venom in their system. Venom comes from our bites but we have to feed the blood to a human. After that, we have to kill the person or they have to die somehow. The combination of vampire blood and venom causes a person to turn. I don't know why or the science of it, I just know that's how it's done. Do you know how you got his blood in your system?"

I thought over her words. I remember biting into his hand, then feeling something sharp on my neck, and then blacking out. Maybe that's how I got his blood. I bit into his hand. I guess it doesn't matter how much vampire blood you have because I couldn't have possibly got a lot of it. I don't remember anything after. I blacked out and then woke up four days later. I wish I knew what happened.

"He had his hand on my mouth so I bit it. That's how I got his blood in my system." If what she is saying was true, then Nate was really trying to kill me, not turn me. He would have fed me his blood if he were trying to turn me. Or maybe he knew I drew blood? "Maybe you're right. Maybe Nate was trying to kill me."

"I could be wrong… are you willing to take the chance that I am?" *I really don't want to take that chance and I don't want to be anywhere near him.*

"He and his friends are probably at school anyway and I need to go check on my family."

"All right, but I'm going with you," she says as she hops out the bed. "This is really a bad idea because I highly doubt that you will like what you see." We put our shoes on and walk outside. The forest is beautiful in the daylight. I can see everything in so much detail. It is amazing.

"Ready to Run? We can move really fast when we want to."

"How do I do it?"

TRANSITION

"There's not really a method…you just do it. Let's go."
Here goes nothing.

…And then we are off. It feels like flying through the woods. It is exhilarating. We speed past the trees at an unnatural pace, yet I can see everything clearly. Running this fast feels like freedom. I am so caught up in how fast I can run, that I don't even notice that I have stopped paying attention to where I am going. Then suddenly, I hit a tree.

"Oh my gosh," I say as I stand up quickly. I didn't hurt myself, but I hit the tree so hard that it falls down and knocks into another tree. It is like a domino effect until one tree is too strong to be knocked down.

"Nichole! Pay attention next time. You cannot close your eyes and run," Jade chastises. Then she starts laughing. "But that was funny."

"Oops, my bad." I might be the first vampire that has ever run into a tree *by accident*. It is pretty funny.

"Come on, and no more running into trees." I roll my eyes and start running again.

Jade leads me through the rocks and trees of the forest. We run miles in seconds. *I wonder how far I was dropped off in the forest?* We are pretty far away from where I live so I guess they traveled far to bury me. When we get close enough to the city to see it, we stop. *Running this fast is amazing.*

"It's amazing that we can see when we are so far away," I say in awe.

"Yea it is… so where do you live?"

"This way," I point to my right. "Follow me."

We run until we get a little behind the tree line, in front of my house. Jade stays quiet while I observe my family through the house's windows. They all look sad, worse than

CHAPTER 7

sad. They look broken. I wish I could go to them and comfort them but I know that would be a bad idea. I watch as Tiffany is bent over the breakfast counter crying, while my mom comforts her.

"It's going to be ok sweetie," my mom says sadly. "I'm sure we will find her." *They will never find me.*

"What if she's gone for good, mom?" Tiffany cries. "What if she's dead?" She chokes on the last word and breaks out into an uncontrollable cry. Tiffany is holding on a bear I had got her for her birthday one year.

"Aw baby don't cry..." my mom says but as soon as she says it, she starts crying. Tiffany sits up and gives her a hug. "I'm sorry, Tiff, I need to be strong for you.

"It's ok, mom," Tiffany cries. "It's ok for both of us to cry." I look to my dad's study. My dad is on the phone yelling at a policeman about how incompetent they are since they haven't found me.

"What do you mean you have no leads? This is my daughter we are talking about! Well, well, you better try harder," my dad says. He slams the phone on its receiver. He paces back and forth while running his hands through his hair. He goes to close his study door and slams it shut. He looks stressed as he continues to pace. Then suddenly, he starts to silently cry and sinks to his knees.

"Where are you, Nicky," my dad whispers and continues to cry quietly.

It is beginning to get really hard to watch them. They are so sad, and in so much pain. I want to just go to them and explain everything. Why can't I be with my family, even though I am a vampire?

"I need to go see them," I say quickly and try to run to the house. Jade tackles me to the ground.

TRANSITION

"No you can't," Jade says. "You cannot go see them! You're a vampire!" I look at my family again. All I can hear are their cries for me.

"Look at them Jade! Don't you hear them crying?" I look away. *I'm going to kill Nate.* I'm going to kill him for doing this to me. I am going to kill him and his friends. I dig my fingers into the ground and bare my teeth. I'm going to kill them just because they didn't help me, and before I kill John, I'm going to laugh in his face like he laughed in mine. I don't feel sad or scared anymore. *I am angry.*

"Don't let the anger consume you, Nichole." How does she know what I'm thinking? "I know you're angry because your fangs are out. Also, your eyes are black. Vampires' eyes turn black when they're angry, when they're about to attack as well as when you want to feed on someone. Attacking and feeding are two actions that aren't really that different though." *That makes sense.*

I look back at my family and my home. They put signs in the front yard that read **Missing, Nichole Roberts, age 18.** They put a number to call and offered a ten thousand dollar reward for anyone who can find me. The picture they put on the flyer is one from my birthday. I look pretty in my black dress, I look happy. *I was happy…now I'm angry.* Nate is going to pay for this.

I turn away from my family and run deep into the forest. When I feel like I've gotten far enough, I drop to my knees and scream. I scream over and over again. My breaths heave in and out. I want to cry so badly. I sense Jade behind me.

"Why can't I cry," I growl. *I have never growled before.* She walks around me and stands in front of me. I look up at her.

CHAPTER 7

"Calm down..." *Calm. Down. Really?* There is no way I am calming down. "You can't cry because you don't have any tears." I...Don't...Have...Tears? Is there anything else I don't have?

"I'm going to kill him...I'm going to kill him and all his friends," I say with a cold voice. *My voice scares me.* "Well, are you going to help me or not?" I don't know what I expect her to say. *Yes...No...Maybe?* She looks out into the forest and is silent.

"Yeah," she says with confidence, "I'll help you. If it were the other way around I would want you to help me too. Let's get those bastards." *But how?* I pull myself together after a moment. There is something I need to do.

TRANSITION

Chapter 8

Jade is going to protest when I tell her what I need to do but I don't care. I need to warn my friend Casey about Nate and his friends. I know that whatever story Nate told, Casey won't believe it. She is in serious danger of angering a murderous vampire and I don't want her fate to be like mine or worse. I don't want Casey to get killed.

"I need to go see my friend Casey."

"Who?"

TRANSITION

"She's my best friend and if Nate kills the people that piss him off, she will be dead... *soon.*" *I know she's giving him a hard time.*

"Oh... so you want to actually make contact with her...absolutely not." Jade crosses her arms. She looks adamant. *She can't stop me.*

I look down at my wrist. I still have the charm bracelet on that my parents bought me. I look at the charm with the picture of my family and me and then I look at the one of Casey and me. I am glad I still have the charm bracelet. It makes me feel just a little closer to them. *I'm sorry*, I think. *I wish they could hear it.* I look up at Jade.

"Let's go," I say.

I run to Casey's house. Jade follows me and nags me the whole way about how this is a very bad idea. I'm not surprised that Casey is at home. They probably let her off school a couple of days to mourn my disappearance. I don't hear anybody else at home so her mom must be at work.

"How will we get in?" I ask Jade. I can see Casey through her living room window. *She looks miserable.*

"I have no clue! This is a really bad idea!" I pace back and forth. How will we get in her house without breaking in? *I have an idea!*

"Do you have a phone Jade?" *Please have a phone.*

"Of course, I have a phone!" I give her Casey's number to call and tell her what to say. Casey picks up on the third ring.

"Hello?" I hear Casey say. She sounds like she'd been crying for days.

"Hi, is this Casey Neal?" Jade asks nervously. *Why is she nervous?*

"Speaking," Casey replies with a sniffle.

CHAPTER 8

"Hi, my name is Jade and I have some information about your friend Nichole, Nichole Roberts." Casey sits upright on her living room couch. "But it needs to be between you and me." She stands up from the couch.

"O...K...," Casey paces back and forth biting her nails. "What is it? Why didn't you call the police?"

"Tell her that it can't be over the phone. Tell her it has to be in person," I whisper to Jade.

"I can't tell you over the phone. It has to be in person. Can I come by your house? I'm not a psycho killer or anything... I'm telling you the truth." I roll my eyes. Casey pauses for a second. She is quiet.

"Fine..." Casey finally says. "It needs to be in the day time though. You can not come over at night."

"I understand," Jade says. "Where do you live?"

"Well, I'm glad you don't know already..." I tune out as Casey gives Jade her address. I'm glad Jade asked Casey what her address was even though we are standing in the woods, right in front of her house.

We wait thirty minutes before Jade walks around the block and then proceeds to walk the sidewalk that leads to Casey's house. The plan is that when Casey opens the door, I am to use my newfound speed to get into the house quickly so no one will see me. Jade finally makes it to Casey's door and rings the doorbell. Casey opens the door.

"Hi, I'm Jade." Casey looks Jade up and down and then steps out of the way to let her in. I take my chance and I run in Casey's house as fast as I can.

"That was some breeze," Casey says as she closes the door. She turns toward Jade and freezes.

"Nichole..." Casey sobs, "Is it really you?" I freeze, too.

TRANSITION

I freeze because I have this undeniable urge to sink my fangs into Casey's neck. I can smell her blood. It smells like cinnamon or something close to cinnamon. Whatever the smell is, it is mouthwatering. I can hear the blood pumping in her arteries and I can see the steady pulse under her skin. My eyes must have turned black because Casey screams. A second later, I feel my fangs protract. Before I can even stop myself, I am lunging at Casey. Jade is the only reason my fangs don't connect with Casey's neck. Jade knocks me to the floor and stands to block me from Casey's path. I recover myself quickly and stand in a crouching position.

"Nichole! What is wrong with you! What's wrong with your eyes," Casey cries. I zone out and stand up straight.

'What the hell is wrong with you, Nate? What's wrong with your eyes!' His eyes....his eyes were so black. I can see the same fear that I had that night in Casey's eyes. I quickly realize what I am about to do to my best friend and my fangs retract.

"I'm...I'm sorry, Casey. I didn't mean to scare you?" Casey drops to her knees crying. Jade is still standing guard. "I'm fine, Jade."

"You're not fine Nichole. You almost killed your best friend. *This* is what I was trying to warn you about." Jade is pissed, I can tell by the way she is looking at me.

"What happened to you, Nichole," Casey says between sobs. She looks at me expectantly. I don't know what to tell her so I say the only thing that comes to mind.

"Nate did this to me." It isn't an answer to her question, but it is the first explanation that I can give. I have no idea what she will think if I tell her I am a vampire. She is my best friend and I don't want to lose her.

CHAPTER 8

"Nate did what exactly," Casey says. *She won't believe me.* I take a deep breath and blurt the answer.

"He turned me into a vampire." She looks lost.

"A vampire..." Casey says with uncertainty. "...And how did he do that and why would you let him? Do you even know what your family and I have been going through the last couple of days?" Casey goes from scared and sad to furious in a matter of seconds. "So you just want to play vampire with Nate! Is he that important to you?" Her last statement hurt me but I don't let it show.

"He's a vampire and I think he tried to kill me but ended up turning me by accident. I didn't choose this! This was forced upon me! It was against my will! I don't even think Nate knows I'm still alive...well sort of alive anyway." Casey stands up and wipes the tears off her face.

"Sorry, I should have known you wouldn't put your family or me through pain on purpose. Well, I would say you were crazy but I just saw what looked like fangs pop out your mouth. What happened to you, Nichole? ...And are you one too?" Casey turns and looks directly at Jade.

"Yes I am. I've been helping your friend with this difficult change. I told her coming to see you was dangerous but she insisted that you needed to be warned about Nate and his friends."

"John and Tyler are vampires too, aren't they?" Casey asks shocked. I nod my head yes. "Oh...wow...ok," Casey says in disbelief. "Tell me what happened, Nichole."

We go to Casey's room and I spend almost an hour explaining what happened to me after I drove from her house to Nate's house that day. Throughout the whole conversation I have to constantly keep my urges to feed on Casey in check. Focusing on not feeding on Casey is harder than I thought it would be. *Jade was right about not going to see my family.*

Casey shakes her head in disbelief as I replay the details of Nate's attack on me. She wants to know how it felt to transition into a vampire, but all I can remember is that it is was dark and it felt like I didn't exist anymore. I tell her how I felt like there was nothing anymore. When I get to the part about meeting Jade, she smiles. I guess she is happy that I have someone to help me. Her happiness fades when I reach the end of my story. I guess that everything I told her starts to settle in her mind because Casey is furious.

"I could kill Nate...if I could, I mean," Casey says enraged. *Me too...*

"What's been going on with my family and this whole situation? I mean, what happened when you all figured out I was missing?" I say anxiously. This is something I really want to know but also something that I know I won't like.

Casey tells me she waited all day for me to come over to her house the next day. She says she called and texted constantly but my phone wasn't working. She got really nervous. At about ten that night my parents called her to tell her that it was time for me to come home. They were shocked when she told them that I wasn't with her. Casey told them that she would call Nate to see where I was. Nate told her that he thought I was with her. *The liar.* She says she went to her mom and told her mom everything. Her mom was so furious, and she called my parents and told them that they should come over to their house. When my parents made it to Casey's house that night, Casey says she told them everything. They couldn't believe that Casey and I had pulled this stunt on them.

They called the police and Nate. The police came over to Casey's house, and Nate showed up shortly after. Casey

CHAPTER 8

replayed the story to the police, my parents and sister, her mom, and Nate again and again. She showed them the text I sent when I made it to Nate's house, and then the questioning turned toward Nate. *Nate's lying ass* told everyone that when I made it over to his house I came in, saw his friends, and blew up at him for having his friends over. He then said I took the necklace off he gave me, threw it down, yelled that I was leaving the house and him, and left to go to Casey's house.

On the next day, the police found my car abandoned in some ally with the keys in the ignition and the driver's door wide open. In the car, they found my phone, my overnight bag, and whatever else I kept in the car. She says that she never believed what Nate said and that she has been giving him a piece of her mind. *Just like I thought.* When Casey finally finishes explaining everything to me, I am having a hard time keeping my anger from not boiling over. *Nate's not going to get away with this.*

"Your family has been devastated," Casey says. "They have been organizing search parties, putting up flyers, and constantly calling the police all day long. They won't even speak to me, Nichole." *I didn't know that...*

"I'm sorry. If I could go back in time, I would have got out of the car when I dropped you off and just spent a night at your house." I will regret my decision to go to Nate's probably for the rest of my now immortal life.

"Looking back at what happened to you," Casey says slowly, "There was no way you could have outrun this. If he didn't get you then, he probably would have got you later." *Yeah, she's right. I wouldn't have even known he was a vampire if I had made different decisions. I would be in the same situation no matter what, or probably worse, I would be*

77

dead. I want to cry...

"We're going to go kill him, you know," Jade adds.

"You are," Casey asks looking back and forth between Jade and me. "How are you going to do that? How do you kill a vampire?" *That's a good question.* Both Casey and I look at Jade.

"You could behead him, or burn him, or stake him in the heart with a wooden stake," Jade says smoothly.

"Don't believe her, she likes to tease me about watching vampire entertainment movies and TV shows." Casey laughs.

"I'm telling the truth..." Jade says offended. *Oh...* "Well the wooden stake part is false." Jade smiles and I roll my eyes.

"That does seem a little cliché," I say, and Casey agrees with a nod of her head.

"Say's the girl who thought we had magical powers," Jade says with sarcasm. Casey laughs.

"So what can vampires do that humans can't," Casey asks curiously.

"Well as far as I know we have extremely heightened senses, we are hard to kill, and we are deadly." After what Nate did to me and after how I reacted to Casey, there is no doubt that we are deadly.

"There are old myths about ancient vampires having powers of telekinesis and probably other stuff, but like I said they're myths. Like I said we don't have special powers," Jade says suddenly, shocking both Casey and me.

"Really," Casey and I say in unison.

"How do you know that?" I ask.

"Even though I've been a loner, I've run into other vampires since I've been turned. I asked questions, got

CHAPTER 8

answers, and then we went our separate ways."

"So, tell us more about these myths," Casey insisted.

"Well, the myths say that some ancient vampires had powers and were able to pass them down to the next vampire they made. Not all vampires were believed to have powers and none have shown any signs of powers either, so it's probably vampire folklore." *Interesting.* "Or maybe the myth was that the strongest of all vampires had powers?" *She doesn't know at all...*

"So, it's all fairytale then. On a more serious note, can we spend a night here?" I ask quickly.

"Sure," Casey says.

"Are you sure that's a good idea," Jade interrupts. "Isn't your mom coming home soon? We wouldn't want this baby vampire to lose control," she says pointing her thumb at me. "I wouldn't want you or your mom becoming dinner for an uncontrollable vampire." I get the feeling she is taking shots at me.

"I *can* control myself! I haven't attacked Casey yet... again anyway."

"Nichole, I'm so happy to see you and also sad because I'm the only one that gets to know you're alive...well somewhat anyway...but Jade's right. You're new to this vampire thing and from what I saw earlier, you're not in control yet. You should have seen yourself. It was like your animal instinct took over or something."

"Ok, well we will see you tomorrow or something if you need to reach us, call Jade's phone...alright," I say sadly. *I'm not ready to leave.*

"Alright," Casey says as she stands up and walks us to the door. "Nichole," she says and I look at her. "You're still my best friend, and I love you."

TRANSITION

"I love you, too." Jade opens the door and we leave. We wait in the woods until we hear Casey's door lock and then we take off towards Jade's cabin.

Chapter 9

"You really need to change out of your clothes,"
Jade says as we are making our way to her cabin in the
forest. "I mean, look at what you're wearing!" I look
down at myself. *I'm still wearing my party dress and
shoes.* I am a little dirty but at least my feet don't hurt
from the heels and I've had them on for five days.

"I don't have any spare clothes and I doubt my
folks will leave the house anytime soon." I do need to
change. I look like a 'missing girl' dressed like this.

TRANSITION

"Come on let's go to the mall and get you some clothes." *To the mall? I can't be seen around here!* "Well, *I'm* going to go to the mall to buy you some clothes. You, on the other hand, are going to wait for me in the woods. If you spot those guys, you need to run back to the cabin. Three on one is not a good combination. Remember, we can see really well and far away. So, if you can see them, they can see you." Even the slightest mention of Nate and his friends have my emotions raging.

"Ok, Let's go." What would have been a fifteen minute drive to the mall is less than a five minute run for us. Jade stops far behind the tree line and looks at me.

"You stay here and I'll be back." I give her my sizes and tell her what I like to wear. I tell her she doesn't have to buy me much, but she just shrugs it off and says she has more than enough money. "Remember what I said," she says and then she is gone. *At least I will be able to get out of this dress soon.*

I look around the forest while I wait for Jade to come back. The trees are so tall and everything is so green. *Jade said we could jump high.* I brace myself to jump and give it a try. I feel a strong power in my legs as I lift off the ground, and for a second I think I am about to fly. I lean my head back and stretch out my arms in mid air. I embrace the feeling of being so high up. Before I get too high off the ground, I grab on to a thick branch on a tree to my left. *Wow, that is amazing!* I crawl up the branch and lean against the tree. I look down to the ground. I am really high up. *I'll wait for Jade up here.*

I find my mind drifting off in thought of Nate. *I want him to pay.* Nate will pay for what he has done to my family and me. I sigh. I will miss being human and alive. *I will miss my family and Casey.* I will miss chocolate pancakes and cheese dip. I will miss my sister growing up into a beautiful young lady. I probably can't have children so I will miss out on having my own family. That thought alone really makes me sad. I wish I could have a family of my own. I've always wanted to get married one day and to have a family. I've always wanted to fall in true and honest love. *Will I be able to find love in this new life?* Do I want it after what Nate did to me? *Of course you do,* I tell myself. Now I know what Nate and I had wasn't love; it wasn't real. Maybe there will be happiness… *What is that smell?*

I look back, opposite the mall, and see a young couple walking a trail in the woods hand in hand. They smell delicious. I can't help myself; I drop down from the tree and land gracefully and with no sound. I run past them and watch as they recover from what they think is wind. I hide behind a tree near them. *They smell so good.* I can just taste them, they smell so good. I creep around the tree so I can see them. Just then, the boy walks up to a tree carving their names in it with his back turned away from the girl. *Perfect time.* I run with instantaneous speed, grab the girl by the neck, and before she can scream I run far away from the boy. She keeps fighting but I am too strong and she can't scream. I feel my fangs grow out and sink my fangs in her neck. *Oh my gosh,* she tastes so good! I lose myself in that moment.

An instinct to defend myself creeps up. I know someone is running towards me. Before I can defend myself, the person knocks me over and I drop the girl. She falls to the ground unmoving.

Jade has finally come back. She is the one that knocked me over. Jade has pissed the vampire in me off because we are fighting on the forest floor, fangs out and all. I almost get close to biting into her throat when she pushes me back and sucker punches me in the jaw. I fall to the ground and my mind finally clears. *What the hell am I doing!*

"What the hell, Nichole," Jade screams. "You almost killed that poor girl!" *What have I done?*

Jade walks over to the girl and checks her pulse. I am frozen looking at the scene in front of me. *I almost killed her!* In the distance I can hear the boy calling her name.

"Jessica! Jessica, where are you," he yells. He keeps yelling her name. He sounds frantic, like he's lost someone he really loves.

"She will be ok, her pulse is fine, she should wake up soon." *What about my fang marks?*

"Will she have bite marks on her neck?" I ask hesitantly.

"Your fang marks are gone. The venom in our bites heals the bite when we pull out." *Oh...how...convenient.* "Let's go take her to the boy. Get the bags." *What? Why?*

I guess Jade dropped the bags when she attacked me for feeding on the Jessica girl. She picks the girl up and I grab the bags. We find the boy easily, especially since he is yelling. Jade is about lay her down near him when he pulls out a knife in shock. Jade is so close to him that when he swings the knife at her, he cuts her deep in the arm. *That's going to need stitches.*

"Stop that," she says calmly while looking at him directly in the eyes. He does. "Put the knife away." He puts the knife safely up. "Jessica got dehydrated and passed out... Alright? Now take her and go home." He nods his head and takes Jessica away from Jade.

"Hey thanks, I thought I lost her. Have a good day," he says as he walks away with Jessica in his arms. *What just*

CHAPTER 9

happened?

"I'm sorry," I say to Jade. She takes half of the bags from me and shakes her head.

"Don't be sorry. It's a part of your nature. Now imagine if we were at Casey's and you let your guard down in your sleep?" *Oh...* "You know, you are really like a baby. You have to get older, in a sense, to be able to control yourself."

I don't say anything as we make our way back to the cabin. I am too ashamed to talk. I can't help it but I am constantly thinking about how great Jessica's blood tasted. If I compare it to the wolf, the wolf is garbage and Jessica is a home cooked meal. I don't want to be this way. Jade says it is a part of my nature, but how can hurting someone be a part of my nature? *Because you're a vampire...* This is Nate's fault! I feel the anger build in me again. It feels like I'm going to explode.

"Calm down," Jade says breaking my concentration. *She can see my eyes...*

I feel so out of control sometimes. It is like I am losing myself and becoming someone new. *I am someone new...* and now I have to figure out who that is. I will get right to figuring myself out after I kill Nate. I look over at Jade and see that there is no longer a cut on her arm.

"Your arm isn't cut anymore." She looks at me questionably. "He cut you on your arm... really badly I might add." She looks at her arm and shrugs.

"Oh yea...it's healed. I didn't even feel it." *That's cool.*

"Oh..." I say intrigued.

We make it to Jade's cabin around eight at night. When

we get in the cabin she dumps all the clothes she has bought on the bed.

"I got me a few things, also," Jade says as I start looking through the pile of clothes that is mine.

Jade has bought me three pairs of skinny jeans, one black, one blue, and one light blue. There are three different color tee shirts—white, black, and red. I also have a few stylish tops, a peach sundress, some underwear, and a short tight looking leather dress. I hold up the leather dress and look at her with confusion.

"We might go to a club or party or something," she explains. *Partying is not on my to do list...* "Oh, and here are a pair of tennis shoes." She hands me a shoebox with white tennis shoes in them.

"Thanks for the clothes." Along with the clothes, she bought me some body wash, shampoo, a toothbrush and some toothpaste, also. "So vampires do clean themselves up?" I feel like I am asking a stupid question.

"Of course! We might not ever smell or get funky because we have no sweat or tears, but we can still look dirty." *That makes sense.*

I go into Jade's bathroom and run the water in the bathtub. Then a thought comes in mind. *Where is the water coming from?* We're in the middle of the woods! I lean out the bathroom.

"How do you have plumbing out here, Jade?" She looks at me.

"I have my connections," she says and continues to read the book she got from her bookshelf. Ok, then. *Still doesn't make sense.*

I go back into the bathroom and look at myself in the mirror. I look different now. I look stronger. I even think I look older, even though I haven't grown in five days. My hair is dirty and I look like I got drunk and slept in the woods. I take my birthday dress off along with my underwear and get in the tub. *I will burn that dress.* I can't believe I bought nice underwear for Nate. I lay in the bathtub and sink under the water. I probably can stay under here all day without drowning. I close my eyes and relax. *How am I going to kill Nate?* I know that Jade told me how a vampire can be killed but how will I get the chance? I need a plan and fast. I lay in the tub, under water, for about an hour. After I wash my hair and myself I put my underwear on.

No pajamas?

Well, I guess I really don't need them. I put on my light colored skinny jeans and the black tee shirt. *No lotion?* I probably won't get ashy anyway. I put a towel on my head to dry my hair. When I finish I brush it out and brush my teeth. *Can't have my mouth smelling like blood...yuck. I'm hungry.* I can't believe I'm hungry. *I just fed!* If I have to go out and hunt some wild animal, I will get dirty again. *I just washed up!* I put my dirty clothes in a bag and walk out the bathroom. I place the bag on the floor and walk over to Jade's bed. She looks up at me.

"What?" Jade asks.

"I'm hungry, and not really for animal." There I said it. I said it to her and to myself.

"Well... I don't feed on humans and I don't think you should either," Jade says evenly. "I adopted you, you live under my roof, and you will abide by my rules. Do you understand young lady?" *What?* Anger flares inside me. *Who does she think she is?* Then suddenly she starts laughing.

"Oh my gosh... you have got to get your emotions in check," she says while laughing. "I really don't feed on humans but that's my personal choice." She pauses deep in thought. "Put the leather dress on, do your make-up, and let's go to a club." I look at her questionably. "You said you don't want animal and I can't let you feed on a human alone."

"Why a club?"

"…Because it's less suspicious if you're in a club full of drunk humans and it's like an all you can eat buffet. Get dressed! I want to party anyway."

"Why are you in such a mood to party?"

"…Because… if we are going to take on three vampires soon, there is a chance we could both die. Might as well have a little fun before then." I roll my eyes. It is set in stone in my mind that they will die and we will live. No exceptions.

Chapter 10

We are ready to go to the club an hour later.

We leave the cabin and I follow Jade to wherever we are headed. We arrive at a club called Red Waters at about twelve midnight. Red Waters is located on the outskirts of Rosenburg. The club looks pretty high-end for a club on the outskirts, but I guess a lot of money comes from travelers.

The Red Waters is a huge two-story building that looks like a small mansion made of stone. It has a two-story balcony that surrounds the entire building. A blue glow illuminates from the balcony. A fancy sign on the outside of the building flashes the name of the club from red to blue.

TRANSITION

We are walking towards the building when Jade suddenly pulls me to the side.

"Ok, whenever you find your meal take them into the bathroom and feed on them in the stall. Do not drain them dry, and do not feed on them until they pass out. When you're finished, look them in the eye and tell them to forget it. You have to look them directly in the eye. When you look them directly in the eyes, you can control their minds. I'm not going to follow you around or go with you to feed because you have got to learn control on your own but if you're in there too long, I'm coming to get you. Got it?" I nod my head in approval. *Yes mother.* Jeez she can be uptight sometimes.

"I got it. I got it. Let's go, I'm starving."

We start towards the club doors that are spilling red light through its cracked opening. There is a huge line blocked off from the entrance by a black velvet rope. The line continues from the front of the club to somewhere in the back. One bouncer stands on each side of the front doors. Every once in a while, one of the bouncers will let a few girls that aren't in line into the club. Some of the people in line groan when it happens. I guess he is judging by beauty or something. The prettier girls get in without having to wait in line. It is either that or it is the raunchiest dressed girls that do. The other bouncer, closest to the velvet rope will, every once in a while, let in a few people that are standing in line.

I look down at my outfit. I am wearing the black, short, leather dress that Jade bought for me. The dress top slants across my torso and then drifts into one sleeve on my right shoulder. It is super tight and it stops just below my butt. I have on the same red pumps that I wore for my birthday, since those are the only heels I have. My hair is loose and

CHAPTER 10

hangs in loose curls. I went for a smoky look with my make up with some red lipstick. It makes me look mysterious and hot. The only thing I am carrying with me is a small black leather clutch with studs on one side of it. Jade is wearing a harlot red dress that is so raunchy it looks like she is going to stand on a corner for cash. She still looks good but I would never wear it. She has on red platforms with black colored heels. Her hair is straight and she has on minimal make up. I take another quick glance at Jade and then myself. If these outfits don't get us in, I don't know what will.

We walk right up to the velvet rope and without a word the bouncer lets us in. The interior of the club is nice. A bar takes up the whole right side of the bottom level. Red glowing light streams from beneath the bar and throughout the whole bottom floor. Stylish black bar chairs accompany the glowing bar while a decorative assortment of alcohol lies behind it. I turn towards the dance floor. It is filled with people dancing to the booming music. The dance floor looks like it has red water flowing through it. I know it's a fancy floor but it almost looks like there is a red pool blocked off by glass in the middle of the club. The walls around the club are red and the borders around the dance floor are black. I look at all the people in the club. Some of them are being very inappropriate and some are so drunk they need to go home. I can smell the alcohol seeping through the skin of every drunken person. I can also smell all the blood running through each and every person's veins. It's almost overwhelming. Well maybe that's an understatement but I can handle it. Suddenly, Jade grabs my arm.

"What," I ask.

"Are you ok? There are a lot of people here."

I think I am doing pretty well with my self-control even

though it isn't easy.

"Yeah, I'm good. I want to go upstairs and look around. This club is beautiful." The glowing lights can put someone in a trance alone.

"Your eyes are more sensitive to detail." *Interesting...*

We walk through the crowd of people toward the stairs. As we make our way to the stairs, some guy grabs me on the booty. *How rude.*

"Hey sexy lady, you want to join me on the dance floor," the man says. The man is wearing a button down gray shirt that is halfway open and black jeans. He is sloppy drunk and looks like he is going to fall out soon.

"Put your hands on me again, and I will break them," I say sternly. For some reason his comment along with his action really pisses me off.

"Calm down, Nichole," Jade says. The man puts his hands up in surrender. Suddenly, Jade grabs my arm and pulls me through the crowd. He had better be glad she pulled me away, because he was about to become my first meal.

In the back left corner of the club is a wide spiral staircase. There are people packed on it from the bottom to the top. We are going to have to squeeze through all those bodies. This is not going to be easy.

We walk up the stairs to the second floor weaving through all the people. When we make it to the top, I see that there are just as many people on the top floor as on the bottom floor. The second floor is similar to the bottom with the exception of the blue glow, instead of red, and a circular bar, instead of a long straight one. The bar is positioned in the center of the room. It forms a complete circle with a small door that allows the bartenders to walk through. All the alcohol bottles are placed tastefully in the direct center of the bar in a wedding cake like formation. The upstairs dance floor is everywhere that the bar isn't and, just like on the first floor, it looks like blue water flows through the area. This is by far the most fancy looking club I have ever seen, or been to.

"Hey I'm going to go back down to the red floor," Jade says trying to get my attention. I am so enchanted by the design of the club I don't notice that she is talking to me. "There was this guy staring at me; he was kind of cute and I wanted to go and dance with him. You be good Nichole. If you need me just whisper my name. I can hear you. Oh, and there are bathrooms on both floors." Jade walks back down the stairs to the red floor and leaves me up on the blue floor.

I look around nervously. *How am I going to do this?* I walk over to the bar and sit down on the barstool. A bartender walks up to me immediately. He has bleached blonde hair, blue eyes, and looks like a male model. "Are you twenty-one young lady?" he asks. His eyes look skeptical as he looks me up and down.

I don't have an ID and, of course, I'm not twenty-one so I will have to do the only thing I can think of. I look him in the eyes.

"Yes, I am, and I'm no young lady," I say seductively. The bartender has this blank look for a second and then it's gone.

"Well then, what can I get for you beautiful," he asks. *Beautiful!* He smiles at me when my face registers shock at the word beautiful. His smile is beautiful.

"Can I get…?" I look at the bar menu. "A red water please." A drink named after the club…*Hmm.*

"Our club's signature drink coming right up." He starts to fix my drink. It is amazing how bartenders can make 'fixing a drink' creative. "I don't think I've seen you before, do you come out to Red Waters often?" I look at the blonde bartender and try to figure out what to say.

"Well…I guess…I mean no. This is my first time here. Is it that obvious?"

He smirks at my response.

"No it's not. I just haven't seen you before. I think I would remember someone as beautiful as you." I smile.

"Thank you." He continues to make my drink as I wait.

"Can I drink alcohol?" I whisper so low that only Jade will be able to hear me. She is somewhere down stairs.

"Try it and see," she whispers back. *Try it and see?* Why must she be so taciturn?

The waiter hands me my drink. The drink has two layers a blue layer on the top that is accompanied by ice cubes, and a red one on the bottom. *Just like the club…*how creative. I take a sip of the drink. It is strong. *How can I drink this?* Being a vampire is so confusing.

I am finishing up my drink when a man in a black shirt and blue jeans sits right beside me. He is nice looking and all but I can tell he is a little drunk. He leans against the bar and gets the bartender's attention. He orders bourbon and then turns to smile at me.

"Hey sexy, what brings you out tonight?" He directs the question to me.

"Hunger," I say. It isn't a lie but I'm sure he takes it the wrong way. His heart beat speeds up a little and his smile widens. There is no way he can know I am a vampire.

"I think you're hungry for me." Ugh… I'm so not hungry for him in particular but I play along. "Maybe we can go somewhere and ease that hunger. What do you say?" He is being so forward that I'm not going to decline. He is going to be my first meal tonight.

CHAPTER 10

"Buy me another one of these drinks and it's a yes." His eyes widen for a second in shock and then he gestures for the bartender.

"Can I help you, sir?" the blonde bartender who helped me asks.

"Get this beautiful young lady another..." He looks at me for my drink's name. I lift the glass.

"Red Water," I say confidently.

"Red Water, please," he repeats.

"Coming right up...and sir," the blonde bartender says grabbing the man's attention. "...She's not a young lady." The bartender turns and starts making another Red Water. The man looks at the bartender in confusion. I almost burst out laughing.

"So, what's your name sexy?" The man asks turning his attention to me. I don't want to give this man my name. First of all, I'm a missing girl. Second of all, I am about to feed on him and I don't want him knowing who I am in case he remembers me somehow.

"Why bother with names... names come with too much baggage," I say with a smile. *That should work right?*

"I like you. You're absolutely right. What happens at Red Waters stays at Red Waters?" *Absolutely...*

I finish my second drink and I don't even feel buzzed. I grab the man's hand and lead him to the bathroom located on the back wall of the second floor. He keeps saying, under his breath, how he has got lucky tonight. I roll my eyes. We go into the men's bathroom and into the big stall. I don't want to go in the girl's, because girls like gossip and scandal is the biggest form of entertainment for them. I don't want anyone peeking in on me and in a girl's bathroom that will surely happen. I guess guys are the same but I feel there is less risk.

TRANSITION

I close the stall door, put my purse on the floor, and push the man up against the wall.

"Yeah baby, you like it rough don't you?" he says.

"Take off your shirt and be quiet," I say looking into his eyes. I don't want anything to get on his shirt. He takes off his shirt and says nothing. "Now I don't want you to move, ok?" He nods his head. I feel my fangs grow and I quickly bite into his neck. *Better than alcohol.* A few seconds later I pull back and my fangs retract. I look at the neck wounds and watch them close. *No evidence.* I then turn my attention to the man. He looks scared. "You will forget what just happened. You got laid and you're pretty happy about it but you can't remember the girl's face." He nods his head and smiles "Now go." He leaves the bathroom.

Another man is washing his hands at the sink when the one with me leaves. I was talking too low, so there is no way he heard me. I lean against the stall door with one hand on my hip trying to look sexy, and probably failing. I make eye contact with the man through the mirror.

"Come here," I tell him. He walks into the stall with me and I close the door. He is wearing a tee shirt so there is no need for him to take off his shirt. I pull his shirt aside and tell him to be still and not to scream. I am about to bite him and then I stop.

"You smell horrible, like you're sick. You can leave and forget you ever saw me." There is nothing appetizing about his smell. As a matter of fact, it is revolting. *What is that about? Am I full or something?*

I leave the bathroom and bump into Jade. "Getting full?" she asks. Not even close, now that I think about it.

"Well, I was going to start on my next meal but it smelled rotten. I mean he really smelled horrible." If I were

96

CHAPTER 10

paying close attention to my surroundings, I would have noticed his scent sooner. There are so many people around that I am trying to block out all their scents. I don't want to lose control.

"You are becoming more vampire every second. Babies grow up so fast," she says pretending to be sad. "He smelled bad because there is something wrong with his blood. He probably has an STD or something." So we can tell when someone has bad blood. "Let me know when you're ready to go. I'm going to go dance some more with that guy I was talking about." Jade goes back down to the red floor.

I spend the rest of the night drinking red water and feeding on three more men before a couple walks into the bathroom. It's no guessing what they planned to do. I ask if I can join them and they say yes. So, I fed on a total of four men and one woman. *What is wrong with me?*

Why am I feeding on so many people and why am I ok with it? Grief floods my emotions. *I will never be the same again.* How can I casually feed on so many people? It doesn't feel like it is wrong until I think about it. I feel horrible for feeding on all those people. I feel like a monster. *It's time for me to go.*

Jade tries to get me to have one dance with her before we leave, but I am having too many conflicting feelings. There is no way I am going to dance. When we leave, Jade and I go our separate ways. She goes home with the guy that she has been dancing with, and I go back to the cabin alone.

When I make it back to the cabin, it is almost three in the morning. There is no telling when Jade will get back from her so called 'date' so I'm not going to wait up for her. I slide off my shoes, lay down on the couch, close my eyes, and then sit up quickly.

"Shoot! I left my purse at the bar," I whisper. I stand up quickly and leave the cabin. I run back to the club in no time. The bouncer quickly lets me back in and I make my way back to the bar upstairs. The club is still crowded when I make it inside. *Wow! People never sleep.* When I get to the bar upstairs, I look around it frantically. I don't see my purse.

"Hey." I yell to the blonde bartender that assisted me earlier and he turns toward me. "I left my purse here. It's a thin leather black clutch with studs on one side." I hope he has it because, if not, Jade is going to be pissed.

"Here it is. I thought you would come back to get it." He hands me my purse.

"Thanks, you're a lifesaver!" Just then a gorgeous man walks to the bar. He is tall and very muscular. I quickly slide into a trance and just stare at him. I blush as he looks at me. "H-H-Hi," I stutter.

"Hi gorgeous," he says. *Oh, he's sweet, beautiful and he smells so good.* I can't tear my eyes away from him. I am sure that I have a stupid, big grin plastered on my face. Who wouldn't have a big grin plastered on their face?

"Thank you...so are you," I say dazed. I'm not even sure the words came out clear. "I'm Nichole...Nichole Roberts." *I can just melt right now.* He laughs.

"I'm Langston... Nice too meet you, Nichole." *His voice is like chocolate.* Langston is such a beautiful name.

"Langston? Like Langston Hughes?" I can't tear my eyes away from his face. He laughs again. He has such a deep laugh. *I can listen to his laugh all day.*

"Yeah, I'm afraid so, my mom loved the man's poems so she named me after him." *An interesting name for an interesting man...*

CHAPTER 10

"So your dad was ok with that?" What am I saying? "I mean, with you being named after another man." He clears his throat.

"My dad wasn't really around to have a say in any aspect of my life." Oh... I shouldn't have asked. Why am I all in his business anyway?

"I'm sorry, I shouldn't have asked." I finally look down at my hands. "That was rude of me." I am prying into this man's life and we don't even know each other.

"It's fine, I don't mind." He lifts my head up with his hand. "Besides, I would answer anything you asked me." His words are just, wow. "Would you like to sit with me?" *Would I...!*

"I would love to." I sit down on the stool next to him. "Tell me more about yourself, Langston."

We talk for about an hour. I am enchanted by everything he says. He tells me that he's a lawyer and that he has just moved to Rosenburg. He tells me that his family used to live here and he wanted to move back to his roots. I ask a lot of questions, some are really personal, and he answers all of them. He finally cuts me off and says it is his turn to get to know me and ask all the questions. I tell him about my family and friends and how I miss them. He asks me why I don't visit them if I miss them so much. I tell him that they don't live in Rosenburg and work is consuming me. I tell him I am an optometrist. I figure I know enough about that profession, because of my dad, that I can fake it.

The conversation with Langston goes on for what seems like forever. I am beginning to think I can love again. *Too soon*, I tell myself. What am I thinking? Langston is a human and I am a vampire. Sooner or later, I am going to get hungry. The sooner part wins out faster than I think. I am hungry now.

"Let's go to the bathroom," I tell him. *He smells divine. Maybe I'll keep him.* He can come live with me and Jade. *He can be my own personal dinner and a show...*

"Let's not," he says. I instantly feel disappointed. "You don't seem like that type of woman and I'm not that type of man either." Aww... he is respectful. How nice. "Maybe we can exchange numbers and go out on a real date sometime?" He wants to go out with me? I want so badly to say yes but I can't.

His refusal irritates me a little. I feel like I am tucking one side of me away and the other side is surfacing. How dare he refuse me?

"Let's go to the bathroom now," I say looking in his eyes and knowing mine have darkened. My vampire instinct to feed is winning over the part of me that wants to be human. His face blanks for a second but he complies.

"Ok, let's go." We stand up and head to the bathroom. We go into the male's bathroom and into the large stall in the back of the restroom, where I have been most of the night. I shove him against the wall.

"Don't scream and keep still." I pull his head to the side and then sink my fangs into his neck. He tastes like chocolate. *Yum.* I don't understand what makes me do this to this man and at this moment and I don't care either. I am enjoying my meal when I hear someone come into the bathroom. I don't care. It's not like they will see me.

"Hi, Nichole," A familiar voice says. I pull back and look down. There is somebody standing near the stall. "I didn't expect to see you here." My mind starts working. *I know that voice...*

I open the stall door and jump back when I see Nate.

CHAPTER 10

Langston falls to the floor and slumps against the wall. I look down at him and gasp. *I drank too much.* I don't know which situation to address first, Langston on the floor or Nate in front of me. How did Nate find me? Nate walks into the stall and closes the door. *What do I do!* I should have never come back for my purse, or at least not alone! Nate walks up to me and I back up until I bump into a wall.

"You look even more beautiful as a vampire," he whispers in my ear. He grabs me by the waist and pulls me up against him. I look down at Langston. "Don't worry about him, we'll deal with him later. Let's talk about us." *Us...?* As far as I am concerned, there is no *us.*

"Nate get away from me," I plead. He starts to kiss me up and down my neck. I pull away from him.

"Why?" he asks as he pulls me back and continues to kiss me. "Don't you miss me baby?"

"...Because you tried to kill me and you turned me into a vampire." I try to fight him off but he is still too strong. *Why is he still so strong?*

"I'm glad I accidentally turned you. I miss you and now that you're a vampire we can be together *forever.*" He starts to pull one of my legs up against his side. "You know, this short dress gives me ideas." I feel my anger rise inside me and I try to kick him in the nuts but he moves out the way. "Oh, no you don't." He pins me against the wall again. "Be a good girl."

"Get away from me," I yell. He steps back to look at me. I want to get away.

"You don't want to be with me baby," he questions looking sadly into my eyes.

"Of course I don't want to be with you! You tried to kill me." He looks at me and his eyes turn black. "But I love you, Nichole," he says as his fangs come out.

"I don't love you, Nate," I say furiously. "Now get away from me!" He looks at me for a second, searching. Then his face goes from sad to angry.

"If I can't have you, then no one can," he snaps and then he sinks his fangs in my neck. *And then there is nothing.*

Chapter 11

I wake up frightened. Why do I keep having dreams about Nate killing me? Is it because I'm scared of Nate? That's exactly why, it's because I am scared of him. Why did I get it in my head that I can kill him, and his friends, with Jade's help?

TRANSITION

I stand up off the couch and pace, the room. I look down a notice that my clutch is on the floor. *What time is it?* I look around Jade's cabin looking for a clock. There is one on her bookshelf. It is eight in the morning. I have only been sleep five hours and frankly I need to go back to sleep, but I am dreading having another dream about him. Am I ever going to get Nate out of my head? I know the answer; the answer is "NO!" No, I'm not. Nate is the reason I am in this situation. He is the reason for everything. I will never be able to forget him. I only hope that, one day, I can stop having nightmares about him.

Jade still isn't back and there is no way I am staying in this cabin any longer. I change into my black jeans and white shirt. I slide on my tennis shoes and walk outside. I look up at the sky. The sun is beautiful and its warmth feels good on my skin. I'm glad that I can go out and enjoy the sun. I wouldn't know what to do if that was taken away from me too. *The sun always made my days hopeful and good.* Not anymore, I think to myself, my days will never be good anymore. The sun can no longer bring my day hope, and it can never make me feel like my days are going to be happy. Everything has been taken away from me and it has taken a great toll on my happiness.

I start walking. I'm not sure where I am going but I am going somewhere. I weave through the forest quietly. I need to accept this new life and embrace it. Otherwise, I will be miserable forever, and forever is a long time. Somewhere deep inside, I feel I will never accept it. If only I can go back in time and change the past. Nate has taken away my future and given me a new one, one that I don't want. He didn't have the right to do that to me. He didn't have the right to kill me or turn me. I am beginning not to feel like Nichole

CHAPTER 11

Roberts; I am beginning to feel like a stranger. *One day*, I think, *I won't recognize who I am.*

I start running. *Where am I going?* I am sure that I am going to get lost since I'm not paying much attention. I don't know until I get there that, *that* is where I am headed. I am near Tiffany's school. *Just in time.* My mom is dropping Tiffany off as soon as I get there. Tiffany gets out the car slowly. Her head is down and she looks as if she has been crying. I can tell she doesn't want to go to school. One of her friends comes and grabs her hand and walks her into school. *That is nice.* I'm glad she has friends to help her through this sad time.

I watch as my mom drives off. As soon as she pulls away from the school, I hear her crying. I wonder how long it will take them to move on? I want so badly for them to have happiness again. I wish I could cry and let my emotions run away with me. Seeing my family is hard. I want so badly to go and show them that I'm not dead. Will they be happy to find out that instead I have been turned into a vampire? I don't know but what I do know is that I will never get to be with my family again. I turn away from Tiffany's school and start running toward my own.

...

This is a very bad idea. I tell myself but it is too late. I am already in the woods looking at the front of Rosenburg High School. I hide behind a large tree so that I won't be seen, and then I peak around the tree to get a look at everyone.

Casey is sitting at a bench by herself looking down. I guess that she is faking being sad since she knows I'm not truly dead. Or she is sad because I'm a vampire. I'm not sure which. Amber walks over to where Casey is sitting. Her usual pep is gone. Casey looks up when Amber approaches.

TRANSITION

"Hey, I know we're not friends but we were both hers and… I miss her too and I'm sorry for your loss." Amber looks down at her hands. She is talking as if I am dead and not just missing. She must think I am. "Nichole and I weren't close, close friends but we were friends and I loved her like a sister. I hope they find her."

"Thanks, Amber." Casey grabs her hand and squeezes it. Amber walks away from Casey and takes off into the school. *I will miss Amber.*

I look toward where Nate and his friends sit. Typical, they are all smiles and laughter. Not a thought of what they did to me expressed in their faces. Anger explodes in me. Shouldn't Nate at least pretend that he's sad? I mean, I was his girlfriend after all! I guess he is either clinging to the 'I dumped him' story, so that he doesn't have to look sad about my 'so called' disappearance but it isn't like we only dated a few weeks! He should at least look like he cares! From the look on his face, I know he doesn't care what anyone thinks about his joyful demeanor. He is the reason I am gone and he could care less. I am certain that he will just kill anyone who suspects him as the reason I am gone.

As I watch them, Tyler looks over at Casey. I always knew he liked her, but what exactly does he like about her? He is a vampire and she is a human. Is she just an appetizing meal to him? I don't know, and the thought of not knowing frustrates me. What do any of them like about any human girl besides the fact that they are pretty food, a decorative meal.

"I'll be right back," he says to Nate and John. They look over to see what he is looking at. I wish he would just leave Casey alone. He doesn't have the slightest chance with her anyway.

CHAPTER 11

"Come on man, you still don't have a crush on Nichole's friend, do you?" Nate says with such disgust that I wonder if Nate ever liked me at all.

"That's none of your business, Nate," Tyler says as he stands up.

"Tyler," John says. "Remember the last time you had a crush on a girl, you tried to have it all and stupidly told her that you're a vampire." John laughs. I hate when he laughs. It isn't a pleasant sound to hear at all. His laugh sounds like he enjoys others' pain. He seems to always laugh when something terrible happens or when something terrible is about to happen. It is a disgusting trait. "She tried to run, and you killed her because she hurt your feelings." John laughs. "What was her name?" I know instantly who they are talking about.

"Ashley something," Nate finally says. *So Tyler killed Ashley Fortune?* Doesn't surprise me after all I've been through with Nate. She hurt Tyler's feelings and died because of it. I pissed Nate off and was turned because of it. Why can't they just break up with us and go their separate ways like regular guys? The worse case scenario with a regular guy would be a broken heart or just hurt feelings. It's completely different if you're dating a vampire, whether you know it or not, the worst-case scenario for hurting a vampire's feelings is death. People think women are emotional but they have never seen or met a pissed off male vampire. Hell hath no fury like a vampire scorned.

"Right, Ashley...I mean," John shrugs, "with you killing her and Nate killing Nichole, we are going to have to relocate soon. Firstly, we are all friends. Secondly, Tyler's girlfriend goes missing and is never found, and then Nate's girlfriend goes missing and is never found. People are going to talk, especially with your crush on Casey. If she gets with you, soon she will go missing, too." They aren't talking loud enough for anyone else to hear. I am the only one that can hear them. I am certain that if someone did hear them, *they* would go missing and would never be found.

"Whatever you guys." Tyler finally speaks. "I really like her and maybe she will be the one to like my vampire status. Who knows?" Tyler leaves Nate and John and walks over and sits by Casey. I wish I could go over there to protect her. Casey looks up when he sits down.

"What, Tyler?" she says. Casey, do not get an attitude with him. Tyler looks momentarily taken back with the attitude in her voice. He relaxes. He probably thinks the attitude comes from the fact that I am missing but I know better. She has an attitude because she knows he is a vampire. She also knows everything that happened to me and that Tyler had done nothing to help me.

"How are you, Case?" Case? So he's using her a nickname? "Are they having any luck finding Nichole?" Casey turns her head away from Tyler and away from Nate and John who look like they are hanging on every word of the conversation. I smirk when she rolls her eyes.

"No." She turns back toward him looking utterly sad. "I feel like it's a lost cause but I don't want to give up. She's probably dead." She breaks out in a sob at the last word. Casey is a good actor. Tyler puts his arm around her in an attempt to comfort her. Casey shrugs it off and stands up.

"I just need time alone." Casey puts her hands up in defense and Tyler nods. I can tell Casey doesn't want to be anywhere near him.

"I understand; you need time to grieve. You know if you ever need anyone to talk to, you can call me." Casey

CHAPTER 11

nods and walks inside the school building. Tyler goes back to sit by his friends. I am proud of Casey. Brushing him off without pissing him off is a good tactic.

"...And he strikes out," Nate says with a laugh. My attention is quickly diverted from Casey's retreating figure to Nate's unbearable smile.

"Shut up, Nate," Tyler says as he sits down. "If it wasn't for you killing her best friend, we would have been together by now." *No you wouldn't.* Casey wouldn't have given you a chance even if I were still alive. She would have flirted and I guess that still wouldn't have been good for her.

"Well, the girl pissed me off, but I can't say I miss her. I'm glad she's dead." So Nate thought he'd killed me... well I have a surprise for him. It is sloppy for him not to know he really turned me. Suddenly, Nate looks back and smiles at Rebecca who is sitting at a table with all her friends. "I got some new eye candy now." John rolls his always-black eyes and Tyler shakes his head. As if on cue, Rebecca walks over to Nate.

"Hi, Nathaniel," she coos and smiles. "Thank you for the necklace. I was so surprised to find it this morning." *My necklace*, she is wearing *my* necklace.

I have to give it to Nate, he moves on pretty quickly. I shouldn't be surprised. He never cared about me anyway. I can't believe he gave her my necklace, but what should I have expected from a sadistic vampire. For a second, just a tiny second, I think about ripping her throat out and taking my necklace back. I quickly dismiss the thought. I don't want the necklace back nor do I want Nate. She can have him and the necklace for all I care. I shouldn't care about anything he does or whoever he likes. He has ruined me and all I want to do is ruin him. Killing Rebecca wouldn't do that. He doesn't care about her either.

"I thought you might like it," Nate says as he rubs his hand down her cheek. I roll my eyes as she blushes.

"I do," Rebecca says. She is stupid to like him, just like I was stupid. "I'll see you later." She tosses her hair with her hand and walks away.

"Yep, we are definitely going to have to leave soon," John says as he stands up. "Aye, what happened to that Landon kid?" *Landon*... I forgot all about him. Did Nate kill him, too?

"Oh, I didn't kill him," Nate says confidently. "I told him he could see ghosts. I think his family sent him to the psych hospital or something." John laughs.

"Really dude? That's classic. He'll be in there for the rest of his life." I am beyond pissed. How could he do that! It doesn't matter; I am going to undo it as soon as I get the chance.

The school bell rings. It must be nine o'clock. I watch everybody go inside the school building; even the three evil vampires go inside. I slide back against the tree trunk. So they like killing, girls, and school. They are vampires! Why do they like school? My guess would be that they like to prey on the girls at school. I wonder if females are the only humans they prey on.

I peek around the tree to see if anyone is outside. Everybody has gone inside the school. *Good.* I run out of sight of the school before I slow down to a walk.

Grief takes over my emotions as I walk. *I don't want to be anything like them*, I think, *I don't want to be anything like Nate.* Nate and his friends are killers. Killing Nate will mean that I am just like him. I'm not a killer even though I am now a vampire. I will try everything in my power to not

CHAPTER 11

become one. *I can still feed on humans and not be a killer right?*

It is hard enough seeing my family and not being able to do anything about their grief and sadness. I can't comfort them; I can't go see them anymore. I mean, I can watch them from afar but I can't go be with them. I can only watch them fall apart. On top of that, seeing Nate makes me want to kill him even more. It makes me so angry that all I can feel is anger and rage. All these feelings of sadness and anger make me feel like I am losing myself. I don't want to lose myself. I know what I have to do to stay sane. It is the only way I will be able to rebuild myself and to remember who I am. *I need to leave.* I need to leave Rosenburg for good.

TRANSITION

Chapter 12

"So let me get this straight," Jade says calmly.
"You went to your old school, where the guys who killed you were at? Are you crazy?" She gets a little louder. "If you could see them, then they could see you!"

As I made my way back to the cabin from my school, I ran into Jade. She says she has been looking all over for me. I guess she feels responsible for me or something. I told her where I had been that morning and she isn't taking it very well.

TRANSITION

"They didn't see me, Jade. Calm down." She is really over reacting. We start to slowly walk towards the cabin.

"How can you be so sure?" I'm sure because I'm here with you right now.

"Just trust me, okay!" I throw my arms in the air. I am still feeling pretty down about everything and I don't feel like getting scolded. Not to mention, I'm not all that in control of my emotions, and Jade is starting to piss me off.

"Alright, fine, I trust you." Jade is calmer now.

"So how was your date?" I am eager to change the subject and from the looks of it, Jade is eager to spill about her date.

"It was great! Of course, it was only a one-night stand because I don't do human/vampire relationships. They always end in death." She gives me a look.

I know all too well that it is the human that ends up dead or, like me, turned. I wonder if there has ever been a human/vampire relationship that went well. I mean, eventually the couple will have to split due to the immortal/mortal thing or the vampire could turn their partner so they can be together forever. I wonder what it is like to live forever with the love of your life. Do vampires even have relationships filled with true love?

"Have you ever known a human/vampire relationship to go well?" I really don't know what I mean by *well*.

"Sometimes the vampire would make the person they love forget them so that the human could live a normal life or they might turn them, so… I guess, yeah. But, if you ask me, both those situations are bad endings. Someone is either heart broken, dead, or completely unaware that they were even in love."

Jade has a point; there is no way *that* kind of relationship can end well. So my best chance at love will probably be with another vampire. That idea doesn't sound good because I doubt I will find a sweet, loving, and kind vampire. I have lost the chance to have a family and now my chances at love don't seem too good either.

"Hey, I'm going to go feed. So meet me back at the cabin." Jade looks pointedly at me. "…And don't go wandering off to visit anybody or school…alright!" I roll my eyes. She needs to calm down.

"Yes, mother." I say sarcastically. "I will head home, straight to my room, and no where else." I can't keep the irritation out of my tone.

"Good… and calm down. You have some serious emotional issues. It is expected because you are a new vampire but eventually you need to control them better." What I need is to rewind time.

She turns and vanishes into the forest. I run, in the opposite direction, towards the cabin and I am back in no time. I walk in and plop down on the couch. Jade is right, I need to control my emotions better and I am beginning to feel like I will never be able to control them. I sigh. *I want to feel like me again.*

Everyday I feel less and less like me, and more like someone else. What if the bloodlust and lack of humanity takes over and I'm nothing more than what Nate and his friends are? I want to get a grip of who I am or was and keep it close. I might not have had a choice on whether I turned or not, but I can at least try to control who I will become in the future.

I close my eyes and doze into a dreamless sleep.

TRANSITION

...

"Wake up girly." I open my eyes and see Jade sitting on the arm of the couch. Why is she waking me? That is the best sleep I have had since I've been turned. No nightmares and no Nate.

"What do you want?" I say sleepily. I am a little irritated because I have no idea when I will get sleep like that again.

"Ouch, your dullness is hurting my energetic mood." Oh my gosh, why is she bothering me? I sit up on the couch and look at her.

"What's going on, Jade?" It doesn't seem like she will be leaving me alone so I might as well amuse her.

"Well I fed and am now full but I have a problem." She pauses dramatically. I wait for her to continue but she doesn't.

"What's the problem?"

"I'm bored!" I roll my eyes as she acts like it is the end of the world. Then I remember something.

"Well, I don't know what to do about your boredom but I have to tell you something." She looks a little disappointed that I'm not entertaining her problem anymore. I take a deep breath. "I need to leave Rosenburg. I can't live here anymore. It's too painful to be here. I can't help but want to see my family and friends. You even said it yourself, that I'm having emotional problems and being here makes them worse. I know I said I wanted to kill Nate and his friends, but I feel like it will make me more like them and I don't want to be like them.

I just want to leave and try to move on from this, and I will never move on if I am here where all my hurt lives. I want to forget about Nate and his friends; I hope I never see

CHAPTER 12

them again. So can we go? I mean when I go will you come with me? We could go to Denver and live at your condo. I mean... if I can stay at your condo with you?" I drift off and stare at her. My rambling episode is over and is accompanied by silence. All she does is stare and listen to me throughout my entire rant.

I don't know what I will do if Jade wants to go separate ways. I don't want to be alone and I feel like I need her... at least, for right now.

"Yeah, we can leave." She smiles. I release a breath. I thought she was going to say I could leave but she is staying. I didn't realize how nervous I was for her answer until now.

"Really? ...And you would leave with me?"

"Of course! I don't know why you thought I wouldn't come with you, or that you couldn't stay at my condo or something." She outstretches her arms. "Let's leave all this mess behind."

I smile a little. She walks over to her bed and sits down with a thud. "I mean, I'm like your mother and I can't let my daughter roam the world by herself. You might destroy a village or something. I can't have that weight on my shoulders." I laugh. "We'll leave in the morning," she tells me.

I am glad that I will leave everything behind soon. I need a fresh start.

TRANSITION

Chapter 13

Jade's condo is just as she has described it, techie.
There are all sorts of electronic devices everywhere
including HD TV's, touch screen everything, game
consoles, music bars, etc. There is even a big fancy
remote that controls almost everything.

When I first walk in, the foyer opens up to a fairly
large living room and kitchen with granite counter tops.
The condo is furnished in a way that makes me feel
warm and at home.

TRANSITION

The color scheme is consistent with browns and other warm colors throughout the condo. In the middle of the living room is an L-shaped beige couch that faces a large HD TV. There is a small square dark wooden table that sets between the couch and the TV. A little farther behind the couch is a breakfast bar with marble counter tops that leads to the kitchen. The breakfast bar will no doubt remind me of my family every time I look at it.

I walk over to the stainless steel fridge, hearing the hum that says it is on, wondering with curiosity what can she possibly have in it. I open up the fridge and turn to Jade who is looking through an iPod for some music. I clear my throat and she looks up at me. I gesture towards the contents of the fridge.

"What? I like to have a drink every once in a while." *Every once in a while?* The fridge is full of alcohol. I shake my head at her. There is almost every type of alcohol in this fridge. It looks more like she is a full-blown alcoholic than a once in a while drinker. I close the fridge.

"If I open the cabinets will there be more alcohol?" I ask sarcastically.

"No…" she says a little offended. "You will find cups and napkins and other accessories." I am a little shocked she doesn't have all the cabinets full of alcohol.

"Accessories?" I repeat as a question. Jade looks up at me.

"Yeah, accessories for the kitchen!" I shake my head at her and lean against the counter top in the kitchen.

Settling on *Flawless* by Beyoncé she walks over to the kitchen, leans against the breakfast bar and winks. I smile at the fact that we have similar taste in music.

"Don't you think you woke up flawless?" Jade says

with a smirk. I look at Jade and we laugh. Well, she has a point. We are immortal vampires with superhuman abilities. Most women don't like to age or wrinkle and we are never going to age or wrinkle.

"So, to give you the run down, there are two bedrooms, two and a half bathrooms, a study where I keep all my computers, laptops, and everything else a study would have, and a game room with a Wii and other stuff."

"Why do you have all this stuff?"

"For entertainment, in case I have a date over, because even though I don't need any of it, I like collecting the things that I've always wanted." I open the freezer and see there is food in it.

"Food?"

"Yeah, I told you sometimes I have dates over and they have to eat something." She laughs. "Come on let me show you to your room."

Jade leads me to a hallway to the left of the kitchen and living room that splits into two. She tells me that her room is down the right hall and proceeds to lead me down to the left. She opens the door to what is my new room.

My room is quite big and houses a big king sized bed with a dark brown duvet. There are way too many decorative pillows that decorate the beautiful bed. There are two dark brown wooden nightstands on each side of the bed with lamps that look more like art than furniture. Above the nightstands are windows with curtains that match the color scheme of the room. The walls hold no decorations. There are two doors, one on each side of the room. The double doors on the left side of the room open up to a walk in closet, and the door on the right leads to the bathroom. The ceiling holds a fan with a light on it. The light turns on and the fan starts to move when Jade flips the switch.

"You can add your own personal touches to the room. It is, after all, yours. I know I said our kind doesn't get along well, but I think we will and I hope you stay with me. As long as you want to, I mean. I enjoy your company."

I didn't realize until now that she likes my company just as much as I like hers. I don't plan on ever leaving. I need someone at this time in my life. I start to feel thick with emotion and I want to lighten the mood.

"So, since we are roomies now, we need a code for when we have a date. I mean, when *you* have a date." Jade laughs. I'm not planning to have a date for a long, long time.

"We do not need a code." She says with humor in her tone. "I'll just be like…'hey, I have a date' and you can just say okay have fun!" I smile at her and roll my eyes.

"Alright… whatever."

"You know that was nice of you to help that friend of yours out before we left." I look at her and nod my head. I told her about Landon and she was all for helping him get his sanity back. Once he was back to normal, we got him out of the psych hospital and told, or rather made his family leave and move to Florida.

"Thanks, and thanks for helping me. He didn't deserve that."

"So, I'm going to leave you to settle in and if the music is bothering you at any point, let me know. Nobody is really ever in here so I usually just leave it on surround sound." I nod my head and she closes the door and leaves.

I take a look around the room again before I drop the bag I have been holding on the floor. I will sort through my belongings later. I hop onto the bed and roll onto my back. I look up at the spinning fan and stare, watching it as it spins

CHAPTER 13

slowly. The bed is comfy and welcoming, which is a change from the couch in Jade's cabin.

I'd finally left everything behind. I left my family, my friends, my city, and my old life. The only thing that makes me happy at this moment is Jade, my new friend, taking me in and the fact that I won't see Nate anymore.

I thought that as soon as I was gone I would feel relief, but all I can really feel is grief. I start counting the rotations the fan makes as my mind drifts to my family again. *One... two...three...* I hate the fact that my sister will grow up without me. I want to be there when she goes to her first dance or when a guy breaks her heart. I want to go through a phase where she steals my make-up and clothes. I would rather fight with my sister everyday than never see her again. I want to feel the warmth of my mother's embrace, or the safeness that my father makes me feel whenever he is around. *Sixty-one...sixty-two...sixty-three...* I will never have anything with my family anymore. I can't risk their lives for my own happiness. I can't be selfish. If I look at this situation literally, I am a vampire and they are food. If you live in a house with your food, eventually it will get eaten and I just can't do that to them... *nine thousand and eighty...*

I break away from staring at the fan long enough to notice light streaming through the dark curtains of the windows positioned on each side of the bed. It isn't afternoon light, which is what catches my attention. I get off the bed, pull the curtain aside, and look out the window at the morning light. *It's morning?* It can't be morning already. We made it to Jade's condo early afternoon.

I turn around and notice a digital clock that hangs on the wall by the door, that I didn't noticed before. The clock reads seven-thirty a.m. I can't believe I have stared at that fan all day and night without moving.

I pick up my bag off the floor and dump its contents onto the bed. I fold all my clothes and organize what little I have into the drawers of a dresser that is in my closet. I pick up my toiletries off the bed and head into the bathroom.

The bathroom is huge. It has a glass shower door and a huge oval Jacuzzi style tub. It even has jets. Everything is white in the bathroom, including the floors, cabinets, and counter tops. I put my toothbrush and paste on the white granite counter top by the sink and place my towels and shampoo in the cabinet above the toilet. *I need to relax...*

...

I don't know what time it is when Jade walks into the bathroom. I am lying in the huge tub. The water that was scolding when I had run it is now tepid.

"Are you going to be in here all day?" I shrug not knowing if she can see the gesture.

"What time is it by the way?" I am losing track of time, all the time, it seems.

"It's six p.m." I don't hide my shock. "Yep, you have been in here all day. Are you... are you sitting in cold bath water?" I just stare at Jade who has her eyebrow cocked.

"No, it's slightly warm, kind of. I think I'm depressed." Let's face it; I know I'm depressed.

"Well if you are going to sit in a bath all day, at least add hot water as the day goes by," she says. I nod. "...And about your depression, you do know you will need to come out of it eventually. I mean if you're going to live forever, at least be happy." I nod again. She has a point.

"Are you at least going to come out with me tonight? I'm going to a club!" I shake my head at her and she makes a show of looking sad. "Well fine, I will see you later then."

CHAPTER 13

"See you later," I say as she closes the bathroom door.

...

When I finally get through sulking in the tub, I get into bed in my underwear. This time, however, I get under the cover. *I really need to get pajamas.* I pull the duvet all the way up to my neck and bury myself in the fluffy pillows. I know I have fallen asleep when I hear Jade come in the condo.

"Hey I have a date!" Jade says loudly while laughing. I can tell she has been drinking. "My roommate is here and that's our code for don't disturb me," she says to whoever the guy is. I don't bother responding. I don't really feel up to talking. They both laugh and I tune them out.

I guess what happened to me is starting to settle inside but I'm not ready to embrace it. It is making me feel worse everyday. I never leave the bed. I lay there for days and in the same position. Every morning Jade will come check on me, every night she has a date, and every day and night I lay in the bed. I'm not sure if she brings the same guy home everyday...I think she does but I don't care much to ask. The days turn into a week, and the week turns into weeks. It has been three total weeks when I hear, or rather smell, multiple people come in the condo. I look up when Jade bust in my room.

"This has to stop Nichole!" Jade is furious. "It has been three weeks, and yes I have been counting. It is time for you to get out of bed and feed...have fun...live...*something*!"

"You said we live forever! I think I can afford to sulk about losing my life for a few years." I flinch at the sound of my own voice.

"Ok fine...you are right." She says irritated. "...But you can't go a couple of years without feeding! You will completely lose yourself when your body's natural instinct is to feed and you attack and kill someone. No… not just someone but maybe you walk in a party and kill everyone because you decided not to feed for a few years!" I just stare at her. She does have a point. "…And you are really hurting my feelings," she says jokingly. I smile.

"Oh my gosh! Is that a smile?"

"Ok…alright, I need to feed. Did you bring dinner home or are you having a party." Jade smiles.

"So…I know you don't like animals, and I respect that. Therefore I brought a selection. Also, I don't know how deprived you are and I don't want you killing anyone. Come on."

I get out of bed and follow Jade to the kitchen. Standing in front of the breakfast bar are five people, three girls and two guys. They all have a dazed look in their eyes. I have to fight the urge to launch at them like a starving person at a buffet. I can see why Jade wants me to feed sooner rather than later.

"Don't worry, they don't even know where they are and as soon as they leave, they will forget everything." I give her a side-glance.

"You have been working hard haven't you Jade." I say looking at the people she obtained for me.

"Well I can't let my only child starve, can I?" I roll my eyes at her. "What kind of mother would I be if I did?" I sigh.

"Would you like the blonde or the brunette? Or do you like her?" She pointed to the girl in the middle. "She smells like chocolate. Or, would you prefer a guy? They are both kind of cute." She sounds like she is trying to sell me something as she goes down the row of people."

"…Umm…"

CHAPTER 13

"Pick two, any two." Jade looks at me expectantly. It really doesn't matter but I have to choose. So, I choose the girl who smells like chocolate and one of the guys because he smells like chocolate too. I wonder how a human can smell like chocolate? Maybe they ate chocolate recently.

"Feed in the kitchen," Jade says as an order. She leads the others out and sends them home.

It feels good to sink my fangs into flesh but it also confuses me. I feed on the girl first and then the guy. Jade watches me as I feed. I guess she is trying to make sure I don't kill anyone. Somewhere in the back of my mind I feel like I am doing something wrong and that I am becoming a monster. If I can feed on a human and feel good while doing it, I am a monster but it is just something about feeding that feels right, it makes me feel strong. When I finish, Jade sends them home.

"I'm going back to bed Jade." I am in my room before she can protest. I do catch her say "Really?" in a sad disappointed way before I close my room door.

TRANSITION

Chapter 14

There is a rumbling sound that wakes me up.
It sounds like someone is trying to get into the condo. I
feel warning bells ring in my head. I listen closely. I
don't hear Jade in the condo and she never had problems opening the door either. I hear someone swear and
it isn't Jade's voice. It is a man's voice.

"Hurry up and open it," another man says. I hear
some more rumbling and finally the door opens.

"Come on, grab anything we can sell."

TRANSITION

I am in the living room within a second. It is pitch black inside the apartment with only the moonlight shining through the now opened door. The intruders close the door, turn towards me, and jump.

"Listen here lady," one of the men says as he holds up a gun. "Get on the floor now." I have been feeling depressed for weeks but now all I feel is rage. I don't like having a gun pointed at me or the fact that the person pointing it is breaking into my home. He is really pissing me off. My emotions run red. "Get on the floor now!"

"Are you threatening me?" I say in a low menacing voice. My voice almost scares me.

"He said get on the floor now," repeats the other man.

"Put the gun down and leave my home...now!" I almost yell the last word. I am trying to control my emotions but I am quickly losing it. *How dare they...?*

"Get her Tom, we don't have time for this," one of the men says to the other.

Tom walks over to me with shear confidence. I guess he thinks I am some weak woman he can subdue easily. When he gets close enough to grab me, he reaches for my arm and I grab him by his neck. I have a tight grip on it and I bring him face to face with me. He fights against my grasp.

"I said, get out of my home," I growl. Then the gun goes off. I still have Tom locked in my grip as I look at the other man. "Did you just shoot me?" I look down and see a hole in my chest. I growl and my fangs extend.

I throw Tom across the room and pull the bullet out of my chest. The other man shoots again and again, hitting his target each time. When I get tired of being shot, I materialize right in front of the man and he screams. I quiet his screams when I grab him by the neck.

CHAPTER 14

"I told you to get out and you didn't," I whisper in his ear. Then I sink my fangs into his neck. I only noticed that I ripped out his throat when Tom runs behind me and hits me in the head with a lamp. The lamp shatters all over the floor and I don't even budge from the impact.

I drop the other guy to the floor and grab Tom. He doesn't have a chance either. I don't feed on him like his friend but I am so enraged that I break his neck and he falls limply to the floor. I stand there looking at the two men on the floor, dead, until realization of what I did hits me.

"Oh...my...gosh." I say in a whisper and sink to the floor. "What have I done?" I bring my knees up to my chest and start rocking back and forth, back and forth.

I don't know how long I sat there, rocking, but I am glad when Jade comes home. I hear her gasp when she walks in. She is dateless, which is good. I can't imagine what would happen if she came home with a guy. She turns on the lights and just stares at me.

"What. Happened. Nichole?" I don't say anything. There is blood everywhere from me and whoever this Tom guy's friend was. The bullets some how popped out when I started to heal and are everywhere.

"Nichole!" She yells. "What happened?" She demands. I shake my head and just keep rocking. Back and forth, back and forth... *What have I done?*

...

Jade has cleaned up the mess I made while I sit in the same spot rocking back and forth. I don't know what she did with the bodies but I am glad when they are gone. I need to pull myself together but I don't know how at the moment. I have never killed someone or two people before. When Jade is finally finished cleaning up she sits down in front of me.

TRANSITION

"Well I guess I'm glad that I don't have carpet. That would have been a hassle." I don't look at her. I am fixed on one spot and I continue to rock back and forth. "It's hard when it first happens but you will be fine." I have nothing to say, I am blank.

I snap out of my trace when Jade's hand comes crashing down across my face, knocking me over.

"Dammit Nichole! Snap out of it and tell me what happened!" I can see fury radiating off of her. "I just spent two hours cleaning up *your* mess! So tell me now."

I have to fight the urge to react to her slapping me. She isn't a threat, she is my friend. I have to breathe because I feel like ripping out her throat just like I did Tom's friend. I look up at her.

"I was asleep. They broke into the condo. I told them to leave. They didn't. The one whose throat was ripped apart shot me. I lost control and ripped his throat out. The other attacked me, twice. I lost control and broke his neck. Then I broke down because I realized I had killed them." I am speaking with clenched teeth. I am trying hard not to get into a physical altercation with Jade.

She stares at me the whole time I speak. Then suddenly, she pulls me into an embrace. We sit on the floor hugging like normal people would if one is comforting the other.

"It's okay, Nichole. We have strong emotions and sometimes people walk into the wrong situation." I don't say anything. I just let her hold me. "It's always hard when you first kill someone." I pull back and look at her.

"You've killed someone before?" It is a stupid question. Of course she has, she told me this already.

"Yeah I have. I didn't have control of myself at the time." She smooths my hair back like my mom used to do.

CHAPTER 14

"Time will heal." *I nod. Time will heal.* "...But a bath will do wonders." She says with a smile.

"I get the hint."

I don't ask what she did with the bodies. I don't want to know either. I just get up and go to my bathroom. I look down at myself and I just now realize that I am in my under-wear. Was I in my underwear when I fed earlier too? I groan. I can't believe I have been walking around like this.

I run scalding water into the tub. I get in and watch the water turn red as the blood washes off of me. The sight of red water is making me sick so I drain the tub and run more water. I add liquid soap this time and just soak in the bubbles and water.

...

With each passing day I feel less like myself and more like a monster. I feel stronger, fierce, and less scared of anything, but a monster. What bothers me the most is the fact that I feel no remorse for the people I killed and it is not because of what they did. I feel no remorse because it just doesn't bother me anymore. I don't care that two people are dead because of me. *I am a monster...*

I no longer lay in the bed every day like I have for three weeks. I shift to moving around the house but never leaving it. I am laid out on the couch one afternoon when Jade walks in the condo.

"Let's go shopping!"

I sit up on the couch and give her a look that says 'I'm not leaving this condo'.

"Oh, come on Nichole! You need new clothes and I need a new dress!" I groan. Maybe it's time to venture around town.

"Alright, I'll go but I have no money Jade." Maybe this

minor set back will call this whole trip to the mall off.

"Look, I have lots of money, so put some shoes on and let's go." I think it over for a second and then agree. One day I will ask Jade where she gets all her money.

...

We go to the Cherry Creek shopping mall. Jade makes me stop by almost every store. She buys me dresses, shoes of all kinds, jewelry, lingerie, shirts, pants, shorts, etc. She even buys me *pajamas* and a robe. If it is a type of clothing item, she buys it for me. We also stop to get hair accessorizes like flat irons and wands. By the time we make it to a store that sells room decorations I am tapping my foot at her.

"What? Don't you need to personalize your room? You know, make it you." I roll my eyes and sigh.

"Not really," I grumble.

"Yes you do. I'm not taking no for an answer. Personalizing your room will make you feel at home and maybe, less depressed." What she doesn't know is that my depression is slowly fading away. I just never want to leave the condo.

It is when we stop at the apple store to get me an iPhone, MacBook, iPad, and cases to go with each that she asks me about Casey.

"So have you spoken to your friend Casey recently?" My somewhat content mood plummets. I miss my friend and thinking about her makes me think about my family. I miss them all.

"Yeah, I talked to her last week, when you left your phone at home by accident." Talking to Casey gives me a fleeting moment of happiness.

"Oh, yeah I was frantic about it. I was like 'where's my phone'," she says nonchalantly. "What did y'all talk about?"

CHAPTER 14

"I told her that I was trying to move on. I said it had nothing to do with her and that she would always be my best friend but this was safer for her and my family." Jade nods her head.

"Did she take it well?" *Did she take it well?* She took it so well that I felt hurt.

"Yeah, she did. She said she understood."

"That's good. I'm glad to hear it. Also, I'm glad you are starting to move on."

We wait in line at the apple store so that she can buy me all these devices. I am really tired of shopping. We already had to make like five trips back to her car just because we had too many bags.

"You know, I really don't need any of this." Jade turns around to look at me.

"Oh be quiet, yes you do! What if you need to reach me and I'm out on a date."

"Who is this guy you have been seeing anyway?" I found out that the 'guys' she keeps bringing to the condo is in fact only one guy.

"His name is Richard, you will meet him soon but only if you have fed. He's tall, gorgeous, and handsome." I give her a questioning look because I know he isn't a vampire.

"I know, I don't really approve of vampire/human relationships," she whispers, "…but he is so sweet and cute. I promise I won't bite him."

"You don't even drink human blood," I say under my breath. Jade gives me a look that says I am right.

"I need you promise not to bite him or kill him in any way." I look at her questionably. Does she really think I will kill her boyfriend?

"Whatever… I promise." I pause. "…But if he breaks

your heart, I will keep no such promise."

Jade shakes her head. "Oh my gosh Nichole." I guess she doesn't approve of that statement.

We stand in line silently. I look around the store and notice an entrance to a bathroom across from it. I am feeling a little hungry and that will be the perfect place to enjoy my meal in peace. I look at Jade.

"You can get this right," I say quickly. I don't give her time to respond. "I'll be back, I have to use the restroom." I walk away quickly, not giving her time to stop me.

I weave through the people in the mall and walk down the hallway to get to the bathroom. When I open the door there is one person in the women's restroom. The woman is probably in her early thirties. I grab her arm, just as she finished up washing her hands and pull her into a stall.

"What do you think you're...?" I drop the bags I have to the floor of the stall.

"Don't talk, don't move, and don't scream," I say looking in her eyes. I pull her hair back and sink my fangs into her neck. I am done quickly and I send her on her way.

I walk out the bathroom and down the hall where Jade is now waiting for me. She has her arms crossed with bags in both of her hands. She is tapping her foot and the look on her face says that she isn't happy.

"What do you think you are doing?" She is furious.

"I was hungry. Did you get the stuff?" Maybe I should have waited until nightfall.

"You should never do that during the day! Or at a mall!" I roll my eyes at her. "Come on let's go."

We don't talk as she drives us back to the condo. When we make it she drops my bags on the floor, takes hers, and heads to her room.

CHAPTER 14

"Jade are you giving me the silent treatment?" She slams her door. I guess that's my answer.

I take my bags and go to my room. I put them on the floor and snuggle under the cover in my bed burying myself in the pillows. *Maybe I am a monster.*

TRANSITION

Chapter 15

A knock on my door wakes me up.

I look up as Jade walks into my room. She is wearing a black wrap dress with a pair of black pumps. Her hair is put up in a flattering bun. She has diamond studs in her ears and she has make-up on.

"You going out or something?" I take a second to take in my surroundings. I can smell food coming from the kitchen. "Is that food?"

TRANSITION

"I invited Richard over for dinner and he is bringing his friend. I would really appreciate it if you will put something nice on and join us." I just stare at her. Is she serious? "I would also appreciate it if you wouldn't feed on our guest and if you would be cordial."

I arch my eyebrow at her.

"We are having a dinner party," I say sarcastically. "Did you factor in the fact that we can't eat...food?" Jade crosses her arms. I can tell she is still mad from earlier.

"You can put it in your mouth and chew and swallow. It will eventually come up. So if you feel it, just go to the bathroom." *So gross. So, so gross.*

"Why? Why would it come up?"

"Our bodies can't handle human food. It's not compatible. So if we eat it, it comes right back up. Are you coming or not?" I sigh.

"If I attend this dinner party and abide by your rules, will you forgive me already?" She sighs.

"Yes I will. Can you get dressed already?" I nod and she leaves closing the door behind her.

I go through my bags that I laid on the floor earlier, and pick out some dressy, high waist, loose grey pants and a thin black sleeveless turtle neck top. I pull out the black pumps that we bought earlier and put them on. I go to the bathroom, brush my teeth, and put on some make-up. I have just finished flat ironing my hair, when I hear our guests arrive. My hair is bone straight. I look in the mirror. I look like a businesswoman who is going out to a club today.

I hear Jade open the door for Richard and his friend.

"Hey Richard," Jade coos.

"Hey baby." I guess they are hugging. "Oh, Jade, this is my friend Aiden. Aiden this is my girlfriend Jade."

CHAPTER 15

"Nice to meet you Jade," Aiden says. Aiden has a smooth somewhat deep voice.

"Nice to meet you too Aiden. My friend Nichole should be coming out of her room soon. She always takes forever to get ready." I roll my eyes.

Jade is making small talk with Richard and his friend Aiden, while I take my precious time leaving the room. I am done getting dressed but I know it will irritate Jade if I take my time coming out of my room.

"Nichole if you don't come out now!" Jade furiously says under her breath so that only I can hear. I smile.

"Oh my gosh…here I come."

As soon as I walk into the living room, one guy whistles and I see the other guy's eyes pop. I smile shyly at the response.

"This is my roommate and friend, Nichole. Nichole this is my boyfriend Richard and his friend Aiden." Richard is the one who whistled.

Jade's boyfriend Richard is a handsome guy. He is slightly built with bright chocolate eyes. His hair was black and cut in a high blended fade. He's about Jade's height but just slightly taller than her. They really fit perfectly together. He is wearing a black polo sweater with a white-collar shirt underneath and black jeans. He's nice looking and dresses well. I look toward his friend and am shocked by how attracted I am to him. Aiden has a light caramel complexion and is very muscular. He is wearing a slightly fitted black tee shirt with a cream zip neck sweater on top and faded blue jeans. His eyes are chocolate also but just slightly lighter than Richard's. His blackish brown hair is cut into a polished buzz cut. He has a kind and handsome face with a prominent jaw line and a smile to die for. They both seem like nice people but I can't help the fact that the one thing I notice most is the smell of their blood and the thrumming of their heartbeats.

"Wow, I guess beautiful women always stick together, right Aiden," Richard says bumping Aiden on his shoulder. Aiden nods his head and continues to smile at me.

"Oh stop it Richard." Jade playfully taps him on his arm. I know she is flirting with him. If she had used all her strength, that tap would have sent him straight through the wall.

I hold my hand out to Richard. "It's nice to finally meet you Richard. I've heard so much about you." He shakes my hand. His handshake is strong and firm. I try not to squeeze too hard.

"Yea, it's great to finally meet you too. I've come over a few times but I never got a chance to meet you. I didn't want to bother you or anything because Jade said you were depressed or something." I shoot a glare at Jade. Why is my business being told to Richard?

"Well yes, my boyfriend just broke up with me. You could say it killed me...I guess." I shrug my shoulders and this time I get a glare from Jade. "I'm better now." *Not really...*I add mentally.

"Hey, I'm Aiden. Aiden Washington." Richard's friend finally speaks up nervously. He holds out his hand. "...But you already knew that," he says pointing a finger at me. Yep, he is nervous.

"Nice to meet you Aiden," I say as I shake his hand. "I'm Nichole. Nichole Roberts." Everyone laughs and then a cloud of awkwardness takes over the room.

"Well I made my special pomegranate martinis." Jade goes around the bar and grabs the martinis. She hands one to

CHAPTER 15

all of us. I take a sip. *Wow, this is good.*

"…and why is this the first time that I have tried these. I love them. Can you make them every day?" I lean against the breakfast bar as I smirk at Jade. She rolls her eyes at me.

"If you wish," she says dismissing me. "I made spaghetti and meatballs, green beans, and garlic bread. I know how much you like Italian food." Jade speaks directly to Richard. "I also made lemon pie." She gives him butterfly eyes.

I roll my eyes again and take a sip of my martini. I have never seen her like this. Out the corner of my eyes I notice Aiden is staring at me and when I look at him, he shakes his head. I guess the lovebirds are bothering him too. He has this happy and somewhat shy smile on his face. Reality hits me just then. This isn't just a dinner party that Jade wants to have with her boyfriend. They are trying to set Aiden and me up.

"Jade," I say rather loudly. Jade and Richard look at me. Aiden has already been staring. "Are you trying to set me up with Aiden?"

The look on Jade's face is priceless. She is shocked and furious. I've never been that bold in my human life but I have a new found courage lately. Richard starts laughing and Aiden looks away in embarrassment. I, on the other hand, feel no remorse for being so bold. If I am wrong, I still won't feel bad.

"Nichole, yes and no, but this is somewhat a double date." I smile at her in a menacing way. "Please don't be so rude." She huffs and Richard comforts her.

The dinner is ready so Jade leads all three of us to the dining room that I never knew about. Inhabiting the middle of the dinning room is a nice sized dark wooden table that can seat eight. The table is already decorated with the food Jade has cooked for the evening. Before we started eating, Jade refills all of our martini glasses. Jade is a different person when she is around Richard. She is like a smitten puppy in love. Like that zoned out melting into a puddle love. She seems more human around him. I'm not really giving the dinner party any attention. I just stare at Jade and watch how she and Richard react to each other. They are in love and anyone can see it. Somewhere deep inside, I hope I can find true love.

"Are you going to eat your food? Or should I be worried?" I look at Aiden as he speaks. He breaks me out of the trance I have drifted off into. Jade and Richard look at me expectantly. They have already started eating. I am the only one that hasn't touched my food.

"Oh just give me time. Jade is the best cook by the way. Me on the other hand," I make a thumbs down.

Everyone laughs at the fact that I say I can't cook. I know how to cook but what's the point of it now? I look at the food on my plate. If I were human, I would have already devoured it. I am skeptical about eating. I don't know what to expect but I am enticed by the food. I take a bite of spaghetti and it takes a lot of will power to swallow. The food tastes foreign. If I have to compare it, it will be like human eating a shoe. Well I imagine it would be like that. *This is so gross.* Out the corner of my eye, I see Jade smile and give me a thumbs up. I don't know how she is acting like she enjoys the food. *She said if I did this she would forgive me. So all I have to do is get through the night. Great!*

"This food is great baby," Richard says. I make a face. This food is *so* not good...to me.

CHAPTER 15

"So... Richard," I say slowly. I need a distraction from eating the poison and I want to get Jade back for forcing me to eat it. , "...do you like vampires?" Jade almost spits her food out. I hit a nerve.

"Hey babe, are you ok?" Richard starts patting Jade on the back as she coughs. I smirk her way.

"I'm fine, just ate too fast or something." She looks at me with a look that says "Please stop." When Richard is done making sure Jade is ok he answers my question.

"I guess you could say I do. I enjoy movies and shows about them. If that's what you mean." I nod my head.

"I like anything with a vampire in it, books, movies, shows, etc.," Aiden says. I keep forgetting Aiden is here but he keeps making sure I don't.

I am blatantly ignoring him. If I pay too much attention to him, I might want to take a bite. I decide to not be rude and project my next question to him.

"So what if they were real? Would you still like them?"

"Who's to say they are not?" I make a face at him that says, what are you crazy? "Wait, wait." He put his hands up in defense and I smirk. "Of course they are not real but I always like to think, just because we haven't found something, doesn't make it unreal." Aiden's response shocks me. I like his response and he doesn't even know how right he is.

"So would you like them if they were real? Or would you try to kill them all? Or would you become one?" Aiden and Richard smile and Jade glares. It is Aiden that speaks up first.

"I really don't know. It just depends on the situation. If they were trying to kill everyone in the world, then yes I would want to kill them all. If they were just another species

145

like humans and they had their good and bad people then they are kind of just like us. You can't say you like every person that you have ever met and you can't say that every person you've met was good or bad."

"It would be cool if vampires were real," Richard finally says. We all laugh except Jade.

"I would like to kill this conversation, and my roommate for starting it." That starts new laughter.

"I would like to kill my ex-boyfriend." Everyone looks at me and laughs and Jade gives me an all-knowing look. "... And Jade you can't kill me...you love me too much."

"I'm sure we all have an ex that we would like to kill," Richard says. Jade looks at him. "Aww honey, it's nothing. I was engaged to my ex and when she cheated I broke it off. The only reason I am so pissed is because she took my mother's ring." Jade gives him a sad smile.

"What's her name? I'll be your hit man or women in this case," I tell Richard. "You might want to give that ring to Jade one day." Jade gasps and gives me a look that says she is pissed. Richard laughs.

"I don't know. Maybe I will one day." Jade gasps again and he looks at her in the most loving way.

"Alright, enough of this mushy stuff...let's get drunk," Aiden says. I raise my glass in agreement.

...

The dinner goes smoothly after that. After I force half of the food down. I have to excuse myself to the bathroom. My body can no longer handle that disgusting stuff. I brush my teeth after tossing up the human food and now I am in the mood for vampire food. I am making my way to the dining room when I see that everyone has ventured into the living room. They are sitting on the L-shaped couch. I can tell that

CHAPTER 15

Richard is aroused or something because his heart is beating extra fast. I am having trouble concentrating on not feeding on our guest. All I can hear is the drumming sound of Richard's heart.

"Well I'm going to call it a night," I say needing to get away.

"Aww come on, keep me company while these two lovebirds get inappropriate." I can tell that Aiden likes me but I can't encourage that. I am a vampire, and he is a human. Not to mention the fact that I have issues with controlling my hunger. Also, to top it off, I just got out of a bad relationship where my boyfriend tried to kill me.

"No. I think I need to go to bed." I go to the fridge to grab a medium bottle of vodka. I need a drink after this night. Jade comes up behind me.

"Nichole, what are you doing? The night isn't over and I think Aiden likes you." She says it so low that I know only I can hear.

"You and Richard are getting a little too frisky and all I can hear is his heart. I'm having trouble not feeding on one of our guests. Also, I don't want a relationship, or a fling."

"Who doesn't want a fling?"

"I don't...besides I'm a virgin anyway." That shocks her.

"What do you mean? I thought..." I cut her off.

"I was going to Nate's house to have my first time with him!" She gives me a sad look.

"I'm sorry he played you like that." *Me too...*

"What are you two ladies talking about over there," Richard says interrupting our conversation.

"Nothing!" Jade and I say at the same time.

TRANSITION

"Ok, go to your room then. By the way I'm glad you are valuing their lives so much that you're going to your room." Not that going to my room will help much but at least I won't be face to face with them.

I start to walk to my bedroom when Aiden speaks up.

"You're going to your room to get drunk alone?" I really don't want his attention.

"Yep that's the way I like it," I say and I disappear before he can say anything else.

...

I sit in my room and turn on the flat screen TV that hangs on the wall. I don't know when Jade installed it but I'm glad she did. I drink my vodka straight from the bottle. I start to get a little buzzed as I flip through the channels. I stop when I see America's Next Top Model. Apparently they have the whole series playing today. I watch as models compete for the 'Top Model' title. I drink and watch, and drink and watch until I am drunk. I have been watching the same show for at least two hours. I am just thinking that I can go on the show and probably win when I hear a knock on my door. I know who it is instantly because I can hear two other people getting busy in the other room.

"Come in." Aiden walks into my room. He has a look of shock on his face. "What?" He clears his throat. I look down at myself...surely I'm dressed.

"Nothing...it's just... your eyes were bright green and now they look...umm...black." *Oh my gosh...* I have to make up an excuse fast.

"Oh...it's nothing, they do that sometimes." He doesn't look convinced.

"Really...?" Why did he come in here?

"Really!" I am getting irritated.

CHAPTER 15

"I didn't mean to offend you. Anyways I rode here with Richard and it looks like we will be here a while. So I thought I would give you some company." I am hungry and irritated; I don't want company.

"Well if I wanted your company, I would have stayed in the living room with you. It was inevitable that they were going to get busy you know. I know they were trying to set us up but I'm really not interested. So if you don't mind..." That is his cue to leave.

He nods his head and I regret what I said but it is for his own good. I can tell he really likes me but we can never have anything.

"Wow, your ex did a number on you didn't he?" That comment flares my anger.

"You don't know anything about what he did to me!" I yell. If I could cry, I would be in tears. "You don't know me at all."

"Well maybe, if you were a little nicer, I could get to know you but you don't seem to want to give me a chance." I roll my eyes. He seems to be hurt by what I said.

I have to fix this so he won't be so offended. I look him directly in the eyes.

"Just forget what I just said. Pretend that I said something nice. We can even be friends. We don't hang out or anything but we're cordial." He is taken aback by what I said.

"What are you talking about?" He pauses. "You know what, you have some issues and you need to work them out. Maybe you will be nice to the next guy who likes you. Have a nice night." He leaves the room and closes the door. *What just happened?*

TRANSITION

Chapter 16

"I'm sure it was nothing, Nichole."

Jade is in the kitchen cleaning up the dishes while I sit on the couch looking back at her. She is dismissing the problem at hand. I told her how the mind control thing didn't work on Richard's friend Aiden.

"...But it didn't work! It has worked before and I know I did it right." Jade sighs and then turns to look at me.

TRANSITION

"Look you were drunk maybe you thought you did it right but didn't." She put her hands on her hips. "Does this have anything to do with you liking him, because he likes you?" She smiles.

I roll my eyes. I do not need this right now. With everything that has happened I can't think about anything else, especially another guy. The last one scorned me to no return.

"Jade." My tone is authoritative. She puts her hands up in surrender.

"I was just being hopeful. You are not ready, I got it. I will stay out of it. No more talk of Aiden."

I hope she means it. I need to get myself together before anything else happens, and to top it off, I don't like Aiden. I think it will be a long time before I like any guy again.

"What do you want to do today Nichole?"

"I don't know. What are you doing today? Are you going out with Richard?" Jade goes out with Richard almost all the time apparently.

"No, I thought we could hang out today." I am surprised.

"Oh, don't look like that."

"Like what?"

"Like all I do is hang out with Richard and not you." I smirk at her and sigh.

"So what do you have planned?"

"I thought we could go for a run and then a swim." I arch my eyebrow at her.

"Really?"

"Really."

•••

I thought Jade was crazy when she said she wanted to go for

CHAPTER 16

a run and a swim, but that is before she led me to the woods. We are going running through the woods but the swimming part is still vague.

"Ready to race?" she asks. I smile at her. I am *so* ready.

"I'm ready." She looks at me and takes off.

Jade is ahead of me but I don't care. Running like a vampire is exhilarating. We run through trees and hop over rocks. We don't run side by side but we weave throughout the forest. We laugh the whole time.

I can see the animals run away because they know we are coming. It is understandable; animals will try to stay far away from a bigger predator that can eat them. The leaves, grass and flowers whip as I run past them. I don't knock into any trees this time, thank goodness. We run through the forest for about an hour before I see the cliff. It is farther in front of us but we will be there in no time. I start to slow down but Jade keeps running, toward the cliff, at full speed.

"Don't slow down! Jump!" She yells over her shoulder.

" Jade what are you…?" She jumps before I can finish.

"Jump!" I hear her yell as she falls. *Just do it…* I tell myself. *Don't be scared.*

I run at full speed toward the cliff and jump. My arms are spread wide and my head leans back as I embrace the air. Below is a river with a small waterfall. *So this is what she meant by swimming.* I pierce the water gracefully. I don't know how deep I go into it but I know I can hold my breath for a substantial amount of time. I don't resurface immediately. Instead, I admire the underwater world. I watch as the fish swim away. They scatter when I get close. I continue to swim underwater for a while. It is nice and peaceful. I let go of all my problems and just relax. When I finally surface, I see Jade floating on her back.

"This is nice isn't it? And we don't even have to worry about anything trying to eat or bite us," Jade says. I lean back to float on my back and smile.

"Yea, this is nice. I would have never done this if I was human." I can see Jade smile. I found swimming in natural bodies of water repulsive when I was human. I don't care now.

"Well, you would have probably died from the fall or drowned if you were human but I get what you mean." I laugh. "I like to come out here to relax. It gets tiring playing human sometimes. I'm not a human. Sometimes I feel more like an animal. I need to run the way we do. I need to jump over extreme heights sometimes. I need to feed. I'm not human anymore and sometimes I need to just be a vampire because that's who I am now. Sometimes you can't fight it."

I just listen while Jade opens up. I understand the struggle she is going through. I am going through it now. She always tries her best to be normal, like humans. She doesn't feed on them and she associates herself with them sometimes. The struggle between wanting to be human again and just being a vampire is a difficult one. At least she shows restraint in feeding on humans. I don't think I ever can. It feels good to embrace the new me, the vampire me, only when I don't think about the human me. I want to always remember the old me, because if I don't, I will become a monster with no regard for human life.

"Yeah, sometimes you can't fight it."

We swim and talk for a couple of hours. There is a lot I don't know about Jade and a lot she doesn't know about me. She talks about how she has always wanted to be a painter.

CHAPTER 16

She says she would probably go to art school or something since she had all the time in the world. She tells me that she is an only child and how it was really hard on her family when she went missing. Her mom couldn't have any more children. She says her parents are doing better. She checks on them every once in a while but she says they are getting older and she dreads the day that they will pass on. She tries to reassure me that my family will get better over time.

I tell her I don't know what I want to do in life. I was going to figure it out when I got to college. The one thing that is stopping me from figuring it out is the fact that I don't know if I am going to college anymore. I don't know what I am going to do. I tell her about my life before that dreadful day that I was turned. I feel like I don't have much to say about myself. I don't feel like I have lived yet to say much of anything. She tells me that I have plenty of time to live.

It is starting to get dark so we decide it is time to leave. We climb back up the cliff, which is just as fun as everything else we did today. Jade jokes about how, if we fall, we will just start over because we won't die. It is easy to climb up the cliff. We run back through the forest. At the speed we are going, we are dry before we get through. Before we go home, Jade stops to feed. She asks if I want to but I decline. I don't like to feed on animals. When we make it out of the forest, Jade and I walk back to the condo at a normal pace. It is dark by the time we make it home.

Jade has a huge grin on her face when we walk up to the door and I see Richard leaning up against it waiting for her. *Back to playing human*, I think to myself.

"You guys look a mess. Where did y'all go?" Richard looks us up and down with mock disgust and laughs.

"Oh, we just went on a run and nature walk," she says

as she tries to hug him. I laugh when he resists.

"Jade...no... you're going to get me dirty." They both giggle and I smile.

"I like you dirty. We could take a shower together," she whispers. If I was human I wouldn't have been able to hear it but I'm not and I did. *Time for me to go.*

We all walk in the condo and I quickly go to my room but that doesn't stop me from hearing Jade and Richard playing around.

I don't take a bath like I normally do. Instead, I get in the shower. I want to clean up fast because I need to feed and I want to give Jade some privacy. I quickly wash up and wash my hair. I dry my hair and leave it in its naturally curly state. I put on the leather dress that Jade bought me in Rosenburg and some pumps and leave the condo.

"I'll be back later." I know Jade will hear me.

I decide to go to a random club. I'm not paying attention to too much of anything. I just need to feed and go home. It isn't long before some guy hits on me. I take him to the back of the club and feed. I go into a pattern of feeding and erasing memory until I am full. I leave the club and go back to the condo. Jade and Richard are asleep by the time I make it back.

I strip out of my dress and shoes and replace them with some pajamas. I curl up in my bed under the cover and slip into a peaceful sleep. Before I drift off, I have a nagging feeling. I am somewhat happy at the moment. How can I be happy after feeding on all those people, after killing two people, and how can I be happy when I know my family isn't? I quickly push those feelings away and sleep. *Who am I becoming?*

Chapter 17

I wake up instantly. Someone is yelling.

Jade and Richard are fighting in the living room. I roll over in the bed and groan.

"Richard why are you doing this," Jade whines.

"Why? Well maybe because I like you and I want to know more about you!"

"You know everything about me!"

"No, I don't! I ask you about your family and you just brush me off!"

TRANSITION

"I don't want to talk about my parents. There is no need to talk about them."

"See you just did it again. What about your past? Huh? Can I know anything about that?" Jade is quiet.

"I thought so. You don't want to talk about that either. You don't want to tell me about you!"

"I just want to leave my past in the past and I don't like talking about my family!"

"How am I supposed to know anything about you if you don't tell me anything? I open up to you! How about you do the same?"

"I open up enough!"

"No you don't." Richard's voice is adamant. "You might as well be a stranger to me! What about your friend in there? Huh? Where did y'all meet? How close are y'all? Can you tell me that?"

"How do you know she wants me to talk about her, even if it has to do with me too?" I can tell Jade is making up excuses but do I really want her talking to Richard about me?

"That's an excuse Jade and you know it!"

"Can't you just accept that you know enough about me?"

"No I can't because I know nothing Jade. NOTHING! What is this to you? Is this just sex to you? Are we even in a relationship or did I imagine it?" Jade gasps.

"How could you say that? Of course we are in a relationship! I've opened up as much as I can Richard!"

"You know what. I can't do this anymore! When you are ready to commit and open up to me, call me." I hear Richard's foots steps echo as he walks to the door and out of it. He slams the door shut.

I roll out of bed and throw on some jeans and a tee

CHAPTER 17

shirt. I slip on some sandals and go into the living room to see if Jade is ok. She is sitting on the couch when I approach her. She looks sad. I sit next to her on the couch.

"Jade...why didn't you do that mind control thing to fix your relationship?" Jade shoots up off the couch.

"Why! What do you mean why! Well let me see maybe because even though I'm a vampire I want a real relationship! That's why but you wouldn't know anything about that would you?"

That is a low blow. She knows what I've gone through. My relationship with Nate was real in my eyes. At least until I found out he was a vampire. I know Jade is just giving me backlash from her argument with Richard but that doesn't stop me from becoming angry at her comment.

"Oh so when it fucking rains it pours! Don't you dare take your anger out on me because you're having issues with your *human* boyfriend. You knew from the beginning that you couldn't tell him everything! Aren't you the one who said human/vampire relationships never work?"

"Fuck you Nichole! You're the last person that should be lecturing me about human/vampire relationships? You know what, I don't even know why I'm talking to you! It's not like you would understand what I am going through. It requires you to have a little humanity!"

I cross my arms. "What are you trying to say? I don't understand because I don't value human life? Well you are wrong. I do value it!"

"Yeah, really? So where did you go last night? Did you go out to have fun or to feed on innocent humans? You're losing yourself everyday!"

"Don't take it out on me because you're having problems and can't control your emotions!"

TRANSITION

"You want to talk about control! Where was your control when you killed those two guys, huh? Why didn't you just do that mind control thing on them!" She took it too far and I am through with this conversation.

I leave the condo and slam the door like Richard. How dare she throw every mistake I've made back in my face. I have been through enough already and I don't need this from her. I walk down the sidewalk. I don't know where I am going. I see Richard sitting on a bench a little further down the sidewalk.

"Hey Nichole, is she still mad?" He looks sad. I feel bad for him. *There's some humanity for you Jade!*

"Hey." I am curt and keep walking.

I walk past him without answering his question. I sigh and turn around. I walk right back up to him and he looks up.

"Yeah, she is still mad. So mad, in fact, she took it out on me." He looks down at his hands.

"Sorry about that." I roll my eyes.

"No need to be sorry. Look, why don't you go buy her some flowers. I think she likes red roses." He looks up at me and smirks. "I know; red roses are so standard." He smiles. "Oh and say you're sorry. Her past isn't a happy one so give her time. It's not an easy thing to talk about." I know Jade will never tell him about her past and family but he doesn't need to know that.

"…But how can that be enough? I don't know anything about her past or family." I sigh. Am I a counselor today?

"Look Richard, she is telling you the truth when she says everything she has told you is everything that matters. If you really like her then you will accept it."

"I love her." I stare at him.

"Don't tell *me* that. Tell *her*."

160

CHAPTER 17

I walk away. I hear him ask me where I am going but it is none of his business. Jade won't see me for a couple of days. I walk until I am back in the forest that we were in yesterday. I just want to be alone. I continue to walk through the forest until I make it to the cliff. I look over the cliff at the river below. It is a long drop. I lay down on my back at the edge of the cliff. I look up at the sky and I start crying. I know tears won't fall but I let myself feel like I am crying.

I don't know how long I lay there at the edge of the cliff but the sky starts to darken. It isn't night that begins to darken the sky but storm clouds. I can see the rain form in the sky and fall. It isn't long before it soaks the ground and me along with it. I pretend that I am crying as the rain falls and travels down my face. Every drop is a tear that would have fallen if I could cry. The raindrops are my substitute tears.

Maybe Jade is right about me, no matter how mad she is. I am losing myself and adapting to being a vampire. At least she is trying to somewhat be human. We are vampires and I don't think there is anyway to avoid what we have become but at least she tries. I, on the other hand, am beginning to give up.

I am fighting a battle between wanting to live and wanting to die. I mean I'm already dead. I look over the cliff and into the water. It looks more welcoming than before. I roll over the cliff and slowly fall downward into the blue water. When I hit the water, I don't swim, I just suck it all in. I suck all the water into my lungs until everything goes black.

...

"Nichole!" I hear someone in the distance calling my name. "Nichole! Wake up stupid." The voice is getting clearer. I feel someone shaking me.

TRANSITION

I open my eyes and see Jade looking at me with an angry look on her face. I don't have time to respond to her because the water in my lungs is making an exit out of my body. I lean over on my arms and cough out all the water. *Why couldn't I just have died?*

I sit up and look at Jade. She tries to help me up and I just push her away.

"Don't touch me Jade."

"Come on Nichole. Stop being ridiculous. I can't believe you tried to drown yourself," she says in disbelief.

"I wish it had worked. I had doubts but I had to try." Jade looks at me with sympathy.

"I'm sorry...ok? I shouldn't have said the things I said. We are emotionally unstable and after Richard left, you were the only person around but that doesn't make it right." I get up off the ground and Jade also stands up.

We are back at the top of the cliff. Jade must have carried me back up it. I look at her and she is soaked. I guess I should forgive her since she jumped in and got me.

"Let's go home Nichole." She starts walking and I follow. I don't know if I am happy that I am still alive or sad that I didn't just die. We make it back to the condo at three in the morning. I don't say anything to Jade on the way back or at the house and she doesn't push me to talk either.

She does give me a look when I grab some tequila out of the fridge but she doesn't say anything. I go into my bathroom and run some hot water in the tub. I strip out of my clothes and get in the tub. I just soak and drink until the sun comes up.

Chapter 18

I break my one unwritten rule and call Casey.

I know I shouldn't have but I miss her. She is the only one from my past life that knows what is going on. I am spiraling out of control and losing my mind. I just think, if I hear her voice, it will help me feel better. I know it is silly to think that hearing her voice will help but I just need something familiar. I just need my best friend.

"Hello?" I don't know what to say to her. "Hello…?" She doesn't have my new number so how can she know it is me.

TRANSITION

"Hey Casey." I hear her gasp on the phone.

"Hey Ni... Hey girl! I thought I would never hear from you again. I thought you said you were trying to move on? I mean I'm glad you called! I miss you." I smile I miss her too.

"I miss you too Case."

"Is everything alright?" She always knows when something is wrong with me.

"I just...I'm just losing myself. I don't know who I am anymore. I feel like I'm becoming a monster and I can't stop it."

"Do you feel like you're depressed?"

"Yes... I mean... I think I am."

"Nichole," she says calmly. "You aren't even trying to move on. I know you. You are just dwelling on what you are missing and on what happened to you. In order to move on you can't keep being sad and pitying yourself. You have to accept what has happened. What if your family knew? Would they have wanted you to be so sad and depressed? No, they wouldn't. I don't want you to be either. I know it's going to take time but you can do it." I wonder how she can be so sure.

"You think so?"

"I know so! Hey, and maybe when I go to college, somewhere away from this town, then we could see each other again! By that time, hopefully you have more control." I laugh. I am glad that she is giving me so much positive energy.

"That sounds like a plan," I say quietly. I never thought I would get to hang out with Casey again but if she lives somewhere else what will stop me? She already knows about me.

CHAPTER 18

"You know, you are what you are. You can't help what you have to do to survive. Just try not to kill people and don't feel bad about embracing it. Just don't let it turn you into a monster and when I say monster I mean a sadistic, evil, killing vampire like the bad guys in vampire movies or Nate." I laugh.

"Ok, I won't. Thanks Case. You don't know how much I needed that and to hear your voice. How's my family?" I can hear her sigh softly, as if she is going to give me bad news.

"They are really sad right now but they will get better. Don't worry. They are speaking to me again. I think talking to me helps them feel closer to you and I will do everything to make them feel better." The smile I had earlier faded. I wish I could do something to make it better for them. Right now, what is best is to stay away for their safety.

"Thank you Casey... for everything. Can you tell my family that if I could see them now, I would tell them I love them and to be happy for me."

"Yes I will. I love you Nichole."

"I love you too Casey. Bye."

"Bye." I hold the phone to my ear until she hangs up.

I lay in the bed and cover myself with the cover. It is the beginning of the day, but I'm not going anywhere. I pull the cover over my head and close my eyes. Maybe I can sleep away the pain.

...

Today is Halloween. I don't look at the calendar or anticipate this day. I am just sitting in the bed flipping through the channels and it seems like every channel is Halloween themed. I'm not going out today. There will be children and families everywhere and I don't want to disturb their happiness. My plans are to sit in bed and watch TV.

The only thing I wish I could do today is eat candy. I want to devour lots and lots of candy but I'm a vampire. Vampires can't eat candy. Well we can but it probably tastes nasty. I wish I could watch scary movies, eat candy, and do all of that with my best friend Casey. After Casey and I got too old to trick or treat, we would go to her house and watch scary movies and eat candy. It is a tradition for us. Today I will try to honor that tradition by just watching scary movies since I can't do the rest. It is still very early in the day so I am just trying to find a channel that has a scary movie marathon when Jade pops in my room holding two garment bags. She is smiling from ear to ear.

"Come right on in why don't you?" Her smile drops a bit when she hears the dullness in my voice.

"Oh cheer up Nichole! It's Halloween." I just stare at her and she places the bags on the bed.

"Aren't you a little old to get excited about Halloween?" I ask.

She rolls her eyes at me. "No I'm not. Besides we are going to an adult costume party." I look back at the TV and start flipping through the channels again. *I am not going to an adult costume party...*

"You mean *you* are going to an adult costume party."

"No we are going, and guess what you are going as!" When I don't respond she keeps talking. "You are going as a vampire!" I look at her and raise my eyebrow. *A vampire?*

"...And what are you going as? A human?" I smile and surprisingly she smiles too and crosses her arms.

"No...silly. I'm going as a witch." I laugh. She's going as a vampire, playing a human, playing a witch.

"A witch? Why not a vampire?" She gives me a look.

CHAPTER 18

"Of course I'm going as a vampire! It's the only day of the year we can be ourselves! Fangs out and all! But we do need to dress the part." I look at the bags on the bed. Those must be our costumes.

"So what are we wearing?" I am getting a little excited. She digs in a bag and pulls out a floor length long, red, lace dress with long sleeves. It is beautiful and sexy looking.

"You are going to wear this dress. I want you to look like an old elegant vampire. I want your hair to be bone straight and I want you to have dark eye shadow and red lipstick. Crimson red lipstick. Lastly you need to provide the fangs and black eyes." she smiles.

"...And what are you wearing?" She pulls out the same dress but in black.

"I'll be wearing this and everything else will be the same for me but just with a different color dress." We are going to look sexy at this party. Jade digs in the bags again and pulls out two sets of vampire fangs.

"I thought you said we could bring out our own fangs." I pout. I was looking forward to it.

"Don't look at me like that. These are for when someone wants you to take your fangs out. You turn around and pull this out of your bra or something. That way you don't have to explain why your fangs don't come out."

"Or we could just say we put some adhesive on them to make them stay."

"Any vampire fang adhesive is easily removable... unless you went to the dentist and had them like super glued on." She has a point but I am sure there is some kind of semi-permanent adhesive somewhere. I don't feel like looking for it so I will go along with Jade's plan.

"Is Richard attending this party with us?" She gives me

a huge smile that says yes he is.

"Yes, he is…and he is going as Dracula! We are his vampire brides." I shake my head and smile. *Of course…*

"Really Jade?"

"Really! Aiden will be there also but you missed your chance with him. He started seeing this new girl. I'm sure you could get rid of her, if you know what I mean, if you like him that is." My smile fades and I narrow my eyes. She is trying to see if I am jealous that he is seeing someone, but I'm not. I also don't have any plans to make this girl disappear either.

"Jade," I say slowly, "…for the last time. I don't like Aiden and I don't care if he is seeing some new girl. I hope they are happy together." This time Jade's smile fades.

"Fine, I was just checking. Anyway, he and his date are going as vampires too. Apparently, our kind make the sexiest looking costumes. Well, other costumes like cats and bunnies are sexy too."

"As long as we aren't going trick or treating, I'm down." Jade smiles and leaves the room. I know she is happy that I didn't put up a big fight over going to this party.

I look back at the TV and start flipping through the channels. *Tonight might actually be fun…*

Chapter 19

The club is blasting with music and people.

There is a huge dance floor and people are gyrating to the music. Different colored strobe lights flash their way around the room casting a glow around everyone and making the party seem fast paced.

People are dressed in all kinds of costumes. The women are wearing sexy bunny, cat, witch, pirate, doctor, and nurse costumes. You name it; they are wearing it in a sexy style. The men have similar costumes but they aren't as raunchy as the women's.

TRANSITION

I glance throughout the club at the different costumes. We aren't the only vampires in the party but from the looks of people's faces, we are the sexiest. What they don't know is that our costumes are real. At least me and Jade's costumes are real. *Richard on the other hand...* He is wearing a white button down collar shirt that he left halfway open to show his abs and fake blood, with black slacks, and black dress shoes. He also has a black cape that is black on the outside and red on the inside. When he picked up Jade and me, I couldn't help myself and I laughed at him. His fangs look amateur compared to ours and he even put fake blood on his face to look like he had fed on someone.

"Baby, why didn't you get me fangs like yours? I would have even liked black contacts!" Richard yells loudly over the music.

"I'm sorry, I wasn't thinking! I should have." She smiles and kisses him on his cheek.

"I don't know how y'all can close your mouth with those things in, but it makes your costume seem more real!" *If only he knew...*

From a distance, I can see Aiden walking over towards us with his date. He looks just as ridiculous as Richard. They are both dressed as Dracula for Halloween. His date is also a vampire. She has a short tight leather dress on with a cape and stripper pumps on. Her fangs are terrible too. She has a long black wig on that hides most of her blonde hair. Her skin complexion is a bit pale which makes her look a little more like the vampires do in movies. *She must not get enough sun.* Although her vampire costume looks as bad as the two Dracula's, her dress is cute and it isn't as raunchy as the other women's dresses in the club.

CHAPTER 19

"Heyyy!" Aiden says as he and Richard did some kind of guy hug. "This is Sarah!"

"Hey Sarah," we all say at the same time as Aiden looks me up and down. *Oh please…*

"Well you too look more like lady vampires than I do," Sarah says to Jade and me. We both smile and she gasps.

"OMG, your fangs are to die for!" *If only she knew…*

"Yeah where did you get them," Aiden asks.

"Hey, hey Jade and Nichole can't give away all their secrets! I might need to use them in the future," Richard says with complete seriousness. Jade laughs.

"I'm going to get a drink," I say and Jade gives me a shocked look. "From the bar," I add. Her sudden relief is unmistakable.

"Why don't we get everyone a drink," Aiden says suddenly. *Why is Aiden inviting himself to get a drink with me?*

"What would everyone like?" They all give their drink orders to Aiden and I walk away without him. He quickly follows behind me.

"You're looking good Nichole," Aiden says as he takes out his fangs. I don't respond. The bartender walks up to me as soon as I make it to the bar.

"What can I get for you beautiful? A bloody cocktail perhaps?" The bartender smiles at me seductively. I smile back flirtatiously. Out the corner of my eye I see Aiden frown. "I'd let you bite me with those sexy fangs." *Really…*

"You promise?" I might make a visit to the bar later… *alone next time.* Just then Aiden clears his throat…*what is his problem?* "I'll take a bloody cocktail." The bartender looks at Aiden with frustration.

"…And what can I get for you?" He isn't as nice to Aiden as he was to me. I laugh under my breath. Aiden gives him everyone's orders and the bartender walks away to fix our drinks. We stand in silence while waiting for our drinks. Aiden stares at me and I stare at the alcohol that is artfully arranged behind the bar. Jade isn't playing when she says he likes me.

"So… you like bartenders? Maybe I should become one." His comment pisses me off. I look at him with a glare.

"Maybe, I do. They ask me what I want and then give it to me. The relationship is as simple as that. Why… do you have a problem with it?" I'm not being very nice but he is here with a date. He needs to focus on her and not me.

"I could do that if you let me." I don't look away from him. I just stare with my eyebrow cocked.

"Don't you have a date? Why don't you do that for her? Anyway, I'm not…" He cut me off.

"…Interested? Yeah I get it. You keep saying that but I guess I'm not listening." I could see the irritation cloud his face. "How stupid of me," he says under his breath.

I don't understand what he wants from me. I haven't been nice so he can't be attracted to my personality. He has a date so what is he doing flirting with me? *I could do that if you let me…* Really well I told him that I'm not interested and he isn't giving me my space. Yea, he's cute…. so what? I'm not interested. Maybe I should tell him to give me space and then maybe he would. Maybe his attraction is completely physical? If it is, he is out of luck in that department. I just don't know and I really don't care.

The bartender returned just then with all our drinks.

"Here you go. You know I'll be waiting for that bite." The bartender completely directs his attention to me, thus ignoring Aiden entirely. "I'll be a willing victim." *Good to know…* "I get off at one. Come see me," he says as he slides me a card with his number on it. I take it and put it in my bra. The bartender smiles at me.

I pick up my drink and Jade's drink while Aiden takes his, Sarah's, and Richard's. He doesn't speak to me as we walk back to our friends and I don't care. As a matter of fact, I am happy he isn't speaking to me. Hopefully that means he gets the picture.

"Were you flirting with that bartender," Jade asks as Aiden and I approach.

"Yeah, I kind of was."

"He's cute," Jade and Sarah say in unison. Their men on the other hand look a little irritated. I'm sure Sarah doesn't know why Aiden looks irritated.

"Oh, you are cuter honey," Jade says to Richard. I roll my eyes. They can be too much sometimes.

I am starting to feel like a fifth wheel, so I excused myself to the dance floor. I drink all of my drink, which is just cranberry juice and vodka; I place my glass on a nearby table and dance my way to the middle of the dance floor.

Dancing is always fun. At least it is when it's not getting me killed. Jade pulls herself away from Richard and walks over to dance with me. We dance for a couple of songs until Richard comes out to the dance floor and steals her. Then, I start dancing with some random guy. While I am dancing, I start to feel like someone is watching me. My senses are heightened so I know someone is out there looking at me. I start to get this eerie feeling that it is Nate watching me dance with another guy again until I notice it is Aiden. We lock eyes and I see him shake his head. I quickly look away and continue to dance with my current dance partner. *What is his problem?*

TRANSITION

Aiden finally makes his way to the dance floor with Sarah. *Good, he is finally taking his date out to dance*, I think to myself. When they finally make it over to Richard, Jade and me, I leave the dance floor.

I start walking to the bar. It is almost 1:00am and I am taking the bartender up on his offer to let me bite him. I make it to the bar and a lady bartender comes up to me.

"What can I get for you?" She is dressed in a butterfly costume with the wings and all.

"I got it." The bartender who flirted with me says to the lady. She walks away. "Ready to take advantage of me?" I smile. I am more than ready.

"I just came to get another drink." He looks at me like he doesn't believe me. I am only mildly lying.

"I get off in ten minutes." He sounds so sure of himself.

"Oh so you don't believe me? Can I have one shot of vodka please?" I smirk at him.

"I'll get your drink but that's not why you came over just a few minutes before I get off." He is technically right but I'm not about to let him know.

He fixes my drink and watches while I drink the shot. After a few minutes, I start to feel a little buzzed. Actually more than a little buzzed and my vision blurs slightly. He keeps working and I sit at the bar and wait for him to get off. While I wait, I start to feel a dizzy and heavy feeling. I shouldn't feel this drunk. When I drank vodka at the condo it took almost the whole bottle to get me even slightly drunk. I lean against the bar for support. The bartender walks around the bar and stands in front of me.

"Ready to go." I don't feel like I can talk so I just nod my head.

CHAPTER 19

He walks me into a room in the back of the building and closes the door. As soon as the door is closed, I fall to the ground. Immediately I know what was going on. I've watched enough movies to know what he did. The bartender drugged me. Rage floods through me. *Well he drugged the wrong vampire...*

"You drugged me?" I proceed to sound scared, but I'm anything but scared.

"It's called roofies baby. I thought this would be hard but you don't put up a fight, do you? Now let's take these fangs out, I don't want you choking on them." He reaches down and tries to grab my teeth. When he can't pull the teeth, he tries to just pull the fangs out. I start to fight through the fog and bring myself back. It will take more than a little drugs to take down a vampire.

"What tha..." He looks at me. I can see on his face that he realizes the fangs aren't fake.

"I have a surprise too." I say wickedly. "I'm not going to bite you. I don't want to fill my body with your vile blood but I will rid you of the world so no human girl will fall into your trap." *So you don't drug any other girl again.*

He tries to yell but I stop him with my hand crushing down on his throat. I squeeze until I hear his spine snap and his eyes glaze over. I drop him to the ground with a blank look on my face. I grab him by his leg and drag him to the back of the room in the corner. I am walking back to the doorway when a couple walks in. They closed the door and jump when they see me. I smile at them. *Time for dinner...*

"Oh look, just in time for dinner." They laugh but they look a little scared too.

"Aw man, your costume looks so real!" The guy says. He sounds a little drunk.

TRANSITION

"It is real. So don't make a sound and don't run." I say looking at both of them in the eyes.

...

When I am done feeding, I leave the room and find Jade outside the door waiting for me. She is alone. Richard, Aiden, and Sarah are sitting at a table farther away.

"Really Nichole?" I try and think of a quick excuse.

"I had to recover from the bartender drugging me." There that should do it. Her face looks shocked.

"The bartender did what?"

"He drugged me Jade. He said he gave me roofies." Jade puts her hands on my shoulders and then gives me a hug.

"Are you ok? Wait, what did you do to him?" I don't say anything. Then the couple I was just feeding on leaves the room, laughing. I told them to wait two minutes and then leave the room laughing. Jade shakes her head. "Well? What did you do?" When I still don't respond she speaks up. "Nichole, I don't condone killing but at least he won't be drugging any other women." *At least she isn't mad.*

We all party some more, that is, until we hear a scream. Jade and I look back and see a girl run out of the room that I had left earlier.

"He's dead! He's dead! It looks like he was bitten by a vampire," she screams. "He's dead," The girl starts crying.

Jade looks at me. I know she is wondering how he looks like a vampire bit him, since our fang marks go away after feeding. Let's just say theatrics got the best of me. I made two little holes in his neck to make it look like a vampire bit him. It is Halloween after all.

"Nichole what did you do," Jade says a little irritated. I just shrug. I think it is funny. "Let's go, this party is getting a

CHAPTER 19

little crazy." *I couldn't agree more.*

•••

We ride back on a party bus with a few of Richard's friends,
which include Aiden and Sarah. I'm not sure when Richard
is going to get his car, but he insisted that we need to ride the
party bus. It could be a fun ride, but Aiden is staring me
down. He is making me feel uncomfortable and irritated all
at the same time. I can't tell if his stare holds confusion, jealousy, anger, or if he is just admiring me from afar but it
needs to stop.

Unlike everybody else on the party bus, Jade and I are
quiet. I think we are both tired of the company and almost
everybody on the bus is obnoxiously drunk. I have had
enough of the noise when Sarah starts singing with the music. She is a pretty girl but that voice is atrocious and I can
hear every wrong pitch. The burden of vampire hearing is
that I can hear the good, the bad, and the ugly. Sarah's singing is ugly.

"Oh. My. Gosh. Please stop," I say a little too loudly.
Everyone looks at me and Sarah looks hurt. "I…. I'm
sorry…I think my hangover has started early." That gets
laughs out of everyone but Sarah still looks hurt. Even Jade
is laughing. I laugh along with them until I see Aiden's
smirk, then I frown. I don't want him to think I yelled at
Sarah because of him. I'm not jealous.

We make it back to the condo and I look at Jade questionably when Aiden and Sarah get off the bus with Richard,
Jade, and me. I know Richard is coming home with us but
what are Aiden and Sarah doing.

"We're just all kicking it," Jade whispers. I frown at
her. "Nichole…"

I don't give her time to finish. I walk straight in the

TRANSITION

condo and right to my room. No way am I spending any more time with anyone. I lock my door, slide into my bed, and go right to sleep.

Chapter 20

I lay on a red picnic blanket with Nate.
We stare up at the sky while holding hands. Nate planned this date. He brought hoagie sandwiches, chips, chocolate-covered strawberries and he even brought sparkling white grape juice. He doesn't drink the grape juice. Instead, he brought a red thermal bottle of some kind of protein drink in it. It smells weird but I don't think anything of it. I ask if I can I try it and he says that I won't like it. I shrug it off. It is a beautiful day and I am enjoying myself. We lay in silence.

TRANSITION

"I think I found her," Nate says, breaking the silent tranquility.

"You think you found who?" I sit up and look at him while I run my hands through his silky black hair.

"The girl I'm supposed to spend forever with." He smiles at me. He reaches up, grabs my hand off his head, and kisses it.

"How do you know it's me?"

"Cocky much? How do you know I'm talking about you Nichole?" I arch my eyebrow up at him. *It better be me...*

"Well unless you are cheating on me..."

"...I'm not, I'm not." He laughs. He has a nice laugh.

"So...?"

"So... what?" I roll my eyes. He's playing games with me.

"So, how do you know it's me?"

"Because I have never felt this way about anyone. I feel like I can trust you." I lay back down on the blanket smiling from ear to ear.

"You *can* trust me," I finally say after a beat.

Nate sits up and reaches in the brown picnic basket. He pulls out a chocolate covered strawberry and brings it to my mouth. I take a bite out of it and he smiles.

"Don't do anything to hurt me or make me mad, alright?" He looks in my eyes like he is searching for confirmation that I won't hurt him.

"Wouldn't dare, but sometimes the people we love can make us mad. So I'm not sure I can say I will never make you mad. You'll just have to forgive me if I do." His lips lift into a loving smile.

CHAPTER 20

"So, you love me?" I blush. I didn't mean to tell him that I love him but it just slipped out.

"Yea, I do, I love you Nate." I say confidently looking into his deep blue eyes.

"I love you too. Still, don't do anything to make me mad. I can be an unforgiving person and I don't want you to see that side of me." I look at him strangely but before I can respond to his statement, he kisses me. It is a deep passionate kiss and it makes me forget whatever it is that he has said.

...

I wake up in my bed and clutch my pillow. I had another dream about Nate. It is the first dream that I have had about him that doesn't involve him killing me. I open my eyes and for the first time, I feel like crying for what I have lost with Nate. Maybe what we had wasn't real but at the time it was real for me. To me, he was just a guy, I was just a girl, and we were just in a relationship. Everything was simple. Yet nothing was.

I loved Nate and I thought he loved me. Who am I kidding...I *love* Nate. I now realize that it is possible to love someone and hate them with every fiber of your being, at the same time. Nate tried to kill me, accidentally turned me, and he also broke my heart. I wonder if he ever loved me. I laugh. *He literally broke my heart.*

Nate destroyed everything in my life. My dad used to say that you shouldn't want to change anything in your past, not even your mistakes, because your mistakes help shape who you are. I don't think my dad ever factored in me being turned into a bloodthirsty vampire. If I could go back in time, I would change everything about Nate and me. I would have kept walking in that hallway and ignored him. I would never have become his girlfriend. Even though I would never have known Jade, I would have my family, I would have my best friend, and I would still be human. He could have made me fall in love with him on account of the mind control thing but at least I wouldn't have gone willingly.

I jump out of the bed and walk into the bathroom. I take one look at my hair and groan. My hair is a curly mess. As soon as I start flat ironing it Jade bombards into the bathroom. I look at Jade through the mirror. She has a huge smile on her face.

"Guess what, guess what!" She jumps up and down clapping her hands. I smile at her.

"What? Did you win the lottery?" She stops jumping and puts her hands on her hips.

"Really? The first thing that comes into your mind is did I win the lottery?" I put the flat iron down and turn around towards Jade.

"What is it Jade? It must be something good by the way you are acting."

"Richard asked me to come with him for thanksgiving and meet his parents," she squeals. I don't want to spoil her moment, so I act as if I am happy for her. I mean, I am happy for her but I don't want to be left alone. *Don't be selfish Nichole*, I tell myself.

It has been weeks since the Halloween party and now Thanksgiving is a week away. I know if she is going home with Richard that she will be leaving soon. I like having Jade around. She is now the closest thing I have to family. I feel less alone when she is around but I don't want to tell her that. If I do she might stay instead of going to meet Richard's parents. Or she might just feel guilty the whole time she is there because she left me.

CHAPTER 20

"Really! That's great! I'm so happy for you." She comes closer and hugs me.

"Are you going to be ok staying here by yourself?" I pull back and look at her.

"Of course I am! When are you leaving?"

"We are leaving the Monday before Thanksgiving." Jade looks at me as if she wants to say something.

"What is it Jade?" She takes a deep breath. This can't be good.

"Well I need you to do me a favor." *What can she possibly want?*

"Sure, what is it?"

"I need you to not feed on humans while I'm gone. You have to promise me, vegan diet only." I roll my eyes at her choice of words. No matter what we feed on, it isn't vegan but I know what she means.

"Fine," I say nonchalantly, "I won't feed on humans while you are gone. How long will you be gone anyway?"

"We will be back that Sunday, Richard has to get back to school." Richard is a law student who attends the University of Denver Law School. Maybe one day I will go back to school. It's not like I have anything better to do.

"Well, I'll miss you," I say with a pout, "...and you said our kind couldn't get along."

"Aw... I'll miss you too roomy and we don't get along all the time." She laughs and goes to her room. I will always be glad that Jade was there when I woke up in that forest.

...

It is Thanksgiving, and the only thing I am thankful for is the fact that I am alive and not dead, buried in a forest alone. I feel anything but happy today. If I were back at home, my mom would be cooking dressing, making greens, and baking

TRANSITION

a Cajun turkey. My grandma, on my mom's side, would be cooking corn bread and homemade macaroni and cheese while my grandpa would be drinking beers with my father. My dad's parents would have come down to visit, with lots of wine, because they can't cook to save their lives. They are more like 'let's go out to eat' type of people. My dad's sister, my Aunt Anna, would have come down for Thanksgiving with her husband and their new baby that she probably had last month. I would have loved to see her and hold her; I don't even know what they named her.

What I would be doing, if I could be home for Thanksgiving, is baking a cake with my sister while watching her sneak and eat the frosting before we can finish frosting it. My whole family would all be laughing and joking around, but not this year. This year, they will most likely be sad because of my disappearance and I will be miserable because I can't be with them. I want so badly to be with them.

Maybe I can go and check on them. *No…no…* I can't. That is a bad idea. I sit up on the couch in the living room, and look around at the empty room. *So alone… so, so very alone.*

Jade is gone with Richard. I'm not desperate enough to call his friend Aiden to come hang out with me. That would be cruel since he likes me and I don't return the feelings. There is nothing to do and nothing I want to do. *Well…there is one thing I want to do.*

I go into my room and slip on some black jeans, a black shirt, and some tennis shoes. *Am I really going to go through with this?*

I grab my phone and some money and leave the condo. *There is no turning back now.*

CHAPTER 20

...

I take a cab to the outskirts of Rosenburg. I don't want to ride all the way into the city because I don't want to be seen. I force the driver to forget my face before I get out of the cab. It is becoming easier and easier to control the minds of others.

I run the rest of the way into the woods outside my house. I stand behind a large tree and peer around at my house. I see my mom, dad, sister, grandparents, and my Aunt Anna and her family. *I was right. They are all here.*

I look around for my new baby cousin. *I just want to see her face.* I find her in my mom's arms. My mom is standing and rocking her back and forth. She is smiling. I am glad my new cousin can bring a smile to her face.

I look to the other side of the house through the study's windows and see my dad and my two grandpas talking.

"I don't know what to do anymore," my dad says sounding broken. My dad's father, Jake Sr., walks around to the chair my dad is sitting in, and puts his hand on my dad's shoulder.

"Son, the only thing you can do is keep trying." I look to the sky and shake my head. I don't want him to keep trying. Trying is useless.

It is my mom's dad, Matthew, who speaks up next. "You can't ever stop trying. I would never stop trying, even if someone told me it was a lost cause." I wish I could tell them to stop. Just stop.

"I just don't know where she could be, she was my little girl, my first born. I can't find her and I can't comfort my other daughter because I am a total wreck over this. I'm supposed to be strong for my family and I can't. I can't do anything!" My dad clears his whole desk with that last sentence.

TRANSITION

Everything falls to the floor.

"Son," Jake Sr. says as he pulls my father into a hug, "You don't have to be strong, I'll be strong for you, and Matthew will be strong for you. We will be strong for the whole family." I always knew that my grandpas would be there for my family even if they were hurting the same. It makes me happy that instead of tearing my family apart, my disappearance seems to be bringing them even closer.

My dad starts to weep into Jake Sr.'s shoulder. "I want her back. I want to hold her in my arms. I want my baby girl." Grandpa Matt hits his hand against the table making me jump at the noise.

"Damn it, I bet it was that fucking boyfriend of hers." My dad looks up at him. Grandpa Matt is smart; he just doesn't know how smart he really is.

"That's what I thought, until they found her car in that ally. I just don't know anymore. I never liked him in the first place but I don't know if not liking him was clouding my judgment," my dad says.

"We need to get off this subject for now," Grandpa Jake says. "Wherever Nicky is, she would want us to enjoy the holiday, or at least try to enjoy ourselves. She wouldn't want us crying over her everyday. Let's try, in honor of Nicky." He is right, I want them to enjoy the holiday and eat enough food for me.

"She would want us to eat enough food for her, as if she were here to eat it herself," my dad says as he sadly smiled. *He knows me well...*

"Anna, you're up? Go back and get you some rest." I look over to where my mom is. She is in the kitchen still holding on to the baby.

"I'm ok, thanks for watching Nicky." *Nicky?*

186

CHAPTER 20

"I can't believe you named her Nicky." I can hear tears in my mom's voice.

"Well, I wanted to honor my beautiful niece by giving my daughter a derivative of her name." I can't believe she did that. I feel so honored to have my cousin, Nicky, named after me.

"I think Nicky is a perfect name," Tiffany says as she walks into the kitchen. I frown. She speaks with sarcasm. "...But what will we call Nichole when she comes back? I'm sure Nichole doesn't want to share her name with that baby. If I go missing, will you give your next baby my name?" My mom gasps and I can see blood rushing to her face.

"Tiffany, go to your room right now! ...And don't say anything like that again."

"Fine! If you want to give up on the real Nicky for this one, then that's on you! *My* sister is not dead and she will come back soon!" Tiffany starts to walk away but quickly turns around. "...And she won't like the fact that, that baby has her name!" Tiffany stomps up the stairs and slams her door. Then she walks over to her bed and weeps into a pillow.

I run my hands through my hair, breathing in and out. Tiffany is hurt and she is taking it out on a baby. To top everything off, I can do nothing about it.

"I'm sorry Anna, she has been so angry lately and I don't know what to do about it." My mom's voice breaks as she speaks.

"No need to be sorry, Kathryn, you lost your daughter and Tiffany lost her sister. It is understandable that she is acting like that." Aunt Anna kisses my mother on the cheek. "I think I left something in my room. I'll be right back." My mother nods her head and continues to rock Nicky.

TRANSITION

I hear Aunt Anna walk up the stairs. I don't know what part of the house she is going to until she opens the door to my room. *Did she leave something in my room?* Realization hits me when she sits down on my bed and buries her face in her hands to weep. *She lost a niece,* I think to myself. No one else knows that Aunt Anna or even Tiffany are crying silently to themselves. I wish I could comfort them, I wish I could make all their pain go away. I guess I can use mind control on them but I don't want them to forget about me and I don't want to risk it if they are immune like Aiden is.

After a while my grandma Connie, my dad's mom, comes into my room and comforts Aunt Anna. It is nice that my family are all comforting each other. I am paying so much attention to Aunt Anna and Grandma Connie that I don't notice when my other grandma goes into Tiffany's room. She lies on the bed and just holds Tiffany as she cries.

"I... Miss... Her... So... Much...," Tiffany says between sobs.

"I know, I know, I miss her too," Grandma Rosie says as she tries to quiet Tiffany. I shake my head. I shouldn't have come here. There's too much pain.

I turn around and sit with my back against the tree. I just sit and listen to my family's conversations and their cries. It is really too much to bear. Some of the conversations they have are sad and some are happy. When I start to hear laughter I stand up and peer over the tree.

My whole family sits at the dining table in the kitchen eating Thanksgiving dinner. They are telling stories about each other and even me. There are smiles on each of their faces but I can still see the pain hidden beneath it. Still it makes me smile that they could have one happy moment even if it is short lived.

CHAPTER 20

My happiness for the moment dies out when I sense someone behind me. I quickly turn around and see Tyler standing not to far away. He starts to run away. *Shit...* I can't let him get away.

Tyler is fast but I am faster. I catch up with him and tackle him to the ground. We fight for control of the other but I quickly gain control.

"Stop it! Tyler, give up!" We both are growling and I can tell my fangs are out.

I grab him by the throat and pin his arms down. "I swear I will kill you Tyler. Stop now!"

"Fine, fine, I'll give up for the moment but we both know you won't kill me Nichole. How are you even alive?" I ignore his question.

"Do you really want to chance it Tyler?" I wish he would because I swear I might kill him now.

So many things are running through my mind. The night of the party and the day I awoke are the main events that come to the forefront of my thoughts. The one thing that sticks out at the moment is the fact that he didn't come and help me the night Nate tried to kill me. I remember how Jade told me that he helped bury me and I am getting even angrier. I am so consumed by my thoughts that I don't even realize he is yelling.

"Nichole please, please don't kill me!" Was he begging me not to kill him?

"Why shouldn't I? I mean it's not like *you* helped me? Remember how I screamed? I bet you laughed." I squeeze his throat tighter and I can feel that I have the power to yank off his head with ease.

"No Nichole! Please don't kill me!" I won't even feel bad about killing him and I can't risk him telling Nate.

TRANSITION

"I'm sorry Tyler, you know what I'm not sorry, but I can't risk you telling Nate that I didn't die." He starts to say something but I stop him. "What I want to know is what happened that night." I have so many unanswered questions.

"Ok, ok, I will tell you anything just stop. You have to calm down a little. Your eyes!" *My eyes?*

"I'm not calming down Tyler, so just give up on it and what do you mean my eyes? We have the same color eyes right now, black. At least now you know how I felt when Nate's eyes turned black."

"No your eyes are red right now. All I know is that when Nate's or John's eyes turn red, they are not to be messed with. Only they have those eyes." *My eyes are red?* The realization that my eyes can be red calms me a little but I don't let go of my hold on him. I see Tyler relax a little.

"Enough bullshitting Tyler. Tell me what happened!" I'm not sure if I believe him about the red eye thing or not.

"Well, Nate was pissed at you, and he told us he was going to kill you. We are vampires, I mean after you turned you should have understood why we didn't come to help you. We knew why you were screaming but we just didn't care. You are a vampire now; you know that our compassion for humans is low." He has a point, I know that about vampires but I don't care, they still could have helped me. If Jade can have a relationship with a human, they could have helped me.

"Well don't you think his reason for killing me was stupid?"

"No, I don't think his reason was stupid." That pisses me off and I squeeze his throat tighter. If I just pull it will pop off. "Stop, please! You're going to kill me. I'm sorry, ok!"

CHAPTER 20

"Keep talking and I'll think about it." There is really nothing to think about but I am giving him a little hope.

"None of us knew you were going to turn. I mean did Nate let you feed on him or something? If he did, that wouldn't be the first time he didn't tell us something. I mean, you're alive so no harm done, right?" *No harm done! Is he serious?*

I am starting to feel the need to feed but there are no humans close around us. What I feel is the need to feed on him. I draw my head back and am about to sink my fangs in him when he speaks.

"Just make me forget that I saw you!" I look at him questionably. *Does he think I am stupid?*

"Excuse me? Do I look like a fool to you?"

"Nate talks about how he can control other vampires, I'm sure you can too." Nothing he says will make anything better but I still need answers.

"Just keep talking." He distracted me from feeding on him but not from wanting answers.

"After Nate thought he killed you, he put you in a trash bag and we buried you in the woods. I swear that is all. Nothing else happened." He makes it sound like killing someone, putting them in a trash bag, and burying them in the woods is nothing at all. It's just a typical Friday night.

"Why should I believe you? You would say anything to stay alive." I have my answers or at least the ones he gave. It is time to end this encounter.

"Wait! If you kill me, Nate will know something is up when I don't come back. We are best friends and he will know something is wrong. You can just make me forget everything and we can go our separate ways." He has a point and I don't want to be bothered with Nate anymore.

TRANSITION

"So how am I supposed to do this mind control thing to you?" I cock my head to the side and stare into his black eyes.

"Well your eyes are already red, so just do it like you would on a human." *I need to test it first.* I stare into his eyes.

"Stop struggling and don't make a sound, I'm going to kill you now and I want you to die with a smile on your face." He stops struggling and smiles. I act as if I am going to kill him and he doesn't scream, he doesn't even struggle.

"How old are you Tyler?"

"I'm 212 years old," he says in a monotone. *Wow he is really old!*

"How old is Nate?"

"He is 511 years old." I am speechless. Nate is ancient.

"So I was dating a fossil? Never mind, why were you in the woods today?"

"I was out hunting and I saw you in the woods. I was on my way back home."

"You were going back to that dump y'all call home?" I can't understand why they are living in that house.

"No I was going back to that big mansion that you can see as you enter Rosenburg." *Mansion!* They live in a mansion and he took me to that dump to have my first time? Maybe that is where he wanted to kill me. No blood on the mansion floor just on the crappy house floor I guess.

"I want you to forget that you ever saw me, and I don't want you to pursue Casey anymore. You don't like her anymore and she doesn't interest you. Don't even speak to her. Also, I don't want you to come anywhere near my family again. Got it?" He nods.

"Got it."

CHAPTER 20

"Now curl into a ball and count to one-hundred slowly. When you are done counting you can continue your journey home." *To your mansion*, I think bitterly.

I let him go and he does as I said. I run as fast as I can. I need to get out of Rosenburg and fast.

TRANSITION

Chapter 21

I keep running as if my life depends on it.

It does. I run through the forest weaving through the trees and rocks. I look behind me. I see no one but I know I am being chased. I can sense it. I can feel it. I run and run. I am breathing rapidly from fear. The only thing I can concentrate on is running. *Run faster...*

I am so focused on what is behind me, that I don't see the tree right in front of me. I run straight into it and stumble over.

TRANSITION

I can feel the shrubbery, rocks, and twigs scrape against and cut my skin. I quickly recover myself and start running again. I can hear footsteps closing in on me. *Shoot... run faster.* Knocking into that tree put me and whoever is stalking me closer than I want us to be. *Run...Run faster...*

I am starting to freak out and my breathing reflects my panic. I hear someone running to my left. *Not another one...* I adjust my course away from both my pursuers. *I have to get away... How could I be so stupid?* I push myself. I need to get away. I am losing ground slowly but surely. I can feel them both gaining on me. I propel myself forward and look back to see how close they are to me. In that one second that I look back, I run straight into to someone. *How did they get in front of me?* I think in horror.

I look up and see that I have run into Nate. I look into his cold black eyes. Those eyes have haunted me for the past several months. Those eyes will hunt me forever. I don't have time to react before he grabs me tightly by my throat.

"Nate...Please," I say even though I am being strangled. He squeezes tighter. His grip on my throat is so tight that I can't speak. I claw at his hand with no prevail. I look into his black eyes and watch as they turn a deep red. The color looks sickly like the color of blood. He smiles, but his smile isn't happy, it is a sick sinister smile that makes me fear for my life. I hear footsteps behind me; the others have finally caught up.

"Please? Isn't that what I said when you were about to rip my head off," Tyler says. I can tell it is him by the sound of his voice. He walks up to where Nate has me captive and looks into my eyes. "You should have, but you were too stupid to see that I was lying. Being able to control other vampire's minds," he laughs, "Only in fairytales." He has the same sinister smile as Nate as he shakes his head at me in disapproval.

"You know I haven't torn a vampire apart in a while. I'm glad Nate didn't fully kill you. It will be so much more fun to kill you a second time, as a vampire." I know that it is John who spoke. He's standing behind me laughing a dark happy laugh.

Nate stares at me. He is staring into my eyes. He isn't smiling anymore. He has a dark look of anger on his face. He has been so silent that I am afraid for him to talk.

"Nichole, you were never supposed to be a vampire. See, I could deal with other guys flirting with you but what I didn't like was you throwing yourself at another guy like I didn't even exist. That wasn't very nice was it?" I just stand quietly and continue to claw at his hands on my throat.

"Was it?" He loosens his grip so I can answer him.

"No...it...wasn't." I am struggling to save my own life. Even though I am a vampire, I want to live. I didn't want to before but now that I'm about to die again, I want to live. "Nate...Please." My voice sounds weak. He smiles at my begging tone.

"Beg me again, I like to hear you beg." I try to scream but it is useless. I am alone. Jade is with Richard and his family and I am alone.

"Please! Let me go!" I know begging is useless and that he isn't going to let me go, but I have to try. I pull at his hands but I can't get free. "Just...do it already!" If I am going to die, it will be my choice.

"Oh, you thought I was going to rip your head off? Oh no, I'm not going to do that." I look at Nate in confusion. His eyes are bright and menacing and his fangs are out. "I'm going to kill you like I did before but this time, I'm going to

make sure you are dead." I whimper. *I am going to die…
again.*

He smiles and I can see two of his bottom teeth grow
into fangs. I can't believe what I am seeing. He has two sets
of fangs and his bottom fangs are smaller than his top. My
eyes widen as he pulls me by my hair to expose my neck. I
don't have time to scream before he sinks both his fangs in
to my flesh.

I am bashing and tossing myself against him but he
isn't there anymore. I'm not there anymore. I am in my bed
at the condo. The realization doesn't stop my screams. I keep
thrashing against the bed. The remnants of my dream still
linger in my thoughts.

Jade and Richard burst through my door. Jade hops on
my bed and pulls me to her in comfort. We are both strong
so my thrashing doesn't hurt her but it would have hurt Richard. She gestures for Richard to stay where he is. I can tell he
wants to come and help. He just stands in the doorway wearing only pajama pants and a concerned looked on his face.

"Shh…shh…shh…it's ok. It's ok Nichole, it was just a
nightmare." I feel like I am crying my eyes out but no tears
shed.

Jade keeps comforting me while Richard just stands
and watches us. It has been weeks since Thanksgiving. In
fact, it is a few days from New Years. I haven't told Jade
about my trip back to Rosenburg or what happened with Tyler but she knows something is wrong. All through Christ-
mas, I put on a brave face but my nightmares gave away that
I was hiding something. I have nightmares frequently and
Jade is no stranger to them. This nightmare, however, was so
vivid and my reaction is even worse.

CHAPTER 21

I am shaking and Jade tries to rub my tremors away. I'm not thrashing anymore but I am sure if Jade lets me go I would freak-out and tear the place apart.

"Shh...shh...it's ok. It's ok. Richard you can go back to my room. I'm going to sleep in here with Nichole, alright." Richard nods his head.

"Nichole if you need anything, anything at all, let me know. I'll check on you two in the morning." I don't respond but I know he understands why. He leaves the room and I listen to him go into to Jade's room.

I want to feel comforted by Richard's presence but I'm not. I don't feel safe. Richard is the protective type but he would be no match for a vampire. I will never feel safe again.

Jade doesn't say anything. She just comforts me. When I start to feel a little relaxed, I lay in the bed and she holds me. It feels silly, her comforting me. I am some supernatural vampire and I need to be comforted. When I start to relax, I drift off into a deep untroubled sleep.

...

I open my eyes, and find Jade staring at me. I try to cover my face with the cover but she yanks it from me. She knows something is up.

"Are you going to tell me what happened over Thanksgiving?" *How can she know something happened? Don't be stupid...of course she knows something happened.*

"What do you mean?" I don't want to tell her. She is going to be mad when she finds out.

"Don't give me that crap Nichole! I know something happened! You were fine, I mean somewhat fine, when I left and now you're not. What happened? ...and don't tell me nothing because I know something happened." I just stare at her in silence but when the silence grows, she is more insistent. "NOW Nichole!" I take a deep breath. *Well here goes nothing...*

"I went to Rosenburg on Thanksgiving..."

"...YOU DID WHAT!" She cuts me off before I can even continue.

"Do you want to wait until I finish, to yell at me, or would you like to get it over with now?" She takes a deep breath and composes herself.

"You know what, I'm going to wait for you to finish." She speaks slowly and calmly but I know she is furious inside. I continue.

"I went to Rosenburg on Thanksgiving to see my family. I missed them a lot and I knew all of my family would be there. Don't worry, I just stood in the woods and watched from a distance. I didn't make contact." She relaxes a little but I know that won't last. I look away when I speak the next part. "Nate's friend, Tyler, was in the woods..." I sneak a peek at Jade and see her eyes widen but I continue. "...He saw me but I attacked him. Since I felt I was screwed anyway I asked him about the night I died and then proceeded to kill him. He told me that if I did Nate would get suspicious..."

"So you let him go!" Jade hops off the bed and runs her hands through her hair.

"NO, no I didn't. He was acting all scared and everything saying that my eyes were red and that when Nate's eyes turn red he's not to be messed with. He said that I could use mind control on him when my eyes were red. So I tested it and it worked. I erased the memory of him seeing me and stuff." I shrug. Jade eyes shoot daggers at me.

CHAPTER 21

"...And you believed him? Nichole, did you even look at your eyes? I've never seen them turn red! Also, I have never heard of a vampire using mind control on another vampire."

"I know that sounds weird but it worked and it's been weeks since it happened." Although I've been having nightmares, I haven't had any indication that Nate and his friends are looking for me.

"Ok, make your eyes turn red." I look at Jade like she is joking. "I'm not joking. Do it, do it now. That way we can put the suspicions that they are searching for you away." I have no idea how to do it. Then a thought pops in my mind.

"When he said they were red, I had this feeling like I wanted to feed on him. So maybe if I could get that feeling with you, they would turn red." Jade rolls her eyes.

"Ok whatever." Jade moves her hair to the side to give me access to her neck. "You know, I just think he played you like a fool." I roll my eyes, get off the bed, and just stand in front of Jade. *This is so weird...*

"You ready?" I can't believe we are doing this.

"As I'll ever be." I know Jade doesn't think it is true but we have to try.

I let my fangs come out and I just stand with my hand on one side of Jade's neck and my face close to the other. I don't feel anything. It is a lost cause. *Tyler did play me for a fool.* For a brief second, I think the feeling to feed is creeping up, then Richard busts through the door. I retract my fangs and quickly turn around. He is looking at us strangely.

"I don't know what y'all were about to do...but can I watch?" He looks serious. Jade and I cock are heads to the side in confusion. He laughs.

TRANSITION

"Richard!" Jade put her hands on her hip.

"I'm just playing baby! No, seriously, what are y'all doing?"

"Jade thought she had a hicky and I was inspecting her neck but I don't see one." There that seems like a legitimate excuse.

"Aw baby, you don't want me to give you hickies?" Jade just pouts her bottom lip and he takes her into his arms. Jade looks up at me and widens her eyes. "By the way Nichole, nice contacts. Getting ready for Halloween already, it just passed?"

I quickly walk into my bathroom. When I look in the mirror, I see red eyes. They are the color of blood.

Chapter 22

"Just let me bite you." I look at Jade like she has
lost her mind. *Is she serious?*

"No! I have nightmares about being bitten. There
is no way you are bringing your fangs close to my
neck." I can't stand to be bitten in my dreams. How
does she expect me to stay calm if she actually bites
me?

"Please? I want to see if my eyes turn red too."
Jade juts out her bottom lip, as if her pouting will sway
me. I shake my head.

TRANSITION

It has been two days since the discovery of my red eyes and Jade has been trying ever since to see if her eyes will turn red too. She has tried everything she can except for actually biting a vampire. That is our conclusion of course that the eyes turn red when one vampire is about to feed on another. It isn't full proof but what other explanation is there? We don't really know anything about why my eyes turn red.

I tried using mind control on Jade. If I could do it on Tyler, surely I could on Jade also. It worked of course but Jade couldn't remember that I did it. I told her to take my word for it but that wasn't good enough. We had to get a camera and record it before she believed it. Well she got her proof and her mind was blown.

All these new discoveries don't make me happy, sad, or mad but they do make me curious. *What else don't I know about my new vampire self?* I have a nagging feeling that only Nate will be able to tell me more about myself since he is the one who turned me.

"Jade," I whine, "I can't handle you biting me! I might freak out and bite you or have a nervous breakdown. Let's go find another vampire and you can bite them." Jade rolls her eyes.

"You know, I've been a vampire ten years and I have never seen a vampire with red eyes." I stare at Jade.

"What are you trying to say?"

"What I am saying is, what makes you so different from me? I mean, we are both vampires but you have this red eye thing going on." I am beginning to think Jade is a little jealous.

"Well, Tyler said that Nate has this red eye thing too. Maybe it's like genetics or something. He made me you know."

CHAPTER 22

"Yeah, maybe you're right. I mean I don't know everything about being a vampire yet."

We are sitting on the couch, in the living room, watching random TV shows and waiting for Richard. Richard and I have become close over time. Richard now considers me as a sister.

He is a good person and I am glad I haven't tried to feed on him. *Progress...*

The silence between Jade and me has stretched. Although we are watching TV, I can feel the tension radiating off of her. I think that even though she seems intrigued by the red eye thing, it also bothers her that she never knew anything about it until now. I am the one who breaks the silence.

"So can I be your maid of honor when you and Richard get married." Jade doesn't really like when I joke about her and Richard's future. I don't think she ever saw their relationship being forever since she is a vampire.

"Only if I get to be yours when you and Aiden get married." *Touché...* I send a scowl her way and she laughs. Her good mood is back.

"That's not funny Jade. I don't even like Aiden. He is neither my friend nor my crush." In reality, I don't really know how I truly feel about Aiden.

"Well don't joke about me and Richard; I don't know about our future yet but I know we will never get married. As a matter of fact, we don't have a future. I'm a vampire and he is human." I always feel sadness when she says that. If Jade will never get married, I will probably never get married.

It is a silly notion, a vampire getting married or even having a successful relationship. We are emotionally worse than women PMSing.

TRANSITION

There is a knock on the door and both Jade and I look up. We both are a little on edge. We don't feel like I am being tracked by my blood sucking ex since the mind control on Jade worked, but I will be lying if I say we aren't a little jumpy from time to time.

"It's just Richard, Nichole." Jade gets up and walks towards the door. I don't know why she is reassuring me? She is nervous too. Jade opens the door and Richard pops in the condo and brings all his energy too.

"Hey, ladies! I brought food!" *Oh great...I have to eat that vile human food?* I hate it because it taste bad and because it will just come up later.

"Hey baby thanks!" Richard gives Jade a kiss on the lips that lasts a little too long. Actually, saying it lasts too long is an understatement.

"O.M.G.," I slowly and dramatically pronounce the three letters and tell them, "Get a room!" I smile at both of them. They are just so cute.

"You know Nichole, if you gave my boy Aiden a chance, you could be doing the same thing." I make a face showing that, that will never happen. Richard walks over and gives me a swift hug.

"What did you bring babe? We're starving." I look over at Jade out the corner of my eye. Why is she encouraging the food thing?

"I'm not hungry Richard, but thanks." I am going to try everything to get out of eating.

"...And what did you eat today? It's three in the afternoon and I don't see any food here or in the trash. You need to eat Nichole, or you're going to waste away." Lately Richard has felt the need to feed us. I guess he feels like it is his responsibly since we never have food.

CHAPTER 22

I look over at Jade and she has already started eating the poison. I get off the couch in defeat and walk over to the breakfast bar. It is a rule of Jade's to never use mind control on Richard. If I could, I would never have to eat the food he brings.

Today, he brought us Chinese food. I get a plate out of the cabinet and start putting very small servings of each dish on my plate. I can deal with small servings. Small servings are good. I am about to walk away, with my small plate of food, when Richard grabs my plate from my hand.

"Come on now, this is nothing. Here let me show you how to fix a plate of food. Look at Jade, she's eating." I look at Jade eating a full plate of food and the words cruel and unusual punishment come to mind.

Richard doesn't pile my plate but he gives me way more than I want, which just happens to be everything on my plate. I sit at the breakfast bar and force myself to eat. I also make a good effort to not vomit.

"So we are all going to the New Year's Eve party tomorrow, right?" Richard looks at both Jade and me, but only Jade nods. "Good, you know Nichole, Aiden will be there." I roll my eyes. Will everyone please stop trying to get Aiden and me together?

"That's good. I hope he brings his girlfriend so that y'all can get off my back." Jade and Richard stare at me with smiles on their faces. I know they will never give up.

...

I stare at myself in the bathroom mirror. I am wearing a purple bodycon dress that has a sweetheart neckline and pushes my boobs to the sky. I also have on sparkly silver platform heels along with my dress. *I can't believe I'm going to the New Year's Eve party...*

TRANSITION

It's not like I don't like partying but going to this party means that I have to deal with Aiden's constant flirtation. *Ugh*...

I run my fingers through my hair. It is bone straight, *the way I like it*. I think about putting curls in it, but I quickly shut down that idea because my hair is naturally curly on its own. I quickly put on some make-up and lip-gloss and turn to head to the living room.

Jade and Richard are already in the living room waiting for me when I arrive.

"About time! I thought I was going to have to drag you out the room!" I roll my eyes. Jade can be so dramatic at times. "...but you look cute. So I guess the wait was worth it." I smile.

"You look cute too." Jade twirls. She is wearing a tight red sheath dress with red ankle strap heels. Her hair hangs in loose curls around her head and her make-up is nice and simple.

"You both look good...now can we please go?" We stare at Richard. "What? I'm ready to go! You women take forever to get ready...and you're always forgetting something. Do y'all have your phone, your purses, ID's, and money?" He ticks off each item on his fingers.

"Oops I left mine in the room," I say shamelessly.

I quickly go back and get my clutch. I really don't need money, my ID, or my phone, but I take them with me to look normal. Anyway, my ID says I am eighteen. I'll have to fix that one day. I walk back into the living room and am greeted by Richard's impatient stare.

"What are you waiting for? Let's go." I am trying to get under Richard's skin and it works. He crosses his arms and Jade and I laugh.

CHAPTER 22

We are riding to the party in Richard's car. It takes Jade a second to decide if she wants to sit in the back with me or in the front with Richard.

"Jade! Just get in the front." I don't care if I sit in the back alone.

"Are you sure?"

"Yes..." Richard and I say in unison.

The ride to the party isn't long. It is ten minutes until eleven when we walk through the doors to the club. There are tons of people dancing around, flirting, and drinking. I can smell a few people who have had a little too much to drink. I am admiring the scenery when Jade turns around to look at me.

"Please...please...no feeding tonight." She stares me down.

"Fine..." I put my hands up in defense. "No feeding tonight." I am a little disappointed but I'm not hungry so I don't let it bother me much. Jade stares at me a little while longer. I guess she believes me because she smiles.

"Good...now let's get a drink."

"Let's..." Jade grabs my arm and we leave Richard to go to the bar.

The bar is stationed on the back wall of the club. It is a simple bar with a black granite counter top and dim lighting hanging above it. People crowd the bar in a desperate need to drown down whatever worries they have in their life.

Jade and I wedge our way up to the bar. A handsome bartender with grey eyes greets us. He quickly takes our orders. He asks for our ID's and I tell him that he doesn't need them because we look twenty-one. Jade and I both order tequila shots. We toast to a new and happy year and quickly throw back the strong liquor. We are on our tenth round of shots when Richard comes to steal Jade away from me. I make a show of pouting my lip when she is whisked away. I look toward the bartender and he walks toward me.

"Another?" *Why not?* It is New Year's Eve. *Why not get wasted like everyone else.*

"Make it a double." The bartender fills two shot glasses with tequila. I am starting to feel woozy. Make that way passed woozy, when Aiden comes up to sit next to me at the bar.

"Hey," he says. I look over at him.

"Hey, Aiden. I didn't know you were here." It isn't a lie, I knew he was coming but I didn't notice that he had arrived.

"Yes, you did. You were just trying to avoid me." He smiles big and wide at me. He has a nice smile.

"No really, I didn't know." I look back at the people in the club. "Where is your girlfriend, Sarah? Shouldn't you be entertaining her right now?" It baffles me how he can come with someone and then give all his attention to me. Also, it's strange that I'm not very nice to him but I am always greeted by his presence.

"For one, she's not my girlfriend. Secondly, there is another woman that has my attention." I look away from him. I have this feeling that *I* am that other woman but I want to play dumb.

"Well I hope she's worth the trouble." I can feel his eyes staring at the side of my face.

"Oh, she's worth it alright and then some." *Oh goodness...*

"Could I have another round?" I call out to the bartender and he quickly put another two shots in front of me. He deserves a tip. I reach for the shot and Aiden takes the other.

"Heyyy." I look at him as he holds the shot up.

"Hey nothing. You asked for one shot, this one is mine." My irritation with Aiden is growing over my buzzed state.

"...but you didn't ask for anything. So technically that's mine." I stare at him and we lock eyes. *His eyes are so...goodness why is he looking at me like that?* I quickly turn away. I don't like how I feel with his eyes burning into mine. It makes me shiver. As a matter of fact, I don't really know what I feel but he can't look at me like that.

"Let's toast. Let's toast to our new friendship." He is so persistent.

"What makes you think I want a friendship with you?" I snap but he just smiles and holds up his shot. I reluctantly give in. "To our new friendship." We tap glasses and toss the shots back.

"See that wasn't so bad." He sets the shot glass back down on the bar and stares at me. "I think you like me but you just don't know it yet." I roll my eyes. *Of course he does...*

"Isn't Sarah around here somewhere?" Maybe if I keep reminding him about his girlfriend, he will stop this insistent flirting.

"For the last time, she was never my girlfriend. I told you there is someone else that I like and it's not her." I am slowly but surely getting angry. What do I have to say or do to get through to him?

"Aiden why do you like me? I've been nothing but rude and I have told you many times that I'm not interested."

"I think you are rude because you like me and what makes you think I'm talking about you?" He smiles and I stand up to leave. He grabs my arm before I walk off. "Wait Nichole, it is you. You are the woman I like. I like *you* ok? What's wrong with that?" I could have easily broken away but his tone is compelling.

We are standing mere inches from each other. We are so close that I can feel his breath on my face, the warmth coming off his body, and I can see the blood running through his veins. I need to get away but I stay in place.

"How can you like me Aiden? You know nothing about me. I might be a serial killer or a crazy person. Or worse I could be really messed up on the inside." He smiles and tilts my head up to look into his eyes. I am trapped in his gaze.

"While all those things could be true, I highly doubt you are any of it. You might be messed up though, but that's because someone hurt you. Let me tell you what I do know about you. I know that whatever pain you have has affected your life drastically, but I can see that you are strong enough to overcome it. I know that you are funny and have some obsession with vampires. And... I know that you don't like Jade's cooking." I laugh and in the background I am faintly aware of people counting down for the New Year. *Ten... nine...* "I know that you have a beautiful smile, but I can't help but think that you are holding back when you smile." *Eight...seven...six...* "I know that you are the most beautiful woman that I have ever seen and I don't think I could ever stay away from you." *Five...four...*

"You know all that," I whisper. I am locked in his gaze. *Three...two...*

"Yes." *One...* He kisses me right on time and I feel myself kiss him back. His lips are soft and mine mold like a puzzle into his. We share a deep passionate kiss and I'm not

CHAPTER 22

sure I want to end it. I start to feel something for Aiden. Or is it something that I already felt but wouldn't let myself unlock. Well it is unlocked now. He wraps his hands around my waist and I pull my arms around his neck thus closing any gap between us. His lips mesh well with mine and it is nice, better than nice. I feel as if I could kiss him forever. I am only vaguely aware of the cheering from the crowd in the background. It is a new year and I began it by kissing Aiden. I have been so rude to him, but he still likes me. Maybe he is right, maybe I am rude because I am denying my feelings toward him. When we finally break the kiss, we pull back. I stare into his chocolate brown eyes knowing for sure that if I could blush, I would.

"Wow..." he says as he gazes into my eyes. I smile. *Wow didn't cut it...can we do that again?*

"Wow, indeed. That was some kiss. I mean that was a great kiss. I mean you have soft lips." *What am I saying?* I think my brain and my mouth are having some kind of word spill. He looks at me questionably.

"Wow...yea that was a great kiss and we can repeat it if you will let me kiss you again but I was saying wow I just saw your eyes change from green to black." *He what...*

My smile fades and I quickly turn away from him. I don't want him to see my eyes. What am I thinking? Nothing, and I mean absolutely nothing can happen between Aiden and I. I am a vampire and he is a human. Not to mention, I *am* kind of a serial killer and a little crazy because of my vampire emotions. He doesn't even have a clue that I am a vampire. This is a horrible lapse in judgment and it will not happen again. Maybe Jade can ride the fence but I can't.

"Hey, what's wrong?" He tries to turn me around but I won't budge. "Look it doesn't matter that your eyes turn black. I think it's cute. It makes you different." I don't turn towards him.

What he thinks is cute is his warning sign. It should have sent warning bells off in his head. It is a sign that I am a predator and he is my prey, but instead he thinks it is cute! He says it makes me different, well yeah it does, and it makes me a vampire.

"Look, the kiss was a mistake. I'm drunk and it's New Year's. It won't happen again. I told you, I'm not interested." I'm not sure if I am trying to convince him or myself.

I walk away. "Nichole..." I hear him utter my name in confusion. *You're not the only one confused...*

Chapter 23

"Nichole." Someone is calling me in a singsong voice. "Nichole."

I grumble incoherent words and peak from under my cover. Jade is staring at me with a big smile on her face.

"What do you want?" I am in no mood to entertain her.

"I saw you and Aiden kiss last night." Her smile fades. "…And I saw how you rudely left him standing there. Why did you leave last night?" Too many questions, and I'm sure she has many more.

TRANSITION

I pull the cover over my head, therefore, obstructing my view of her. My effort is useless because she yanks the whole duvet off the bed in one swift move. I sit up, cross my arms, and glare at her.

"Sooo, what was it like? Does he kiss well? Were his lips soft? Did you enjoy it? Why did you leave?" So, so many questions...

I don't even want to talk about it. I did enjoy the kiss, more than I wanted to. I feel something for Aiden but what I feel or he feels means nothing. We should have met before I became a vampire. How the kisses felt when I kissed Nate and how they feel when I kiss Aiden are so different. Aiden's kiss makes anything Nate and I had feel unreal. When Aiden and I kiss, it is passionate and real. I would be lying if I say I don't want to kiss him again but I can't. When Aiden pointed out that he saw my eyes turn black, it just reminded me how much he doesn't know and will never know about me. It reminded me that he is a human and I am a vampire.

"The kiss was good...really good and I left because I'm a vampire." There, that's good enough. She should understand what I mean.

"That's not good enough!" Jade is whining now and I roll my eyes.

"Jade what do you want me to say? His lips were soft and he is a good kisser. When we pulled away, he noticed my eyes were turning black. We are incompatible. He is human and I am a vampire." I plop back on to my bed and Jade lays down beside me.

"You know, just because you are a vampire doesn't mean you have to be alone or without love. You don't have to be with another vampire either. You were thrown into this life and I think you should stop punishing yourself for it. If you like Aiden, then tell him. Be with him." *Oh yeah? Then we can start planning our wedding and picking out baby names.* Why does she not get the 'I'm a vampire and he's a human thing'?

"What do you want me to do? I'll just go up to him and say, hey I'm a vampire and my ex was the one who turned me against my will. He was trying to kill me and that's why I have issues? Oh and by the way I like you and I hope you can get over all of this." I am laying the sarcasm on thick.

"Well…not that. You shouldn't tell him *that* at all but you could still have a relationship with him." I sigh no I can't.

"What would be the purpose Jade? He is going to grow old and I am going to look the same. How will I explain that?" I can tell Jade doesn't really have much to say. She knows all of this. I'm sure that she thinks of it every day she is with Richard.

"There's nothing wrong with being happy for now." I understand what she is trying to say. I can possibly be happy with Aiden even if it is only for a little while. The problem is that all that happiness would be a whole big lie. We would never have a real relationship with all the secrets I hold. On top of that, being in a relationship with me would be putting his life in danger.

"I couldn't be in a relationship with a human if I am constantly feeding on humans. It's like a conflict of interest don't you think? Or like dating your food." I look over at Jade and she shrugs. She doesn't see it my way at all.

"Well then, stop feeding on humans and switch to a vegan diet." My eyes widen at her response. A vegan diet is not appealing. Animals taste like tofu compared to humans. Jade senses my displeasure of her statement. "Oh, it's not that bad. I bet you would feel less like an evil creature of the night if you did."

She has me pinned with that last statement. I do feel like an evil creature of the night when I feed on humans. No matter how great feeding on them is, I always feel torn with the way I feel about it. Her words still hang in my head. Even if I choose not to be with Aiden, I should probably still try to abstain from feeding on humans. It will be good for me.

"Maybe I will try to feed solely on animals." Jade looks at me with a vibrant smile. I know exactly what she is thinking. "That doesn't mean that I am going to give Aiden a chance." She pouts. "Look Jade, I did just get out of a relationship that ended my human life, and on top of that I'm not sure that I want a human/vampire relationship. Let me continue to settle into this life." The look on her face says that we put the Aiden situation to rest. I am relieved. I don't need the extra stress anyway.

"Does this mean that you're not going to try to do the vegan diet thing?" I think about it before answering. *Why not?*

"No, I will try it. I don't like feeling like a monster. Who knows? It will probably be good for me." I am beginning to like the sound of a vegan diet no matter how it tastes.

"Maybe you and Aiden can be friends." I sigh. Jade isn't going to give up but I can settle for being 'just friends' with Aiden. Distant friends that is…

"Yeah, maybe."

"…And maybe I can find you a vampire boyfriend. That way you're not dating your food." I give her a sideways glance and cock my eyebrow up.

CHAPTER 23

"Oh yeah, you can feed on vampires...but technically, vampires are not your food." Apparently, everything is my food.

...

I am rummaging through my clothes when I hear Jade open the door. I thought only Richard was coming over until I hear four heartbeats instead of one.

"Jade what is going on?"

I know that one of the other people has to be Aiden and I just don't want to face him. It has been a couple of days since the New Year's party and I have been trying to avoid him.

"Oh, it's just a group hang. Don't worry." *Don't worry?*

I don't want to face Aiden. The last time we saw each other or talked was that party. I left him after kissing him with no explanation of why. I even said things to hurt him and now I have no choice, I have to face him.

"Who is all here Jade?" I am feeling frantic.

She doesn't respond but there is suddenly a knock at my door. *Oh no...* I listen for a heart beat but the ones I hear aren't behind my door. It must be Jade. I slowly open my door and I am rewarded with relief. It is Jade.

"Well, Richard is here along with Aiden, Sarah, and Sarah's friend Jack." My mood darkens at Sarah's name and who is Jack? I know I shouldn't feel any kind of jealousy but I can't help it. *Why is my life so messed up?*

Jade must have seen my feelings painted on my face. "Why... are you jealous Nichole?" She has a smile plastered on her face. I answer her with the door in her face.

"That was not cool Nichole." She sounds like she is smiling. I will never live this down.

219

TRANSITION

I tear through my drawers and through my closet looking for something to wear. I certainly couldn't go into the living room in my lingerie. *That would surely give the wrong impression.* Wait, I pause. *What am I doing?*

I am beginning to think that I am giving *myself* the wrong impression. I calm down and pull out some light blue jean shorts and slide them on. I find a black tank top and put that on also. I don't need to look cute, especially if I'm not giving Aiden a chance. I brush my hair, put on some purple fuzzy house shoes and make my way to the living room. *That's right.* Go in there looking like you could care less.

As I walk into the living room, I am greeted by Jade's look of confusion at my attire and Aiden and Sarah's close proximity on the couch. The feelings that flood through me are not good ones. I know I shouldn't care but I do. *Why do I care?*

I walk over to the couch and sit down by the person that must be Jack. Aiden's eyes never sway from my movements. I don't understand why he even acknowledges me because it is obvious he is here with Sarah. *Again*, I think, *why do I care?*

"Hey, Nichole. It's nice to see you again," Sarah says. I am sure Sarah doesn't know about me and Aiden's kiss or else she wouldn't have been so friendly. I'm sure not feeling friendly. I am feeling like feeding on a blonde Barbie for the afternoon and her name is Sarah.

"Hey, Sarah." I fake a genuine smile. "It's nice to see you too." I am lying through my teeth. It isn't nice to see her.

"Hey I'm Jack." Jack holds out his hand for me to shake it. "I haven't had the pleasure of meeting you yet. I met Jade a while back but I have heard a lot about you." Jack seems sweet but he is not attractive. At least not to me.

CHAPTER 23

"I hope you heard all good things." I give Jack my best flirtatious smile and I hope Aiden sees it. I know Aiden and I won't be together but I feel betrayed that he brought Sarah.

"Yeah, of course, all good things. You're as beautiful as they've described." I wonder who has been describing me.

"Awww, you're sweet." I am laying the flirtatiousness on there, thick. "So how do you…"

"…What have you been up to Nichole?" Aiden says suddenly cutting me off. Jade and Richard are just sitting on the couch staring like a fight is about to break out. I turn my head so that I can look Aiden in the face.

"Nothing much." I am being nonchalant. I turn back to face Jack therefore abruptly cutting Aiden off. "So how do you and Sarah know each other?"

"They're twins," Richard cuts in, "fraternal of course."

"Isn't that cool?" Jade chimes. I can tell they are trying to cut the tension in the room with a knife. "Anyways I'm starving. We ordered pizza and we got some movies. We can choose from something scary, something romantic, or some action? Which is it?" Almost everybody says something different. It is Richard who offers a solution.

"How about we watch the action movie and then the scary movie. That way if the ladies are scared we can end the night with a romantic movie to take your minds off the scary one." Everyone agrees.

"So this is chat time until the pizza get's here," Jade says happily. I am beginning to think Jade loves human group hangouts.

"I can't wait til the food arrives. I'm starving." I look at Jade when I say the last part. I am rewarded with her scowl. She understands what I mean. "So is this like couples night or something?" I need to know. Jade looks at me as if she knows I am about to say something to embarrass her.

"Yeah, kind of," Richard says. Jade elbows Richard. I guess he wasn't supposed to say that. "What?" He is unfazed and unaware.

"Are y'all trying to hook me up with Jack?" Jade puts her face in her hands and just shakes her head in embarrassment.

"Well yeah, I thought you and Jack were a good fit. I know Aiden and I are," Sarah says with enthusiasm. Any amusement in my face is gone. So Aiden and Sarah are definitely together.

I look at Aiden and he stares back. What is his problem? How can he have said those things to me and then bring Sarah here. He is a liar. Apparently all guys are. Nevertheless, I'm not being set up by anyone ever again. Also, I don't want to force pizza down my throat. It was one of my favorite foods when I was human but now it's nothing to me.

I stand up, tension radiating off my body. Jade stands up also and we step to the side. Everyone can still see us but they definitely can't hear us.

"Nichole, what are you doing?" I can tell Jade is angry. She wants me to cooperate and I'm not going to do so. No way am I staying at this group date thing.

"I'm going to get my shoes and I'm leaving before I have myself a blonde chick for dinner. Or before I feed on her, her brother, and even Aiden." I hope my warning is enough to get her to let me go.

"I thought you didn't like Aiden?"

I roll my eyes. "No, I said that we could never be together because of my condition." I fold my arms. "I do kind of like him but it doesn't matter because I'm a vampire and he is with Sarah." She folds her arms.

CHAPTER 23

"He's not technically with her, he just came here with her." Like I am supposed to believe that.

"Whatever Jade, I'm leaving before I feed on Barbie." Jade is trying to look serious but she is struggling with amusement.

"Ok, Nichole," She is smiling now, "...go before you eat Barbie." I silently laugh and shake my head as I walk into my room.

"Where is she going?" I hear more than one person ask including Aiden.

"Oh, she has a work emergency." *A work emergency!* Jade really? She can't come up with a better excuse.

"...a work emergency? It's Sunday," Aiden says. I laugh as I put on my sneakers.

"Where does she work," Sarah asks. Sarah is being a little nosey. Nobody answers her.

"Was it something I said?" I feel bad for Jack; He has been thrown into our secret drama.

"No, no." I hear Jade exhale harshly. "She just has to be somewhere, alright." For a minute it sounds like everyone accepts what Jade has told them until Aiden interrupts the silence.

"I'm going to go talk to her." I hear Jade protest but he is already at my door, knocking. "Nichole, can I speak with you please?" I am debating jumping out the window but that would be childish. *Think. Think fast.*

"I really don't have time..." He is rattling the door-knob. *I really can't get out of this can I?*

"Nichole, I know you don't have anywhere to be so just open the door and talk to me." He whispers into the door. I sigh and open the door.

Aiden walks right in and closes the door behind him.

TRANSITION

We just stare at each other for a while. I don't understand why he is even trying to talk to me. He is here with Sarah and his attention should be on her, not me.

"What's up?" I ask nonchalantly and with a smirk. Aiden just stares at me and shakes his head. He takes a deep breath before he speaks.

"Nichole, you are so confusing. You kiss me and then walk off saying it was a mistake..." I cut him off.

"...*You* kissed me." He glares at me. I did kiss him back, but I am trying to make it seem like I didn't.

"You kissed me, too, Nichole." I run my hand through my hair and take a deep breath. *Here we go...*

"Ok," I say softly, "I kissed you. What now?" I look him straight in the eyes. I know this conversation will not lead us into a 'happily ever after.'

"I don't know. You're hot and cold all the time. Well you're cold most of the time and hot one time, but still." I laugh, he isn't wrong. Deep down I wish things were different. I wish I could have been human and met Aiden. We would have been good together.

"You're not wrong," I say. This time he laughs and then his face turns serious.

"I'm not dating Sarah. We are just friends. I mean she likes me but...I guess I might be leading her on." I don't know why he feels like explaining but I am glad he does.

"You shouldn't lead her on unless you like her." He crosses his arms. I can tell he is unhappy with my statement.

"So you don't want a relationship with me?" I can see the hurt in his eyes. I have been mean for so long that I can just shoot him one hundred percent down but I want to give him hope even though I shouldn't.

"It's not that." I look him square in the face. "I am in

224

no position to be in any relationship. If you knew what I went through in my past relationship, you would understand." It isn't a lie. I wonder how he would feel if he knew he liked a vampire. "I'm just not ready and honestly, I don't know when I'll be ready. Let's just say it ended so badly that I lost myself and now I need to find myself." He nods when I finish speaking.

"I understand…but that doesn't mean I'll stop trying." I roll my eyes and smile. The feelings I am starting to have for Aiden just keep building.

"You know, I honestly don't think I want you to stop." There is so much nervous tension in the room that I think I am going to explode.

"So how about for now, we can be friends? I would love it if we could do that and I mean real friends not that I'll see you when I see you stuff." I am about to speak when he starts to speak again. "I mean let's exchange numbers and we will just have a buddy relationship…. for now." I laugh and nervously move around. I'm so glad that I can't blush anymore because I would be a bright red. "What do you say?" I can't say no.

"I would like that. Just friends though. None of that friends with benefits stuff." I arch my eyebrow at him and put my hands on my hips. He mocks me by arching his eyebrow.

"I wouldn't disrespect you in that way. If there were any benefits, you would be my woman." This guy is going to make me change my mind about just being friends. *Why do I have to be a vampire?*

"Alright you're crossing the line. No flirting with your friend." The conversation is beginning to get a little awkward. So we just hug it out and then he leaves the room.

TRANSITION

Chapter 24

I am sitting at a bar ordering shots of vodka.

I left the group hang, keeping to my story of having somewhere to go. In this case I have to go hunting… animals…since I'm trying Jade's vegan diet again and to a bar so that I can drink my feelings about Aiden away. I am on my third shot when I get a text message.

Hey friend…I was just thinking I don't know how old you are. I hope you're not 12 or something.

I don't recognize the number.

TRANSITION

Nichole: *Who is this?*
Aiden...who else would it be?

I don't know what to say. I don't want to tell him I am eighteen but I don't want to lie either. Since Jade is going to help me get an ID that says twenty-one...I decide on twenty-one.

Nichole: *Oh...I'm 21. How old are you anyway and how did you get my number?*
Aiden: *I'm 23 and I got your number from Jade. Hope you don't mind, friend?*

Of course Jade would give my number to Aiden. Aiden is about five years older than me. I don't know if I am bothered by it or not. I don't really know what to text back. I am surprised that he has texted me at all.

Nichole: *Not at all. So are you a lawyer like Richard?*
Aiden: *No, but I'm in law school with him.*
We are not lawyers yet.
Nichole: *So you are smart and cute?*
Aiden: *I thought you said no flirting with your friend? So you think I'm cute? Good to know.*

He is right. I did say no flirting with your friends. I should really stop texting him. No good can come from us texting. The bartender walks in front of me and asks if I need anything. I order two more shots of vodka. I am going to need it while battling through the maze that is mine and Aiden's friendship. I am taking my shot when I get another message.

CHAPTER 24

Aiden: *Still there?*
Nichole: *Yea, but I don't think this is a good idea.*
Us texting and stuff.
Aiden: *You're being cold again... and friends text, a lot.*
I'm just trying to get to know you more.

I run my hand though my hair. I am beginning to think that a friendship with Aiden isn't going to be a good thing either.

Nichole: *Can you let me know when y'all leave the condo?*
Aiden: *Nichole...*
Nichole: *Please? ...and I'll catch up with you tomorrow.*
Aiden: *Alright, I will. TTYL*

I let out a breath that I don't know I am holding. I was hoping that he wouldn't put up a fight about me ending our conversation. For some reason, I am starting to feel alone with all the people I am cutting off. So much has happened since my birthday and so much is still happening. I know that if I hadn't gone through what I did, I would have never met Jade, Aiden, or even Richard. Everything good happening in my life now just feels like bad timing.

I have a few more shots before I leave the bar. I am feeling a little buzzed as I walk out into the cool air. I'm not ready to go back to the condo since I haven't received a text from Aiden saying that everyone has left. While I am walking, I feel someone following me. *Don't be stupid man*, I think. It really isn't safe for women to walk around at night by themselves but of course, I am a vampire.

I start to walk slower so the man can catch up with me. I don't feel like having a long drawn out stalking situation.

TRANSITION

When the man gets close enough, I turn around and grab him by the neck.

"Why are you stalking me?" I growl. The man starts moving his hands. I keep my grip on his neck until I realize he is doing sign language. I let go and he abruptly pulls my card-sized pocket book out his pocket. *I left it...*

The man gives me the pocket book and starts to sign something. I don't know what he is saying. I feel bad for how I reacted. He was just trying to bring me my bag. The man starts backing away and I can tell he is trying to get away from me. I grab him by the shoulder and halt his movement. I want to fix what I have done. I look the man directly in the eyes.

"You did a nice thing, you brought me my bag and I am very thankful."

"I would have just strangled him." A chill runs down my spine. I know that voice. It is a voice that once brought happiness into my life but it is also a voice that haunts my dreams. For one brief moment, I feel like I am in a dream and that I am going to wake up soon. That moment is quickly fleeting.

I slowly turn around and am being greeted by my worst nightmare. Blue eyes stare at me from ten feet away. *This can't be happening...*

I can't breathe. I can't speak. All I can do is stare. *How did he find me?* Deep down I know him finding me has something to do with either Tyler or Casey. They are the only ones that know that I am still somewhat alive. I know Casey wouldn't have told anyone but Nate is a vampire and we have ways of getting information. Tyler on the other hand shouldn't have remembered that I am alive, but since I don't have too much knowledge on using mind control on vampires, it could have been him that gave me away. No matter how he found me, Nate is here.

"What are you doing here Nate?" I try my hardest to appear unfazed. I don't want him to see how scared I am.

"I came to find you baby." How on earth did he find me? There are so many places I could have gone but he finds me here? It doesn't make sense.

"*Baby?* I haven't been your baby since you tried to kill me. Or should I say since you killed me since I'm no longer human." He smiles and I want to smack that smile right off his face. "How did you find me Nate? How did you even know I am still alive?" I cross my arms and give him my best glare. He puts his hands in his pocket before he speaks.

"Well when someone you killed and buried is no longer in their shallow grave…there are only a few options. A dead person can't necessarily walk away can they? There were no body remnants so no animal dragged you off to feed on you and there was no news about a found dead girl. The only viable option is that I turned you by accident." He still doesn't answer the most important question so I repeat it really slowly.

"How... Did... You... Find... Me…?" He smiles.

I feel him move before he does but it is too late. He is directly in front of me. We are inches apart. I am stunned into place. I have nowhere to go and no way to get away.

"Don't run…" His face is inches from mine. Being a vampire doesn't help me any. I feel just as weak as I was human. "Baby…I will always find you, no matter where you run…but if you need to know, vampires are great trackers. I tracked the scent you left in the woods in front of your parent's home. I knew if you were alive, you would have visited them. I missed you." *He what?*

TRANSITION

I guess going home for Thanksgiving was more of a bad decision than before.

"You mis..." He cut me off with a kiss. Nate is kissing me but I just stand frozen in shock. *What does he think he is doing?* Before he can realize that I'm not going to kiss him back, all the rage and anger comes rushing through my veins. *How dare he...*

A low deep menacing growl came rumbling through my chest. It is a warning, telling him to back off. He pulls back and stares at me in shock.

"Man, you're so beautiful. Did you just growl at me?" So he finds me amusing. I want to literally tear the smile he has off his face. I feel my fangs slowly revealing themselves. I will show him how it feels to get bit by a vampire. Maybe he would like to feel the bite of my fangs before he dies.

"Oh no you don't...put those beautiful fangs away. I'm not here to fight you Nichole. I'm here to apologize. I'm sorry I did what I did. Can you forgive me?" Forgive him? I lose it.

"Can... I... Forgive... YOU?" I feel myself shaking. I don't retract my fangs. Instead, I bare my teeth at him. "You tried to kill me Nate! I should rip your throat out this very second." He doesn't seem fazed by my outburst. He laughs.

"We are the same now, can't you see. I'm glad you didn't die. I mean I should have noticed that you drew blood when you bit my hand but I was being careless. My carelessness paid off though. Look at you." He gestures toward me with his hand.

"We are not the same and we will never be the same. You're a monster." I will never be like Nate.

"I'm a monster?" He laughs darkly. "Tell me Nichole, how many people have you killed? Ten? Twenty? Or have you killed more? Our vampire line is known to be the strongest and the most deadly. You can't tell me you haven't killed anyone." I'm not about to tell him any truth about me.

"I haven't, so obviously I'm not from whatever line you're talking about." He grabs my arms and pulls me closer.

"You are a product of the Sadune vampire lineage and I know you have killed. Tell me how many?" I easily pull out of his grasp. He can't hold me hostage like before. Like he said we are equal.

"Fine, I have killed three people." I'm sure he will be happy to know that I'm not as monstrous as him. "They were all criminals so I did the world a favor."

"Well, I have to say that I am a little disappointed. I thought that you would have done better, but the fact that you think you did the world a favor just justifies that we are the same. Those people could have changed and became better people. *You* decided to rid the world of them." He is right. I didn't have to kill those people. I am a monster. I could have even used mind control on them so that they would be better people, but instead I killed them. *What have I done?*

"I'm a monster..." I start shaking my head and backing away from him.

"No, you are magnificent. You are like me in every way." He pulls me back to him. "Come here baby and let me see those ravishing bottom fangs." *Bottom fangs?*

"Bottom... Fangs...?" This is too much. Everything is too much.

He caresses my cheek waiting for me to show him my so-called 'bottom fangs' and I smack his hand away. I hit his hand with so much force that I hear some of the bones crack. I know they will heal soon but it gives me great pleasure knowing I broke something of his.

"Don't touch me Nate." I am growling. "...And I don't have bottom fangs." I want to rip off his head.

"I'm going to let that go because I know you are mad...but baby, we can be together forever now...and you do have bottom fangs. All vampires in our line have them. They are lethal to all other kinds of vampires." My mind is boggling. I have two sets of fangs and whatever else he just said about vampire lines is taking me over an edge that I don't want to go over. This is all too much.

"Huh?" I don't know what to say. I don't even know what to think. I need to get away.

"See, you need me. There is so much I can teach you. There is so much you need to know. Come on baby...let's go home." My mind isn't turning anymore. I am full of rage at his last words. Does he think I will ever go with him? I bare my teeth and grab him by his neck in rage and he proceeds to do the same. His eyes darken to their monstrous black color.

"Nichole," he says as a warning. "I don't know what you think you are doing but I would let go if I were you." I laugh darkly through my clenched throat. He isn't messing with Nichole the human anymore.

"Nate," I say mocking his tone. "I wouldn't have come looking for me if I were you. This act you are putting on, like you love and miss me, is hilarious. As I recall, you were getting tired of me anyway. Why shouldn't I just rip your throat out with my so called bottom fangs?" His face darkens at my words. We are on equal ground now. "Don't think I could do it? Try me." I am no longer the weak human that he took advantage of. We are both vampires and according to him we are equal.

To my astonishment, he lets go of my neck and his

CHAPTER 24

eyes go from black to blue. He stares into my eyes. "You know, I really did love you, Nichole." I don't believe a word he says.

"Nathaniel, you wouldn't know love if it slapped you in the face." I know it is now or never. Either he will kill me or I will kill him.

"Is that how you feel?" I nod my head and ready myself for what will come next. "I'll be seeing you soon Nichole," he says before he breaks my hold, and with the speed of lightening runs off.

I stand in the same spot for about an hour. I am in utter shock. I feel as if I can't decipher a dream from reality. This surely has to be a dream or a nightmare. Nate didn't kill me and I didn't kill him. *What is going on?* I start to feel light snow falling down on to my face and body. I look around. If I couldn't see him, surely he couldn't see me and I don't see him. *Where did he go?*

I keep standing in the same spot until I get a text. I look down at my phone and see that it is from Aiden.

Aiden: *Hey we are leaving.*
I'll catch up with you later friend.

My night can't get any worse. It is at its worse.

...

When I arrive back at the condo, I walk slowly to the door. I am in a trance. I hear laughing coming from the inside as I unlock the door. As I walk in Jade turns toward me.

"Nichole where have you...?" She finally gets a look at my face. "Nichole what's wrong." Jade springs from the couch and walks over to me. I look at Richard.

TRANSITION

When he gauges my expression his facial expression changes to one of worry.

"He found me." That is all I say and it has Jade radiating shock and fury.

"This isn't good," Jade finally says after a beat.

"No, no it's not." *This is very bad.*

Chapter 25

"I'm going to go to him." I stare Jade directly in the eyes. This is my decision.

I'm not using mind control on her. I just want to show her how serious I am. I'm not going to put anyone in danger. Not Jade, Richard, and not Aiden. That's what I will be doing if I don't leave. I will be putting my new friends in danger. This is not their problem. Nate is not their problem. They shouldn't have to deal with any of this.

"No!" Jade looks at me with a stricken look on her face. She doesn't want me to go.

TRANSITION

"I'm going to go to him," I say slowly. She needs to understand why. "If I don't he will come back here and who knows what he will do to you, Richard, or Aiden. I mean the guy tried to kill me because I danced with another guy! He would torture Aiden slowly and probably just kill you and Richard." *What will he do to my family?* "He knows I'm alive now! He might harm my family!" I am sure I am the one with the stricken look now.

My family; my mom, dad, and my sister are all in danger now. My imagination is starting to run wild. I can't let him hurt my family. I will do anything to keep them safe. Safe from me and safe from Nate.

"...But he might kill you...," Jade says as she paces my room. *Might*...I am sure he will.

Jade and I convinced Richard that my ex wasn't a psycho stalker or serial killer, which in fact he is. It seems that he believed us but he won't leave the condo. Richard retired to Jade's room so he can be here to protect us, but in reality, he is the one who needs protection. Both he and Jade do. Jade and I went to my room so we could talk. We listen closely just in case Richard decides to eavesdrop.

"He probably *will* kill me, Jade." There is no probably about it. I am convinced that Nate doesn't have a loving bone in his body. Even though I know that my end is truly coming, I don't want put anyone else in danger. This is my fight, not theirs.

"Nichole...you're like my best friend now. You *are* my best friend, even though we haven't known each other long. I don't want you to die!" Jade stops pacing and looks me directly in my eyes. She is trying to show me how serious she is. I look away from her.

CHAPTER 25

"I won't put anyone else in danger." There is no way she can stop me. My mind is made up.

"I'm going with you." I snap my head in her direction.

"Absolutely not!" There is no way she is coming. Three against two is not a good outcome. I am going to have to make Jade stay here. I look Jade directly in the eyes and she quickly turns around.

"NO! No, Nichole! You will not use mind control on me!" I can hear the anger in her voice. "Promise me! Promise me you will never use it on me!" I sigh. She is my friend. I shouldn't have even tried.

"Fine, I promise." I don't want to fight with her. If this is our last moment together, I don't want us to argue.

"Say it!" Jade sounds calmer but hurt. *I shouldn't have tried.*

"I promise I will never use mind control on you. I'm sorry." Jade turns around. "You can't come with me, Jade." From the look on her face, I know there is no way to keep her from coming.

"I'm coming and that's that. You won't face him alone." Jade crosses her arms. *She doesn't get it...*

"You don't get it, Jade," I say exasperated. "I'm not going to face him. I'm going to him. He will either take me under his wing or kill me." She gets it now and her face shows it.

"So you were just going to show up on his door step and say 'Hey I'm here, do what you will?'.... Why would you do that?" I put my hands on my face. *Maybe I'll leave tonight...*

I remove my hands from my face and Jade lunges at me. Suddenly, everything goes black.

TRANSITION

...

I snap open my eyes, take in a deep breath like I've been deprived of air, and quickly sit up. *What just happened?* I look around and meet Jade's gaze in the living room. *What did she do to me?* The only thing I can remember is her lunging at me. After that, nothing.

"What did you do to me?" I am furious. Jade doesn't show any emotion.

"I snapped your neck," she says nonchalantly. *She. Did. What?*

"You... Did... What?" I am in shock. *She snapped my neck...She snapped my neck...* I can't wrap my mind around her words. Last time I checked...when you snap someone's neck, they die. So she basically killed me.

"I snapped your neck." We just stare at each other for a while. She can tell I am pissed and she is the one who breaks the silence first. "I knew you would be fine. It's like the time you drowned when you jumped over the cliff. You'll always wake up. You're immortal." It is like the words go into one ear and out the other without even bypassing my brain. *She snapped my neck...*

"You snapped my neck?" It isn't a question but I say it like one.

"I didn't want you to leave. I had to get Richard to go home. I used mind control on him." I see sadness in Jade's eyes. She never wanted to use mind control on Richard. "I need to be in the same room with you at all times. You're not leaving without me." So instead of asking me to just stay, she snapped my neck?

"You snapped my neck?" This time I say it slow and low, letting the words sink in.

"Yes, Nichole...I snapped your neck. You were only

CHAPTER 25

out for thirty minutes." She crosses her arms and stares at me. Fury is building up inside me.

"Well would you like me to return the favor?" I speak with vehemence. *How dare she snap my neck...?*

"No I would not. I won't do it again." I rub the back of my neck. *Everything feels fine.*

"Don't worry. You'll heal. It's kind of like you're Wolverine..." When I don't speak, she clarifies. "...From *X-men*." I've seen *X-men*.

"I know who Wolverine is..." I say with irritation.

"Nichole, can you just forgive me? We need to think of a plan." I'm going to forgive her...*eventually*. I don't speak. "Nichole!"

"Ok...what's the plan?" I pause. "Since we're both going to our death now...we need to make it look like we tried at least." I am still irritated by what she did but my words are true.

"Nichole!" I roll my eyes and look out the window. Daylight is creeping.

"I don't know if you know this or not but last time I checked, there are three of them and two of us." Last time I checked, three is more than two and two is less than three. Those are not good odds.

"I know, but we are going to try...we have to." I look away from her. There is no way we are going to make it through this.

"I know that before, when we were back in Rosenburg, I thought we could kill him together but I don't know anymore." Jade stands up.

"Look Nichole! We are going to make a plan and we are going to succeed. You are my friend and I am yours! I'm not letting you do this alone! I'm not letting you just walk into your death. We are going to get Nate and his friends too! I need you and you need me!" I look back at Jade.

"Why do you need me Jade?" She sits back down. My phone starts ringing. I ignore it.

"You're my friend and the only person that I can be my true self around. ...*and* the only person I can talk to. Also, vampire life is so lonely. So when you find a true vampire friend, you keep them. We are not a loving species." I laugh. My phone rings again. "Are you going to get that?"

"No, It's probably just Aiden." *I do not have time to deal with him too.*

"At six in the morning?" It is early. Whoever it is will just have to wait.

"It doesn't matter. We have more pressing issues than a ringing phone." Jade smiles.

"So we're going to do this together?" I return her smile.

"Yeah we are." I stand up to give Jade a hug and she stands to hug me back. "Just don't snap my neck again." I am still mad about her doing it.

"I won't." My phone rings again. *Who is calling me?* "Just get it and we will start making plans when you get off."

I get up and walk toward my room. My phone is sitting in the middle of the bed. *I will just turn it off.* That way it won't be a distraction. I reach for the phone and see it is Casey calling. *Why is she calling?* A sickening thought comes to mind. *What if he hurt my family already?* I go to dial Casey's number, when my phone rings again. I answer it.

"Oh my gosh, Casey, is everything alright?" I am breathing heavy. I know her calling early this morning can only mean something bad has happened. Jade is at my doorway, at the mention of Casey's name, but I don't turn

CHAPTER 25

towards her.

"I knew that you had to have contacted either your family or Casey. I guess it was just good judgment on my part that I chose to check Casey first." The voice on the phone isn't Casey's voice. It is Nate's.

"What have you done to her, Nate?" I hiss into the phone.

"Down baby vampire...I can hear your fangs divulging. You know your family got lucky. I was thinking of what I could do to them that would hurt you the worse. No matter, I have Casey. Maybe I'll play with your family later." *My family...* I'm going to kill him. I'm going to kill him and smile while doing it.

"What do you want, Nate?" I thrust my hands through my hair. *My family... Casey...*

"Now you have a choice. Either you come to me and exchange your life for Casey's. Or I come to you and you get to watch her die." *What am I going to do?* I feel like I am out of options, but I don't want him to hear it in my voice.

"How do I know that you're not going to kill her either way?" I should just tell him I am coming. I am playing a game that I've never played before.

"You have no room to negotiate. I'll make you a deal. You meet me at the place I buried you so I can put you where you were supposed to be all along.... or I wreak havoc on Casey, your family, and this whole town...and I think I'll do it in that order." I can hear him smiling.

My mind is racing. It is trying to formulate a plan to save everyone. If I go and just let Nate kill me, he will probably kill Casey and my family. There is only one thing to do.

TRANSITION

"Fine, what time do I need to meet you?" This is going to end with his death, not mine.

"Good girl. You have just saved your best friend and family. Meet me at six tonight. I'll give you the rest of the day to reflect." *Oh how nice...he is so generous*, I think sarcastically.

"Thanks so much," I say with heavy sarcasm as I hang up the phone. I am beyond pissed. I turn towards Jade.

"We're going to kill him," she says. It isn't a question. It is a statement. She heard the whole conversation. I nod.

"We're going to kill him."

Chapter 26

"So you have to take the head completely off to kill a vampire. Like pull it off or cut it off and you should burn the remains also. I mean you could just burn the vampire without taking off the head but he might fight a little and die later." *Sounds easy enough*, I think sarcastically.

I have never taken someone's head off or even set someone on fire. I mean the fire part sounds easy but decapitating someone sounds hard.

TRANSITION

Even in biology, I had a hard time dissecting dead animals. Now, in order to save my family and friend, I have to rip off a vampire's head and then set him on fire. I can't believe what I am about to do and Jade makes it sound like it is nothing. Well, it is something alright.

Jade and I are currently driving to Rosenburg. Well, Jade is driving and I am riding. I feel too on edge to drive. All I can think about is saving my family and Casey. Casey is like my family and now I put her in danger by communicating with her. She would have probably been in danger anyway, no matter if I told her or not, but I still feel responsible. He went after her first just because she knew what I had become. I hope she isn't hurt or worse, dead. The thought saddens and enrages me at the same time.

I look out the window as Jade continues to talk about how to kill a vampire. I hear the gist of it but tune out the rest. My mind is racing, thinking of everything but nothing at the same time.

We leave the condo an hour after Nate's call. I don't want to wait until six to get to Rosenburg. I need to be there way before Nate expects me. I don't want to play by his rules. Playing by someone else's rules could mean failure but if you play by your own, you know the game and you can win. *And I want to win.*

I can still hear Jade talking in the background. I know that I should be listening, but I am too deep in thought about everything. I turn toward Jade as a thought comes into mind.

"Nate said that our vampire line had bottom fangs that were lethal to all other types of vampires." Jade glances at me with a confused look on her face. It sounds so crazy... *I know.* Talking about vampires is strange in itself and now I am asking if there is a possibility that there could be more than one type of vampire? I would look at me crazy, too.

"He said what? Last time I checked there was only one kind of vampire…and that kind was *vampire*." I don't know why he would have lied about that. Maybe he knows something she doesn't. I mean, there are different types of humans. There are white, black, Asian, Hispanic, etc. Why can't there be different kinds of vampires, too? I shake my head. Vampires already have different ethnicities. Having bottom fangs, if I do, can be like a different trait that I have that other vampires don't. In reality, I have so many questions and no answers.

"…But what if it is true? That means that you have a disadvantage and I have an advantage." I can tell she doesn't like the sound of that.

"So, if it is true, and I'm not saying it is, Nate could just bite me and I will die? Or you could target that one guy and get him out the way. Wait, out of the three is Nate the only one that's like you. I mean if it's true." Jade is starting to sound so confusing but for the most part, I understand her.

"Well, I'm not sure. Tyler, the one I ran into at Thanksgiving, is definitely not like me. I think John is like Nate." If John is like Nate and me, then Jade has a huge disadvantage.

"So, I'll wait, where no one can see me, until the right time, or until you need me. Then you try to take out Tyler first, since he seems to be the weakest out of the group." That sounds like a good plan. "Oh! You can just bite Tyler and then we will work on the other two." My eyes widen. So I guess Jade is buying the bottom fangs story. Either that or she is being sarcastic and this is not a time to be sarcastic. This plan is not a stable one. I feel like we are way out of our element.

TRANSITION

"So you think the bottom fangs thing is true," I say arching my eyebrow.

"I don't know. Try to make them come out." I don't even know where to start to make these so called 'bottom fangs' appear. I take a look in the mirror and smile. My two bottom teeth that I've heard people call "canines" look a little too sharp but I think they are supposed to be. Who am I kidding? I know nothing about teeth, let along vampire teeth. I sigh.

"Jade I don't know how." I don't even know if they exist.

"Well then, we can't bet on that. So the plan is for me to hide until the right time. Tyler get's taken out first. In the mist of that, we have to save Casey. Then we try to take out Nate and John. I'm sure you want Nate so I will take John. Let's just hope that the bottom fangs thing isn't real." *Yes let's hope...* Because if it is, then I will have to save Jade and Casey.

...

We park the car at the borders of Rosenburg. Hopefully when all this is over, we will make our way back to the car and just drive off but there is also a big chance that we aren't going to come out of this unscathed or even alive. I just hope Casey will.

"Alright, where are we going first Nichole?" I take a good look around our surroundings. I don't know how the day will play out. I arrive early so that I can have an advantage but I feel unprepared. There is no other road for me to travel down. This is it. This is what I have to do. Even if I leave my family and Casey to their death, which I won't, I will still be on the run from Nate. I would rather die protecting the ones I love, than die a coward.

CHAPTER 26

"I want to go check out my house to make sure my family is ok." I don't trust Nate, so I can't take his word that he has left my family alone, for now at least. If I can just see that they are ok, then that will bring me a little comfort.

"Alright, let's go," Jade says as she puts her long black hair into a ponytail.

We run at inhuman speeds towards my house. Running is still exhilarating but I can't bask in its beauty. There is nothing beautiful about today. The sun could have been shining but dark ominous clouds obscure it.

We finally make it to the woods outside my old home. It makes me sad that I can't go into the one place where I grew up. I scan the house, looking for my loved ones in each window.

"Does everything look ok?" I stare into the house before answering Jade.

My family looks ok. They are all at home. My mom and sister are in the kitchen making lunch and my dad is in his office working. I am taking this last look at them. After today, I might never see them again.

"Yeah...everything looks ok." *I love you,* I think, wishing my family could hear my thoughts. "Come on, let's go." I turn to face Jade. I want to stay and enjoy the view of my mother, father, and sister but I can't. I have to keep them safe.

"Where are we going?" I take a deep breath. This is not going to be easy.

"We're going to the place I died."

...

We start walking slowly toward Nate's house. Well not his house but the dump I was killed in. I am vaguely aware of Jade protesting behind me.

249

TRANSITION

"...Nichole do you hear me? Nichole!" I turn towards Jade. "I said... why are we going there? Isn't that where they live? Are you trying to get us both killed? I thought the plan was to kill them. This is not a good plan." My mind is focused on one thing, killing Nate.

"They don't live there, Jade. They live in a mansion on the outskirts of Rosenburg." I am going to face my fears and I am going to start by visiting the place of my death.

"I'm not sure this is a good idea Nichole. Even if they don't live there, they still might be there." *None of this is a good idea...but this is what I need. If they just so happen to be there, we can end this right now.*

I turn and keep walking towards Nate's house. I guess Jade decides not to argue because she stops talking and just follows me. We walk in silence. I am mentally preparing myself for what will come next. There is no escaping our fates now. Either Nate and his friends are going to die or Jade and I are. That is the reality of this situation.

We have finally made it to the small house where I died. There is no one in the house. *They aren't keeping Casey here.*

"No one is here, Nichole."

"No, no one would be here. This is where they bring their victims." If Jade is in shock, she doesn't make it known.

We walk up to the house and try the doorknob. It is locked. I twist the doorknob until it breaks. *It's not locked anymore.* I walk into the house that will haunt my dreams forever. It looks the same as it did before. *Empty...*

My emotions are swimming as I look around the house that holds my last human memories. Even if Nate isn't here, being here will make me stronger. If I can face what happened here, I can face Nate. This is where they would bring their victims. *Victims*... I was just one of many probably.

I walk down the hall. I walk toward the back room on the right. I walk towards the room where my life changed. I open the door, walk in, and sit on the bed. I breathe. In and out, in and out, in and out. This room held me captive. This room held the scared me, the weak me, the old me. I am no longer that girl. I close my eyes and let her go. It is time to embrace the new me if I want to save the ones I love. Although the old me is gone, I will always hold her in my heart. I will leave my fear and uncertainty here in this room. I open my eyes. *I'm not scared anymore; I'll never be scared again.*

"Nichole..." Jade says as she walks in the room. I stand up.

"Yeah."

"Are you ready?" I finally make eye contact with her.

"I'm ready." *More than you know.*

TRANSITION

Chapter 27

The sun descends and the moon rises, giving the only light that illuminates the darkness. Wind blows silently as if it is trying to tell me a secret. Our steps are quiet, we move like the wind walking along the forest floor, as we make our way to the hole I crawled out of just a few months ago.

We whip past the trees, rocks, and grass like we are floating in the air. The animals in the forest are neither seen nor heard. They are hiding, but I know they are out there. I can hear the steady pace of their hearts and the blood flowing in their veins.

TRANSITION

We make it to our destination. No words spoken, no sentiments given. There is just quiet contemplation and preparation churning in our minds. I look at Jade and she nods. She quickly turns and climbs the tall tree, near me, looking like a spider silently climbing up a wall.

I turn my attention away from Jade. She is now invisible to me. I will neither give away nor tell her whereabouts. She is a secret, one that I will pretend not to know.

I look around through the darkness of night, taking my place, waiting for this game to begin. My stance is confident. My mind is calm. I survey my surroundings, like a predator who feels threatened, bracing for an attack. My eyes land on remnants of the trash bag that once held me inside. I laugh, *Nate will have to do better this time if he wants to get rid of me.*

Nate is going to come into the forest confident and cocky. He doesn't realize that the girl he is coming to kill isn't the same one he had attempted to kill before. She is a vampire now. He doesn't know that I am going to refuse to back down. I make myself a promise that I am going to leave here with Jade, Casey, and my life. The only remnants that are being left here are three sets of ashes.

Time ticks by as I stand silently in the forest. I wait and Jade never makes a movement or a sound. I can easily forget her presence.

I wait and wait until I hear the faintest sound of footsteps. I snap my head in the direction of the sound. The forest doesn't hide their arrival. Nature is on my side. I stay calm, waiting for them, until I hear a slight whimper.
Casey...

CHAPTER 27

Rage boils inside me but I make sure I am relaxed on the outside. I refuse to show any emotion, so I push my feelings to the back of my mind.

Four silhouettes appear in my line of sight but they are still so far away. I bend down to the ground and pick up a thick stick. It isn't too thick; I can close my hand around it. I begin to twirl it around and around like a baton. The figures keep getting closer and closer until they are at least thirty feet away. I smile but they don't return it. They just stare at me. Three pairs of black eyes and one pair of brown eyes focus on me.

"Well, is this a staring contest? Or are we making a trade? My life for Casey's." I speak in a genuine tone. I want to dissuade my opponents from my real intentions. "I mean that's why we're all here, right?" Finally I get a smile out of Nate.

"Always a pleasure to see you, Nichole." I stop twirling the stick and blink dramatically.

"That's it? 'Always a pleasure to see you Nichole?'" I speak mockingly in his formal tone. "That's all you have to say. I mean I'm handing myself over to you in exchange for my best friend and that's all you have to say, Nathaniel." I make eye contact. They don't intimidate me anymore.

"You're not really..." Nate begins speaking but I cut him off. This is my play until I let him have a turn.

"...I mean if I didn't hand myself over, you would have never gotten to me. So I'm doing you a favor." I smile at them again. Nate cocks his eyebrow as if in shock but keeps his smile on his face. I can tell he is getting irritated.

"We would have gotten to you. Remember, I found you in Denver? You didn't even know I was coming. There is nowhere you could have hid." My smile fades. He is right but I wouldn't have gone down without a fight. I could have just run away and he would have never found me.

"No you wouldn't have Nathaniel. That's why you kidnapped my best friend. You needed leverage to get to me. You wanted to play a game…and we are playing the game right? I'm here, aren't I?" Nate crosses his arms with a look of disdain on his face. "By the way, John, it's nice to see you again. I love the eyes. I finally figured out why they are black all the time," I say sarcastically.

John is holding Casey hostage. I finally take a good look at her. She looks scared. She is shaking from head to toe. Her black hair is everywhere and her brown eyes are wide. I can't tell if she has been fed on but I don't doubt it. Those bastards probably didn't even erase her memory. She makes eye contact with me and mouths the words help me. I look away. I can't help her if I can't concentrate on the task at hand.

"Yes. Well, I would say it's nice to see you too but that would be a lie…" John says confidently before I cut him off.

"…Since when are you against lying?" I laugh an angry laugh. "Tyler, I would say that it is nice to see you again but we've already run into each other recently." I am greeted by a confused look on Tyler's face. Nate looks back and forth between us. I only look at Tyler. "Remember? Thanksgiving?" Tyler put his hands up as Nate glares at him. From the looks of it, Nate didn't know I wasn't dead on Thanksgiving.

"Nate, I swear I did not see her. I would have told you if I had." Nate turns back towards me. I guess he believes him.

"Oh, Tyler, don't be modest. You told me to erase your memory, remember? You also told me that my eyes turn red and when they do, that's when I can control other vampires. Well, I guess you wouldn't since I did. You told me everything I wanted to know." Nate looks furiously at Tyler. He is pissed and I just smile.

"I'll deal with you later. Tyler. Right now, we have some business to attend to." *Business...right...*

I jut my lip out at Tyler in a mock pout. "Did I get you in trouble?"

"Enough Nichole!" Nate says with force radiating in his voice. I turn towards him with a livid look on my face. *How dare he yell at me?*

"Let me ask you something...Nate," I say in a clipped tone. "Did you ever love me or was it all a lie?" He starts to speak but I continue. "Let me answer that. You didn't. It was all a lie." Nate arches his eyebrow at me. I put my finger up. "No wait, I do want you to answer it." I begin to twirl the stick again. All three of their eyes follow the action.

"I did love you..." *He did not...*

"...Liar!" I cut him off again. I will only let them speak when I want to hear what they have to say. "I was just your plaything and you didn't even get to play with me." I don't hide the meaning behind my voice. The night I went over to Nate's so called 'house', we were supposed to have had our first time together. Instead, he tried to kill me.

"How do you know I didn't?" I don't hide the fury burning between my eyes. Although I know that nothing had happened after I blacked out, he is trying to say something did.

"Oh, Tyler told me what happened that night, among other things." Nate glares at Tyler once again. Tyler keeps quiet. From the looks of it, Tyler is skating on thin ice with Nate.

TRANSITION

"I did love you, Nichole." I glare at Nate. I'm not falling for his lies. His tone doesn't even express love. He is just trying to bait me. He probably thinks I am some weak-minded woman that will fall for the four-letter word like a mouse in a trap.

"I'm sure," I say with sarcasm. "That's why as soon as I was gone you went running to that bitch Rebecca. If you loved me, you would have at least mourned me!" The corners of Nate's lips curl into a smile. It isn't a pleasant smile. It is one that says I am right about him not loving me.

"You knew about that?" he says.

I ignore his question and asked one of my own. "Did you kill her, Nathaniel? Not that I would care if she were dead. I just want to know. Maybe I'll make a stop by her house when we are finished here. Maybe I'll kill her." Nate looks taken back by my comment. I guess he is surprised that I can be so cold and cruel. I'm not really going to stop by her house, but I can care less about her.

"Maybe I should keep you, Nichole. I think we will be good together." I scoff. *Is he serious?*

"We would be good together in a world where vampires don't exist. You know what, not even then."

His smile quickly fades. I can see the wheels moving in his brain. He knows he will never have me. Tyler speaks up then.

"You know, you're not running anything, Nichole…" His comment angers me. I launch the stick I am holding, like a baseball, and it hurdles towards Tyler and plummets into his chest, where his heart lays. *He can't speak unless I want him to.*

Of course, it doesn't kill him and I knew it wouldn't but I just had just about enough of Tyler. It did, however, cause him to fall back against a tree. A growl creeps up in John and Tyler's chest. Nate just smiles in response. At least one of them likes my skewering techniques. Tyler stands up and takes the stick out of his chest. Almost immediately, his chest starts to heal.

"This is between Nathaniel and me, Tyler," I say in a calm voice, "You two are just his dogs and are only here to bend to his every command. So why don't you let the real vampires talk, okay?"

Tyler and John's fangs come out and they look as livid as I feel but they don't attack me. They are his dogs and Nate hasn't given the command yet.

"Nichole, I don't know what you think this is, but we are not negotiating. It's either you or Casey and right now we have Casey. You can either walk over here calmly or we will rip her throat out and still kill you." *Oh would they...*

"Let me ask you something, Nate." I start pacing a small space and then turn my back completely to them. "When I'm dead, how will I know that you didn't kill Casey?" They probably think that I am too stupid to realize that there is no way they are keeping their word. *Their word means nothing...*

"I guess you wouldn't, Nichole." Nate laughs and so do the others. That is confirmation that they aren't going to keep their word. I can see now that they think they have trapped me. *Good*, I think, *let them think that.*

"At least I tried right," I ask. Nate shrugs. "What about my family, Nate?"

"Dead..." John says. I turn around quickly and snap my head in John's direction. The word sits in the wind, in the silence. Nate doesn't contradict him. *Wrong thing to say...*

TRANSITION

Suddenly, I get the craving for a vampire named John. My fangs slowly creep out and I know my eyes are a blazing red. Let the game begin.

"What are you going to do with those baby fangs Nichole?" John is trying to rile me up. I cock my head to the side and give him a fake smile.

"First, I'm going to tear your throat out, then I'm going to rip you into tiny little pieces and finally, I will burn your bodies until they are ash. Nothing will be left of you."

Tyler and Nate start to walk towards me with Tyler in front. John stays behind to hold on to Casey. I am in front of Tyler in a flash. I grab him by the neck and fling him through the forest. I don't look where he lands. Nate is charging at me then and when he gets close, I backhand him into a couple of trees. It is then I realize I am too late. John takes Casey by the neck and disposes of her the same way I did Tyler. The only difference is that Tyler is a vampire. He can fall from any height and get right back up. Casey, on the other hand, is human. She flies and knocks in to a tree about fifteen feet high. Her body bounces off the tree and lands to the ground with a thump. There is a scream, but it isn't her's. She doesn't make a sound, she doesn't move. The scream, is mine.

"Nooo, Casey!" *No…Casey…What have I done?*

I turn my vehemence on John. All I can see is red. I am vaguely aware of Jade hopping out the tree and attacking Tyler. Nate and John are only slightly distracted by her appearance. They both charge me. John is closer. He reaches me before Nate with his fangs and red eyes on display. It's funny, he thinks he has me. That is, he thinks he has me until I quickly snap his neck. He drops at my feet at the exact moment that Nate lunges at me.

CHAPTER 27

Nate knocks me over and we both fall onto the cold forest ground. I slip from Nate's grasp. He is struggling to get a hold of me but he can't quite get a good grasp. I kick him off me and stand up. As soon as I get to my feet, he grabs me by my hair and hurls me backwards. I skid along the forest floor like a rock across water and then crash into a tree. The tree rips in half and falls over. I quickly recover myself and stand up bracing myself for another attack.

"Is that all you got, Nate? You fight like a girl. No, you fight like a human!" My comment enrages him.

Nate charges toward me and I do the one thing my mom taught me how to, I ball my fist, pull my arm back, and sock him in the jaw with all the strength I can muster. The punch has so much force, that this time he flies backwards. He doesn't fly back as far as I would like but the punch throws him off balance.

I look over towards Jade. She seems to be holding her own with Tyler. Their fight looks like a dance. I can't help her. I have to focus on Nate. This time, I won't let him charge me; I will bring the fight to him. I run towards Nate as he begins to get to his feet. I grab him by his hair and toss him backwards. He falls to the ground and I run at full speed to the spot he lands. I get on top of Nate and am about to sink my fangs into his neck when I lose my advantage. He flips me over holding me captive. He smiles a triumphant smile. I start to realize that I can't break free. For a brief second, I think I have lost the fight. His head is closing in toward my neck. His fangs are bared. Then, Jade comes running and knocks him off of me. The impact causes Jade and Nate to fall and skid across the forest floor.

Nate recovers from his fall and is about to attack Jade when Tyler catches up with her. Jade and Tyler began to struggle with each other again. Jade is slowly but surely overpowering Tyler. Soon, I know he will meet his end.

Nate looks back and forth between Tyler and Jade to me. I guess he decides that I am the bigger threat. We run towards each other and collide. We are both fighting to get an advantage on the other. Nate reaches for my neck but he misses it by a thread. I don't see his leg and that is my mistake. He kicks my feet from under me and I land on the ground. Nate quickly pins me down. His face is close to mine. His red eyes are staring at my red eyes. His hands hold mine captive above my head.

"You're still that weak little girl, aren't you?" *Weak...?*

"You know how you said we are equal now." He decides to amuse my question and nods. *All I need is a distraction.* "Well you were wrong, Nate." *Take the bait...*

"How was I wrong Nichole? The only reason you can't fight back is because I have the upper hand." *That's what you think...*

"You were wrong, Nathaniel, because I'm a lot stronger than you." I feel it in that second that I am stronger. I don't know why; call it a rush of adrenaline or something. I just feel stronger.

I maneuver my leg from under him then kick him in the chest and off of me. He doesn't go far but it gives me the chance to stand up. He rushes toward me and I lunge at him, knocking him down and locking him to the ground. My knee digs into his torso pushing it down to make sure he doesn't get up. I lock his legs between mine to keep him from kicking me. I have one hand on his neck while the other grips both his hands. I'm not letting him get away this time. I am ending this fight now and forever.

CHAPTER 27

I look into Nate's blood red eyes. I wonder how he deceived me so easily before and how had I fallen into his traps. I have no feelings for him, I feel no sympathy for him, and I want him dead. I realize in that moment, that I never truly loved Nate and that there is no way he truly loved me. It was all a lie. Even though I know that what we had was all a lie, I can't help but ask him again.

"Did you ever love me, Nate?" I speak softly and calmly. I already know the answer but I want to hear it again. His eyes widen at my words.

"I thought I loved you once, Nichole. That ended. We aren't capable of love." His words enrage me. I don't expect them and they catch me off guard.

"*You* aren't capable of love!" I tip my head back and for the first time, I feel tiny fangs making their first appearance. Nate starts struggling when he sees them. They aren't lethal to him, but he knows what is going to happen next. "Didn't you ask to see my ravishing bottom fangs?"

I tilt his head to the side and then launch my fangs into his neck. I used the sharp blades that are my fangs, to tear into his neck like he once did mine, ignoring his protests. I grab his hair and pull until I dislocated his head from his body.

I sit up on my knees looking at Nathaniel Blackwood's body torn in two pieces. I feel relief in knowing that he is gone for good. A red haze comes over me and I start to rip him apart even more. I tear off his hands, arms, legs, everything until he is just scattered pieces of my former ex-boyfriend. I stand up, reach in my pocket, and take out the lighter that Jade has given me, out my pocket. I set Nate's remains on fire. *Now for the other two...*

TRANSITION

I walk calmly toward Jade and Tyler with red eyes in tow. Tyler kicks Jade to the side and takes off when he sees me. I am going to chase him until I hear groans coming from John.

"Don't worry about it..." I say before Jade attempts to chase after Tyler. *He is nobody in this group.*

Jade and I walk over to John and tear him apart as soon as he opens his eyes. He doesn't have much time to fight back. We light his remains on fire. *Good riddance to you both...*

I look over to where Casey's body lay. My fangs retract and I am overcome with grief. I walk over to her and drop to my knees. Her eyes are closed and her body still. I pick up her limp body and hold it to my chest. *What... Have... I... Done?*

"Casey!" I cry but no tears will come. "Casey!" I start rocking back and forth. *What have I done?* My breathing becomes erratic. *My friend...* Casey is more than a friend. She is my family. She is like my sister. Now she is gone. "No, No, No Casey. You have to be ok." I rub her raven black hair. "I'm so sorry, Casey. I'm so sorry." I am losing it. I am mentally losing it.

Jade walks closer towards us and kneels down when she is directly in front. She looks sad. I can't place if it is for Casey or me or both. Jade reaches up towards Casey and I recoil Casey's body from her grasp. I don't want her to take Casey from me.

"Nichole..."

"No, no, no. I'm sorry, Casey, I'm so sorry. This is all my fault." *I did this to her. It's all my fault. I did this.*

"Nichole..." I am ignoring Jade. I don't want to hear what she has to say.

CHAPTER 27

"I should have listened to you when I first met Nate. You told me he couldn't be trusted, but no, I brushed it off. I kept thinking you said that because you thought all guys were liars. I should have listened. I should have listened and you would be alive." I sit there rocking and talking to my dead friend's body.

"She's alive Nichole." I look at Jade. *What...?*

"W-What? ...b-but she's not moving and she, she... look at her." Casey's body is twisted and broken. I try not to focus on the blood seeping from her body. I don't feel the need to feed when I see it. I just feel sick.

"Listen, Nichole, you're so blinded by your emotions that you can't hear her heart beating." I stop rocking and listen closely. I can finally hear her faint heart beat. It is weak, almost non-existent, but it is there. *Barely.*

"W-What do I do? Should I...should I turn her? I mean...what would you do?" I look in Jade's eyes pleading for an answer.

"I should tell you "No," Nichole. I should, but, if it were me, I would. It's a selfish thing to do but I couldn't just let someone I loved die." *I can't let Casey die...she's like my family.*

"I can't do it, Jade..." I start breathing heavy and look Jade in the eyes. *Please understand...*

"I understand, Nichole. It's ok if you can't do it." She doesn't understand. It's not that I can't turn her but that if I tried, I feel like I will kill her for good. I'm not *that* in control of myself. I am too scared to even try.

"No, you don't get it," I whimper. "I can't do it because I'll kill her." Understanding flashes in Jade's eyes.

"You want me to do it?" I nod. Jade looks as if she is contemplating whether or not she is going to do it. I have a

TRANSITION

feeling that she isn't until she reaches out for Casey. I hand Casey's body to Jade.

I watch as Jade drips some of her blood into Casey's mouth. She then moves Casey's hair away from her neck. As her fangs come out, I turn my head. I don't want to see her bite Casey. Just because I'm not looking doesn't mean that I don't hear the skin break, or the sound of Casey's neck snapping. There is no more heartbeat. I keep my head turned away when Jade finally sits up.

"Now what," I say in a hoarse voice. My head is still facing away from Jade, from Casey, from everything. *Breathe Nichole...* "Now what do we do?"

"Now we wait, while she transitions."

Epilogue

Dawn is approaching as the man slowly walks over to the vampire lying motionless on the ground. He tilts his head and looks at the creature in disgust. He has made it his life's duty to obliterate the creatures from the earth. He has lost his family to these creatures. He hates vampires.

He pulls out a large machete type knife from his belt and nudges the vampire's face with the toe of his boot. The vampire groans but doesn't wake. His knuckles go white as he grips the knife with all his strength.

267

TRANSITION

He is frustrated. It took him longer than he liked to take this vampire down. It is normally easier to take this kind of vampire down but the vampire put up a good fight. It just wasn't good enough.

He paces in a circle, trying to calm himself. He kicks some small rocks and broken pieces of trees across the forest floor. When he feels he is calm enough, he walks back over to the laying vampire and kicks it harder. This time the vampire's eyes fly open. The vampire growls and releases its fangs. It recognizes the man.

The man crouches down beside the vampire. His elbows resting on his knees as he stares down at the beast. The vampire realizes that it can't move. It is paralyzed. The vampire let out a new string of growls. The man arches his eyebrow at the vampire.

"What did you do to me?" the vampire asks. His tone is angry. The man plays with the knife in his hand.

"I gave you a paralytic," the man replies. He smiles at the vampire. "Creative, isn't it? It took me a while to make. The vampire body burns through alcohol and drugs so fast, so I couldn't just use any old paralytic. I needed to make a drug that would last a while." The vampire keeps growling but the man continues. "It took me a while and I had to test it on *your* kind a lot." The man looks down at the vampire but he avoids eye contact. The man is all too familiar with their tricks.

When the vampire doesn't respond, the man continues.

"I've killed a lot of your specific line. You Poltrunes are easy to take down." The vampire growls and snaps at the man. The man slowly lifts his finger and shakes it left to right. He is warning the vampire. The man takes on a more serious tone; he has purpose for tracking down this vampire.

EPILOGUE

He needs to find another. "Tell me, Tyler, where is he?" Tyler laughs.

"If I tell you, does that mean you'll let me go?" Tyler knows all too well that if he can't move, he is going to die today.

"Now let's be honest, do you really think I'm going to let you go? How many innocent people have *you* killed? How many families have *you* ruined? How many people have you *turned*?" Tyler tries again to break free of his invisible hold. There is no use. Whatever concoction the man has made holds him captive.

"I'm going to kill you when I get free." The man's face is blank, empty of emotion.

"You're not going to get free, Tyler. The injection I gave you will last for an hour. It's enough time for me to get what I want and to kill you." The man squares his shoulders and twirls the knife in his hands. Tyler's eyes follow the action and he growls.

"I'm not telling you shit," Tyler says through gritted teeth.

"I will get what I want, one way or another, Tyler." The man reaches into his bag that hangs on his belt and pulls out a syringe filled with a purple liquid.

"Giving me another paralytic won't help you any. I still won't talk," Tyler says. The man smiles.

"I thought you vampires had heightened senses? Well, I guess not. If you had noticed before, the first injection I gave you was clear. That was the paralytic. This, however, is not." Tyler stares at the man and wishes that he could just make eye contact. He wants to get away. He wants to be free.

Tyler thought he had made it away from danger when he and his friends lost the fight to Nichole but he had just run into an old problem. This man who is about to inject him with a purple drug is a vampire hunter. His name is Chase. Chase had started hunting vampires when Nate had killed his family while making Chase watch. Nate liked to play this back and forth hunter game with Chase yet, Chase never caught Nate. Chase has got really good at it, too. No vampire has ever killed him but he has killed many vampires. Namely, he has killed many of Tyler's vampire line–The Poltrunes.

"What is it?" Tyler asks with hesitation. He knows it can't be good, whatever it is. Chase holds the syringe in his hand and stares at it as he talks.

"Oh, this," Chase says sarcastically. "This is another drug I made. I'm going to inject you with this and it will cause you great pain." Tyler gulps. If Chase can make a drug that can paralyze vampires, this drug probably works, too. Tyler tries to stall.

"What kind of pain will it cause me?" The man looks down at Tyler again avoiding eye contact.

"Stalling are we? Well, this specific drug, and I have *many*, will give you an excruciating burning sensation. It will be like you're on fire."

Tyler tries in vain to break free but he can't. The man snaps the cap off the syringe and quickly sticks Tyler in the neck. He pushes in the purple liquid and the effects of the drug are instant. Tyler begins screaming and groaning. He feels like he is bathing in fire.

Chase stands up and walks around to a tree. He turns his back to Tyler, ignoring the screams of the vampire. He leans against a tree. Chase reaches into his pocket and pulls out a cigarette. He hooks the cigarette in the corner of his mouth and lights it. His whole demeanor is one of disinter-

EPILOGUE

est. He can care less that a vampire is in pain behind him. He blows smoke into the air as he looks back at the vampire. The effects of the drug will wear off in five minutes. He knows that he will get the information he wants soon.

Tyler wants to die. He has never felt pain like the pain he is feeling now. He knows that he will do anything not to feel this pain again. He will give the man what he wants and he will die. The thought depresses Tyler. The burning feeling starts to fade and he knows it will be over soon.

When Tyler stops screaming, Chase walks back over to him. He kneels down again and starts playing with the knife again. Chase is itching to decapitate Tyler.

"So, I'm guessing now you will give me the information that I desire?" Chase's voice grows deep. "Where is he Tyler?"

"He's dead." Tyler's admission shocks Chase.

Chase has been searching for Nathaniel Blackwood for a long time now. Nathaniel has been playing games with Chase. They've had their run-ins and Nathaniel always left Chase injured but not dead. The game would continue until Nathaniel was dead. Nathaniel was a strong and ruthless vampire. Chase wanted to be the one who killed him. Now that he knows he is dead, he feels happier knowing his family's murderer is gone. He only feels a little disappointed that he wasn't the one to end Nathaniel's life. However, his curiosity is piqued. Who killed Nathaniel Blackwood? Then again, he feels that Tyler is lying. He thinks Tyler is trying to protect his master. He pulls out another syringe with the purple liquid. Tyler's eyes widen. Tyler doesn't want to go through that again.

"I think you're lying to me, Tyler. Are you trying to protect your friend?"

TRANSITION

"No, no I'm not lying. He's dead. He is. I saw him die myself." Tyler is speaking quickly. He wants to avoid the burning pain.

"What about John? Where is he?" Chase wondered why he found Tyler alone without his two companions.

"He's dead, too." Tyler isn't sure if John is dead. He didn't actually see him die but if Nichole could kill Nate, then she could kill John. John is most likely dead. Chase rests his chin on his hands. He is taking in all the new information he just learned.

"They're both dead, huh?" Chase cocks his head to the side.

"Yeah, they are both dead." Tyler's eyes are wide. He knows he is going to die but he isn't ready for it.

"Interesting. Who killed them?" Chase needs to know if there are other hunters out there. So far he is the only one he knew.

"A vampire." Tyler is going to give the man whatever information he wants.

"I might have to thank this vampire before I kill it. Well your cooperation has been helpful." Chase says it as if Tyler had a choice in the matter.

Chase takes the knife and rests it against Tyler's neck. Tyler closes his eyes, not wanting the last thing he sees to be the knife coming down upon him. Chase lifts the knife and is about to strike when a thought comes into mind.

"I have another question to ask before I kill you." Tyler opens his eyes. He doesn't know what the man has to ask him now.

"If I don't answer, will you inject me with that purple stuff?" Chase laughs.

EPILOGUE

"Of course, I will." Chase speaks as if Tyler should have already known he would.

"What's your question?" Tyler asks in defeat.

"Did Nathaniel make any other vampires?" Chase will kill any vampire he made since he didn't get a chance to kill Nathaniel himself.

"Who do you think killed him?" Tyler's statement is an answer to two of Chase's questions. Chase now knows that Nathaniel did indeed make other vampires and that one of them killed him. Although Chase is thankful to this unknown vampire, he is still going to kill it and any other vampires Nathaniel Blackwood created.

"Interesting," Chase says with an uninteresting tone. "How many did he make?"

"He made one, by accident." This information is even more shocking to Chase.

"Nathaniel Blackwood made a vampire by accident?" Chase's voice is full of wonder and confusion. Vampires don't normally make other vampires by accident.

"Yes."

"…And he only made one vampire?"

"Yes."

"Interesting. What is his name?" Chase is going to find this vampire.

"*Her* name is Nichole Roberts." Tyler has completely given up. The answers to Chase's questions just spill from his mouth.

"*Her*? Sounds like Blackwood had some trouble in paradise." Tyler knows Chase has hit the situation right on the mark with that comment.

"You could say that."

TRANSITION

Chase looks away pretending to be in thought. He wants to catch Tyler off guard when he cuts off his head. Suddenly, he brings the knife down forcefully through Tyler's neck. He doesn't struggle to cut it clean off of Tyler's body. He wipes the knife off on Tyler's clothes and set the vampire on fire. He stands up, watching the vampire burn.

Chase doesn't need any more information from Tyler. Anything else he needs, he will find on his own easily. Chase walks away from the burning remains of the vampire and begins his search for Nichole Roberts.

DEDICATION

&

ABOUT
THE AUTHOR

I dedicate this book to my father and mother who not only supported me but who also motivated and encouraged me to write and publish this novel. Thank you both for the long talks and for the hours you spent reading and rereading my novel. Thank you for your financial support. Thank you for pushing me to achieve my dreams no matter what obstacles were in my way. *David and Kim Walker*

To my little brother, I also dedicate this book. Thanks for your input and for naming one of the characters. When I see the character's name, I think of you. *David Eamon Walker*

To my grandparents, thank you for looking forward to reading anything and everything I write. It encouraged me to want to finish so that I could get your reactions to my story. I also thank you for all your financial support. I couldn't have accomplished this without you. *Jewell Walker and David E. Walker, Sr., Herbert Smith, Ethel Adway*

To my love, Kearie Saine, thank you for your support and for listening to me whine when I got writer's block. Thank you for bouncing off crazy ideas in an effort to cure it. *Kearie Saine*

To ALL of my aunties, uncles, and cousins, you know who you are; to you I also dedicate this book. Thank you for supporting my dreams. There are too many of you to list, but I love you all. *My family*

Paige N. Walker first found a love for writing through poetry. She began writing poetry when she was only in elementary school and has continued to write it ever since.

In 2008, she published her first book, a poetry book, entitled *Emotions*. Paige then went on to college and graduated from the University of Arkansas at Pine Bluff with a degree in Biology. Though she loved the sciences, she had a passion for books, reading, and writing.

She began writing her first novel Transition in 2014 and subsequently publishing it with College Boy Publishing in 2015. She continues her passion for reading and writing to this day.

For more info books by Paige Walker go to

paigewalkerauthor.com

To order other titles visit

www.CollegeBoyPublishing.com